Winona

Ticket to Ride

WINONA KENT

Print ISBN: 978-1-7773294-3-3
eBook ISBN: 978-1-7773294-2-6
Please visit Winona's website at www.winonakent.com
Please visit Blue Devil Books at www.bluedevilbooks.com

WHAT PEOPLE HAVE SAID ABOUT *TICKET TO RIDE*

If you haven't discovered Jason Davey yet, you're in for a treat. Rock star, private eye, and the target of a deadly and malevolent force seemingly attached to his band's anniversary tour like a demonic limpet. Delightful and compulsive reading!

Iona Whishaw, award-winning author of the *Globe and Mail* bestselling Lane Winslow Mystery series

Ticket to Ride **is a captivating and original mystery with a cast of quirky characters and a likable protagonist who entertains a belief in ghosts and guardian angels. Jason Davey proves a clever sleuth with a wicked sense of humour and a tenacity that never wavers even when confronted with increasingly life-threatening situations. Winona Kent writes with a deft hand, melding suspense and comedy in a thoroughly entertaining mix that will keep readers entranced until the very last page.**

Brenda Chapman, author of the Stonechild and Rouleau police procedural series, the Anna Sweet mystery novellas, and the Jennifer Bannon mysteries for middle grade

It's time to tune up the band as guitarist and amateur sleuth Jason Davey returns for another deadly ballad! Fans of music and mysteries won't want to miss out.

A.J. Devlin, author of the award-winning "Hammerhead" Jed ex-pro wrestler turned PI mystery-comedy series

What a perfect character: popular jazz musician/private eye…everybody's perfect job, right? Well, yes! Until someone with a big grudge tries to kill you! That's when this whodunnit gets very interesting... WHAT HAPPENS NEXT?? Perfect for a tv series, because Winona Kent does what a good crime writer must do; she puts you in the room next to the characters! Write on Ms. Kent !!!

Willy Ward, songwriter, vocalist and broadcaster

Ticket to Ride **crackles and sparkles, pulling the reader along with a heady mix of mystery, mysticism, murder and music.**

M.N.Grenside, author of thriller *Fall Out* and award-winning TV producer

ALSO BY WINONA KENT

The Jason Davey Mysteries

Lost Time
Notes on a Missing G-String
Disturbing the Peace

Other Novels

Marianne's Memory
In Loving Memory
Persistence of Memory
Cold Play
The Cilla Rose Affair
Skywatcher

ACKNOWLEDGMENTS

I'd like to thank my mother, Sheila Kent, who passed away (aged ninety-five) while I was writing this book. Mum was a frequent source of inspiration, insight and knowledge—whether she knew it or not. She will be missed.

I'd also like to thank my sister Stella Kent and my husband Jim Goddard, who put up with me while I retreated into myself to finish this novel. Writers tend to be solitary, focused creatures who function extremely well in their own company. Stella and Jim are hardy souls who understand, accept and assist this aberrant behaviour with good cheer and infinite patience.

And finally, I'd like to thank Brian Richmond for his continuing enthusiasm, wonderful story sense and clever suggestions.

Thank you all!

The things I hate about touring:
It's not my bed.
It's not my shower.
It's not what I usually have for breakfast.

CHAPTER ONE

My parents were the founding members of Figgis Green.

I'll forgive you if you don't remember them. But an amazing number of people do—and still refer to them, fondly, as the Figs.

The Figs were a folky pop group that was huge in the 1960s and '70s and less huge—but still touring regularly and putting out albums—in the '80s and early '90s.

Mandy Green—my mum—was the main singer and my dad, Tony Figgis, shared vocals and played lead guitar.

Their best-known song was "Roving Minstrel," a catchy thing about a faithless suitor and his careworn lady, tormented hearts, lessons learned and a really fortunate ending. It was their anthem, and they always closed their shows with it.

It was Mitch Green—mum's brother and the Figs' bass guitarist—who'd first floated the idea of a 50th Anniversary Tour.

"There's something wrong with your maths," said my mother. "We first got together in 1965."

"The 50th Anniversary Three Years Late Tour," Mitch said, cleverly.

"The Lost Time Tour," I said.

And the name stuck.

The only trouble was, my dad, Tony, had died in 1995.

"You can take his place," said Mitch. "If Mandy doesn't mind."

I am actually a musician and I do actually play the guitar. Quite well, in fact. I have a regular gig at a jazz club in Soho—the Blue Devil—with three mates who join me on tenor sax, organ and drums. My professional name is Jason Davey.

Plus, I had the added bonus of being completely familiar with the Figgis Green catalogue—I grew up with it.

"I don't mind," said my mother. "As long as no one else does."

There were no objections.

And so, in September 2018, we started rehearsals for our thirty-four-day, eighteen-stop Lost Time Tour of England.

#

My uncle Mitch was younger than my mother by two years, with a shock of untidy white hair that always made me think of Albert Einstein. He'd taken to wearing spectacles to help him read, and his waistline was somewhat more portly than when he was with the original Figs. But, like everyone in the group, he'd never allowed himself to appear unremarkable. And he'd never really stopped performing. After the Figs broke up, he and my Auntie Jo took over a well-appointed pub in Hampshire, and Mitch played in a band that offered once-a-week live entertainment to its customers—much of it featuring Figgis Green standards. Once a showman, always a showman.

In the twenty years since the Figs had last performed, Rolly Black—my dad's cousin and the group's drummer—had moved to the States and built his own studio and filled it with instruments and had made a second career for himself scoring music for films and TV. He'd always had exceptionally long hair—which was now salt-and-pepper grey—and to mark his return, he'd braided it down his back and tied it up with a green velvet ribbon. He'd also arranged for his original silver Ludwig touring kit to be flown over, complete with its customized bass drum featuring the Figs' leafy logo.

The original Figs had two rhythm guitarists. The first was Rick Redding, who was hired after mum and dad put an ad in *NME*. Rick was easily the buccaneer of the group, a romantic hero, rough in both reputation and demeanour. He'd been thrown out of the band in 1968 after he'd assaulted my dad.

After Rick left, Ben Quigley came on board. Ben's life was similar to Gerry Rafferty's, but without the six haunting minutes of "Baker Street." He was a sensitive soul who always shied away from the attention Figgis Green brought him. Ben wasn't interested in joining our Lost Time tour. So Mitch recruited Bob Chaplin, a "friend of the band."

I found Bob to be rather ordinary and no-nonsense, though he was an excellent player. He favoured white short-sleeved shirts and jeans, and his hair was short and on the curly side. He reminded me a lot of Bruce Springsteen in his "Dancing in the Dark" days.

A week-and-a-half into rehearsals, our fiddle player, Keith Reader, walked out, claiming "philosophical differences." He'd done it before, in 1989, for the same reason, so I'm not really sure why anyone was surprised.

In any case, the day was saved by Bob, who suggested his girlfriend, Beth Homewood, as a replacement. Beth had done folk, rock, country, classical... Weddings. Commercial functions. Studio sessions. And she was available. I was a bit sceptical, worrying about her formal training—not that it was compulsory, or even recommended. Keith was the only one of the reconstituted Figs who'd had any kind of lessons.

"Royal College of Music," Bob said.

And Beth was in.

She turned out to be brilliant, learning the two set lists and two encores in less than a day.

Beth was a good twenty years younger than Bob. She'd begun rehearsals with long, light brown, wavy hair, which she'd plaited loosely behind her head. By the time we opened the tour, she'd morphed into Eileen from the Dexy's Midnight Runners video that Julien Temple directed, with her hair tucked messily into a scrunched-around kerchief. She wouldn't have looked amiss in the chopped-off blue-jean coveralls they all wore in the film, but onstage she went for a Judy Geeson *To Sir With Love* look—a crocheted white mini-dress with a flesh-coloured lining and matching flat white shoes.

My mother was seventy-seven and her hair was silver-white. She had essentially the same cut that she did when she was fronting the Figs all those years ago. Except, of course, that her hair was thinner now, and her face was fuller. She was a bit heavier than she'd been back in the day, too, but that was to be expected as well. She'd happily embraced a cushiony comfy grandmotherly look, and it suited her.

It turned out some of our songs had to be transposed to fit mum's vocal range, which had diminished a bit over the five decades since she'd started singing them. But other than that, she was still in fine form.

As for me, I hadn't toured in nearly ten years. The last time I'd gigged around England was 2009, the year my wife, Em, died. I'd been on the road with my own band, desperate to "make it," playing concerts in pubs and clubs and converted churches and renovated city halls and repurposed Corn Exchanges. And staging late night turns at so many music festivals I'd lost count.

Between then, and now, I'd run away to sea and worked as an entertainer on board a cruise ship. After that, I'd gone travelling and then I'd come home to England and made a brief living as a busker while I tried to find a more permanent gig.

And then I'd landed the residency at the Blue Devil.

I arranged for a leave of absence from the club and found a temporary stand-in to keep my band employed and my post-tour career in safe hands.

My prep was pretty basic. I packed up my guitars and got a haircut. I'd just tiptoed over fifty, and I have to admit, I was very nearly talked into colouring the silver filaments that had begun to infiltrate my very untidy, dark brown hair. I resisted.

So that was the band: mum, me, Mitch, Rolly, Bob and Beth. Our venues were booked. Our faces were on the tea towels.

We rehearsed. We perfected our show.

On Friday, September 7, 2018, we went out on the road.

And two weeks later, on Friday, September 21, as mum and I were on our way in to the Duke of York Theatre in Leeds for our sound check, we were very nearly killed by a gargoyle.

#

The Duke of York, if you don't know it, was built roundabout 1880 and is Grade II listed. Outside, it's high Victorian red brick and stone and inside it's red velvet and Gothic plasterwork and gold leaf, all lovingly restored to bring the old music hall up to modern-day standards.

The renovations were largely focused on the interior, which was probably why nobody'd bothered to double-check the stability of the three stone figureheads perched outside on the lintel over the stage door.

It was 4:30 in the afternoon when the middle one broke free and crashed to the pavement, narrowly missing me—I'd stopped to tie up a shoelace—and my mother, who was hunting in her bag for her security pass. The dislodged head sent out a spray of jagged stone shrapnel as it smashed into pieces at our feet.

Mum and I looked at one another.

"Bloody hell," she said.

I knew what she was thinking, and she knew what I was thinking.

We made a point, after each show, of going out into the foyer to say hello to people from the audience and signing their programmes and whatever else they might have brought with them. It's something the Figs always did, back in the day, and my mother wanted to continue doing it for our tour. The venues weren't huge, and the fans—some of whom had travelled quite a long distance—loved us for it.

Two days earlier, in Sheffield, as the last of the autograph-seekers and well-wishers straggled out, I'd spotted a woman who seemed to be hanging back. She was tall, with long dark brown hair, and she was wearing a loose black top and a spectacular flowing ankle-length brown and black skirt. She had a gold chain hanging around her neck, at the end of which were a couple of gold medallions. It looked like she was waiting for a moment to talk to us alone.

"Hello," she said, to me, and then to mum, who was on the point of going back to her dressing room. "Please—I wish you to stay for a moment. I would like a quiet word."

I'm always a little bit leery of fans who want to have a "quiet word." You never know what they might consider to be earth-shatteringly important—the fact that you played three wrong notes in the middle of one of their favourite songs or, God forbid, you decided to use a different guitar from the one that was on *that* recording in 1985. Or your input was required to settle a long-standing argument about why there were two versions of one particular tune—the one on the 1968 album and the one on the flip side of the Top Ten single that came out the following year. Because they sounded decidedly different and the general consensus was that the album version was far superior. And they wanted to know what *you* thought.

I waited. My mother waited.

"My name is Kezia Heron," the woman said. "I have been following you for many, many years."

There was something delightfully old-fashioned about her. I couldn't quite put my finger on it. The Figs attracted all kinds of followers, and I suppose because of the sheer nature of most of their songs, those followers were bound to have one foot firmly planted in the distant past. This woman looked and sounded as if she'd embraced that particular concept hook, line and sinker.

"I have the gift," she said, confidentially. "I am able to see into the future."

"Are you," said my mother, wholly unimpressed.

I knew her opinion of seaside amusements and end-of-pier fortune-tellers. I knew that opinion included, with very few exceptions, anything remotely to do with the word 'psychic'.

"I am compelled to speak with you," said Kezia, looking at me. "I bring a warning."

My mother was exercising supreme patience. She would never say anything horrible to a fan, but she wanted very badly to leave. Our shows ended late and by the time we got back to our hotel, it was usually well past midnight.

I'm more open-minded about the occult and the paranormal than my mother. "What sort of warning?" I asked.

"There will be troubles. I am certain of the word 'dropping'."

"Dropping," said my mother.

"Yes, dropping."

"As in, falling down?" I asked.

"I hear the word," said Kezia. "Over and over again. And I feel it as it happens. A dropping."

"Is this dropping going to kill us?" mum inquired. "Because if it is, perhaps we'd better cancel the rest of the tour and arrange for a refund on the hotel deposits and the transport."

Kezia smiled. "I understand. Many people are unwilling to accept the words I offer. I am in your presence only to convey the message, which is extended with graciousness and humility and great caring."

"Thank you," I said. "We do appreciate the warning."

"We are all wanderers on this earth," Kezia replied. "Our hearts are full of wonder, and our souls are deep with dreams. I wish you a peaceful night."

#

My mother maintained an amused silence as we went backstage to change out of our gigging clothes. We had two dressing rooms at our venues—one for mum and Beth, and the other for Mitch, Bob,

Rolly and me.

"You don't have to say it," I said.

"And I shan't," she confirmed.

"I'll keep an eye out for possible hazards."

"I should think you would be doing that anyway," my mother replied, deadpan, opening her door, "as the only reason I brought you along on this tour was to look after me."

#

Beth, Bob and Rolly had repaired to our hotel's bar—which stayed open late—for a nightcap with the crew. Mitch, mum and I went up to our rooms.

I made myself a mug of hot chocolate. A bonus when you're touring is accommodations that come with electric kettles and packets of expensive tea and an equally-impressive array of coffee pods and packages of sugar and whitener and, if you're lucky, hot cocoa mix.

I finished off the last of a G&B Dark Chocolate and Ginger I'd bought that morning and had a bedtime ciggie, blowing the smoke down the sink drain in the bathroom. I switched on the telly and read over the comments that my followers had contributed to my latest Instagram post. I "liked" them all, answered a couple of them, and then fell asleep watching Cliff Richard and the Shadows drive across continental Europe in a refurbished double-decker bus.

#

How do you conduct your life when someone's told you to watch out for something that may or may not have anything to do with a vague premonition of "dropping"? Do you walk around staring at the sky, wondering if a large chunk of blue ice is going to detach itself from a passing jet, plummet to earth and impale itself in your skull? Conversely, do you keep your eyes permanently fixed to the ground in case a sink hole suddenly opens up and you end up tripping into a cavern created by a leaky water pipe dating from the Roman occupation?

If you're my mother, you discard the entire thing as nonsense and carry on without a second thought.

If you're me, you remember the guardian angel who saved your life six years earlier and you very definitely believe what you've been told.

CHAPTER TWO

In 2012, I was an entertainer aboard the *Star Sapphire*, an aging cruise ship doing round-trip weekly voyages from Vancouver to Juneau, Skagway, Glacier Bay and Ketchikan. I was addicted to Twitter and I picked up a follower who immediately appointed herself as my guardian angel. Her name was Jilly.

I had no idea how old Jilly was or what she looked like. Her avatar was a shooting star with a rainbow tail. In my imagination she had long blonde hair and intense blue eyes and she wore long skirts and suede boots like Stevie Nicks. She sent me private messages telling me all about myself. Half the time she was wrong, but I didn't have the heart to tell her. When she was right, she was absolutely right.

Since she maintained she was an angel, I'd asked her—jokingly—what she'd died from.

Knocked down by a car, my love. A distracted driver, not paying attention, overworked and exhausted. His wife had just lost her job and one of his children was very ill. I forgave him immediately…which of course expedited my admission to Guardian Angel School.

That had made me smile. *You go to school for these things?*

Of course! We attend classes and study Angelic Theory. We must write three scholarly papers. And we must earn our halos and wings in an assigned practicum.

Is that all I am to you, Jilly? An end-of-term job placement?

Ah no, lovely. Once placed, we are with you for life. Unless of course there's a major falling out or disagreement…in which case we can negotiate a reassignment.

Some people took their constructed Twitter personalities very seriously.

She went on to warn me that something bad was going to happen aboard the *Sapphire*.

And when the bloody ship caught fire and sank, Jilly saved my life. The *Sapphire* had lost all power and was foundering in the sea. Jilly stayed in touch with me—impossibly—on my mobile. There was no electricity and no WiFi, no phone signal, and we were miles from shore. And yet, she stayed online and navigated me out of the depths of the ship and up through a disused hold into the back of the Showcase Lounge and then outside through a door that I was later told didn't exist.

For her efforts, she was awarded her halo and wings.

And then, of course, she disappeared, and I never heard from her again.

But, because of Jilly, I wasn't a sceptic. I wasn't confident in my own intuitive abilities (in spite of Jilly's encouragement), but I definitely believed that other people had a gift for it, and if they felt they had something important to share with me, I was never going to be dismissive.

#

Plummeting gargoyles aside, our sound check that afternoon in Leeds was uneventful. Every venue has its own limitations, excesses and quirks. Which was why, at 4:30 p.m. on the day of every show, we trekked onstage, took our positions, switched on and ran through our individual line checks, gain structures and volume settings. And then, together, we played a couple of songs from the set lists so Tejo could fix the overall mix.

Tejo's full name was Prakash Thejomaya, and it was his job to make sure our voices and our instruments sounded good—not only in his headsets, but through the front-of-house speakers (for the audience) as well as the rear-facing stage monitors (for us).

He had quite a menagerie of instruments to monitor on top of our vocals. Aside from our guitars, Beth's fiddles and Rolly's drum kit, we'd thrown a jaunty banjo into the mix, an Irish tin whistle, a Celtic drum, a mandolin, an autoharp, some maracas, and an accordion.

Yes, my mother played the accordion.

She'd wanted me to learn, but I'd refused.

I know my limits.

#

A couple of hours later, at our pre-gig dinner, mum and I were presented with a large cardboard box, taped shut and tied up with a big green ribbon.

"What's this?" I said.

Beth had a huge smile on her face. "Open it and see."

My mother appropriated one of the catering knives and sliced through the tape.

Inside were broken chunks of masonry.

"It isn't," mum said.

"It is," Mitch replied.

"More or less," Rolly added.

"He's called The Mad Hatter," Beth said. "He's got an identical twin at St. Peter's Church in Winchcombe, which is said to be the inspiration for Lewis Carroll's Mad Hatter in *Alice in Wonderland*."

"Resin?" I inquired, picking up one of the larger pieces. It didn't weigh enough to be made of stone.

"They wouldn't let us have the original," Mitch said. "Something about the theatre being listed and the need to preserve its history by restoring damaged artifacts."

"Fortunately," Bob added, "the Duke of York's gift shop sells absolutely bang-on replicas of its world-famous stage-door grotesques."

"Which smash up reluctantly," Rolly said. "But mic stands do make quite good hammers, in a pinch."

Mum lifted the rest of the pieces out of the box and placed them on the table. It was like a 3D jigsaw puzzle. But, in short order, she'd got them fitted back together.

The result was a man with a lopsided grimace, exposing a row of top teeth with one missing, and bulging eyeballs with holes where his pupils ought to have been. He was wearing a squashed top hat and he was leering at us like some kind of unhinged madman.

"He looks just like Keith, doesn't he?" mum mused.

Keith's membership in the Figs had always been marked by contentiousness and conflict, and when he'd finally stormed off during rehearsals, it had been with very bad grace, and nobody really missed him—least of all my mother.

I was about to take a photo for Instagram when our tour manager, Freddie Pope, intercepted me.

"I wouldn't," she said. "Theatre management's asked us not to say anything publicly about the incident. Liability, amongst other things."

Freddie's the daughter of a high-profile 1980s music promoter. She planned our itinerary and arranged our hotels and was always on hand at Reception to check us in and out. As well as being our tour manager, she also looked after the merch table—and our wardrobe.

I didn't dare disobey her, lest she neglect to get my gigging clothes cleaned and I ended up having to walk onstage smelling like a steroid-soaked bodybuilder.

"I won't," I promised.

#

One of the original reasons gargoyles—or, more technically grotesques—were added to the exteriors of medieval buildings (and, in this instance, a Grade II listed Victorian music hall), was to ward off evil spirits.

Which didn't appear to be working, in my case.

I came offstage that night experiencing what I recognized, with a sinking feeling, were the first twinges of a cold. I don't know about you, but with me, whenever my immune system starts to kick in, I feel like my brain's being zapped. It's like a volley of warning shots—rapid-fire ordinance that immediately sends me to the medicine cabinet for zinc lozenges, Vitamin C and Lemsip.

But I didn't have any of those with me. And nothing was open by the time we got out of the theatre. So, back at the hotel, I ordered three glasses of orange juice from Room Service, had my usual late-night ciggie, and went to bed hoping for the best.

#

When I woke up the next morning, I knew it was going to be one of the worst colds in the history of mankind.

Unfortunately, they seem to be a standard thing when you're on the road. You're in and out of all those hotels, cafes and restaurants. You're mingling with potentially-contagious guests backstage before the show. And even more potentially-contagious fans in the foyer afterwards. I wondered if Kezia's prediction of "something dropping" might also have included snot, which was most definitely making its presence known by the time my breakfast of poached eggs and toast and another three glasses of freshly-squeezed orange juice arrived.

There wasn't time to go looking for medication; we had to check out and get on the bus. Lincoln, our next stop, was about ninety minutes away.

#

Our bus was one of my mother's gifts to the Figs, prompted by too many old memories of touring in overcrowded vans with unreliable engines. Downstairs, it had a kitchen (tastefully decorated in white, fully equipped with a fridge, a coffee maker, a microwave, a kettle, a toaster, and a sink with hot and cold running water), a TV connected to multimedia, WiFi, a toilet, comfy sofas and reclining seats.

There was a steep little staircase at the back that twisted around, like the steps in an old red London Routemaster. The steps landed you on the sleep deck, where there were eight bunks and a roomy master bedroom (complete with an ensuite loo furnished with a heated floor, a fresh water toilet and a shower with variable temperature controls).

The longest journey on our itinerary was only about three hours, and none of the trips involved overnights. But the leader of the band was definitely making sure we got there in style.

Runny-eyed and miserable, I was the last to board that morning. And I was very glad that, upstairs, we had all those beds.

"Get yourself some Otrivine," Neil, our lighting guy, suggested, as I staggered down the aisle.

Neil Sparks had the perfect last name for someone in charge of our lights and electrics. His dad was a physician, and Neil himself had originally followed in his footsteps and qualified as a GP. But he didn't like it. His heart was in music. And after about five years he gave up his medical practice and got himself a gig with a rock band—probably the oldest rookie stage hand on the circuit—unloading trucks and hanging spots. From there, he'd become a Lighting Assistant, which meant he was the guy making sure everything was plugged in the right way. Then he'd learned how to run a desk and had become a Tech.

And now he was our Lighting Director. And our Band Physician (which wasn't a bad thing when three members were in their mid-seventies and a fourth had the worst cold in the history of mankind and could barely stand up).

Neil was sitting in one of the comfy chairs at a table about halfway along—facing forward, as he'd have otherwise got motion sickness. Honestly, not a very good thing for a roadie.

"Can I get it in tablets?" I said.

"I'm afraid not. Nasal spray only."

I have an aversion to squirting anything up my nose. It makes my sinuses scream—like that pain you get when you eat ice cream too quickly or you jump into a swimming pool without holding your nose and the water shoots straight up into your brain. But, at that point, I was open to anything that would make me feel better and—more importantly—preserve my singing voice and prevent streams of guck from splashing onto my guitar onstage.

I carried on past the little kitchen and up the stairs to the sleep deck. They didn't call it the "Artist and Entourage" bus for nothing. I was obviously part of the entourage—but I had the added perk of being the son of The Artist, so I immediately availed myself of the private bedroom at the very back with its double memory foam mattress and it lovely comfy pillows.

I heard and felt the rumble of the engine, and we were away.

I wasn't allowed to smoke, so I spent the next two hours alternately dozing (with tissues stuffed up my nose) and interacting with my followers on Instagram, many of whom fretted over the state of my health and offered interesting cures, including green tea (a possibility), a dozen oysters (not so much), fresh garlic in a glass of milk (definitely not) and putting a cut-up onion in my socks (your feet end up smelling like Burger King and you still can't breathe).

As we were approaching Lincoln, I checked my private messages. Ongoing chats with friends. One or two women hoping to get into bed with me (not likely, but I was enjoying the virtual foreplay). And a new one from someone called anon77865, who hadn't messaged me before and who didn't have a photo.

I'm very pleased you and your mum weren't killed by that unfortunate gargoyle, they wrote.

I am too, I messaged back. *And thank you.*

It was a good thirty seconds before I remembered I'd agreed not to post anything about the Mad Hatter anywhere.

How did you hear about that? I asked.

Don't you recognize me, my love?

How could I possibly recognize them? They didn't have a picture. And I'd never chatted with anon77865 before.

Sorry, I wrote back. *I don't.*

But now they weren't answering.

I waited.

Finally.

Sorry my love. Just touching up my appearance.

The avatar had changed from the generic grey Instagram head to something else. A shooting star with a rainbow tail.

And the name had changed too.

Jilly? I wrote. *JILLY?*

Yes. It is me.

Hello, I said.

I couldn't possibly convey the depth of my feelings at that exact moment. What do you say to a guardian angel who's been MIA for six years? It was like rediscovering a long lost friend…only much much more emotional.

Welcome back, I wrote.

Thank you, my love. It's good to talk to you again. Although you've never been far from my thoughts.

I should hope not, I said. *Being your assigned practicum and all.*

I've always been watching over you, Jason. I told you, once placed, we are with you for life.

Part of me really did want to believe that she was what she claimed. Part of me still couldn't explain how she'd managed to stay in touch with me—on my phone—while the *Star Sapphire* was in her death throes.

But the larger part of me—the one where my common sense lived—was urging me to think otherwise. This was just Jilly, a very creative human being with a brilliantly over-active imagination.

No matter. She was back in touch. And I was loving it.

Do you know about the warning mum and I were given? I asked.

What warning, lovely?

I told her about Kezia Heron visiting us after the show in Sheffield.

She predicted something would drop, I said. *And it did. Spectacularly. I wanted to contact her to tell her that her prediction had come true. But she didn't leave us any details.*

I shall make some inquiries, Jilly promised.

Thank you, I said. And then, I asked her again: *How did you know about the gargoyle?*

How do you think?

That was Jilly. Infuriatingly obscure when it mattered the most.

Is something else going to happen? Is that why you've come back?

I'm back because I felt it was time, my love.

I believed her.

She'd got me safely off the *Sapphire.*

I'd never have found that door without her, and that was the truth.

I'm here to help you. And now you must prepare yourself for Lincoln.

What do you mean? I asked.

But she was gone.

CHAPTER THREE

My mother loved old hotels. The more ancient, the better. And if some venerable old monarch was reputed to have stayed there in regal isolation during an outbreak of the plague, her eyes positively lit up.

The only trouble with old hotels is that they've invariably been retrofitted to bring them in line with current standards. So you end up with a single lift in a dark corner that only holds one person and half a suitcase. And the long-dead monarch who rode out the Black Death probably wasn't relying on WiFi (which often didn't work) and didn't care about indoor plumbing (no hot water in the cleverly retrofitted bathroom) and didn't likely smoke and therefore it wouldn't have mattered to him that the windows were painted shut.

Old hotels also seem to suffer from uncooperative reservation systems, previous occupants who take their time checking out and staff who go on unscheduled breaks.

Which was, apparently, why our rooms weren't ready in Lincoln.

"I understand there's a bar on the second floor with a view of the marina," Mitch said, helpfully. "It offers a Caesar salad with real anchovies for £8.50 and a nice selection of burgers. I'm in for lunch."

"I don't like hotel restaurants," I said. "They're overpriced. And everyone looks like they're only there because they have a meeting in one of the function rooms in twenty minutes' time."

"Or they've been roped into a day out with Great Aunt Lucy," said Beth, "and the hotel's a two-minute walk from a little shop that sells lavender bath salts and loose face powder in a shade you can't find anywhere else, that she really must visit."

"Not coming, then?" Mitch said, to both of us.

"I'm going to look for lavender bath salts," Beth replied. "For my Great Aunt Lucy."

"I am unwell," I replied.

"Suit yourself," said my mother.

"But I am hungry," I said, appropriating the lift.

I ordered the salad and a cheese and chutney sandwich. I took a photo of it for Instagram, assured everyone that I was still alive (although very congested) and then, afterwards, I went out in search of cures for the common cold.

My quest took me past the Pantheon, the theatre where we were playing the following night—another listed Victorian edifice with any number of opportunities for bad things to happen. Scenery crashing down from above. Lights coming loose from their overhead tracks. Great wodges of centuries-old decorative plaster disassembling themselves from ceilings and walls. Gargoyles.

I'm sure she hadn't meant it that way—or had she?—but Jilly's comment about preparing for Lincoln had all my internal alarm bells ringing.

Fortunately, there were no gargoyles.

Not outside, anyway. I did make a point of looking. The stage door was ordinary and unobtrusive and didn't have anything hanging over it at all.

I found a Boots down the road that supplied me with Lemsip capsules and Otrivine, and a little further along, a health care shop that specialized in natural and homeopathic cures. A nice lady in a white lab coat inquired about my symptoms.

I told her.

"You'll definitely want these, then," she said.

She loaded me up with bottles of oregano oil and Vitamin C and zinc and echinacea.

"And this," she said, handing me a box of loose-leaf green tea. "Packed with oxidants and polyphenols which will help boost your overall health as well as help eliminate the harmful bacteria and free radicals which have taken your body hostage and rendered you susceptible to every virus known to man."

Well, she didn't say exactly that—but I knew it was on the tip of her tongue.

I was back at the hotel an hour-and-a-half later. My room was ready by then, so I went upstairs and acquainted myself with Number Nine in my ongoing tally.

Our rooms usually included king-size beds and pillow-topped mattresses (featuring the promise of superlative repose), posh bottles of nice-smelling things in the bathroom, fuzzy white bathrobes and matching slippers. And, if we were exceptionally favoured, blackout curtains, a little fridge, and a kettle with an assortment of powders you could mix up into a late-night or early-morning beverage.

Number Nine had the heavy curtains but no fridge and no kettle. No matter—I'd bought myself one in Bristol.

The green tea from the health shop came with elaborate brewing instructions and a china cup with a lid that I could sip from while I digested the cost of it all.

The nice lady in the white lab coat had also assured me that the tea would help lessen the anticipated inflammation in my chest and soothe the irritation caused by a sore throat. I didn't have that yet—but I had absolutely no doubt I would before tomorrow.

I dosed myself up and drank my tea.

And then I checked my messages.

No Jilly.

There were plenty of comments though, all of them public—including another forty suggestions for curing my cold, several alarmed individuals hoping I didn't die before we got to their town (they weren't the only ones), and quite a few observations concerning my lunch, most of them lamenting the fact that I went for a cheese and chutney sandwich in a posh hotel eatery instead of something more befitting the surroundings and the *per diem* I was being paid.

All those cold cures must have started to take effect because at some point I felt I needed a lie down, and then I drifted off to sleep.

When I woke up it was dark outside, the blackout curtains were still open, and my mother was texting me wanting to know if I still planned on joining them for a curry at the restaurant across the road.

#

The following morning I had an even worse cold and—on top of that—a cough. Not the best thing for a performer sharing lead singing and guitar duties onstage. And we had a show to do that night.

I'd hung my breakfast order on my door handle, opting for yogurt and granola instead of eggs, some freshly-brewed coffee and another three glasses of orange juice. While I waited for all of it to arrive, I had a shower, and then I lingered for a bit longer in the bathroom while I turned up the hot water and saturated the mirrors with steam and inhaled as much of it as my lungs could stand.

The downside of steam is that it only works for a little while. But I loved how it felt—and so did my face.

For two weeks I'd been standing under glaringly hot stage lights, suffering through dressing room air and tour bus air and, worst of all, hotel room air. I'd been in and out of nine different bedrooms, battling climate control and, more often than not, hermetically-sealed windows. All of these had played merry havoc with my skin. I was beginning to look as old and weather-beaten as my dad's old Gibson Sunburst.

My granola and yogurt were duly delivered and, while I ate my breakfast, I checked my messages. Again.

Where was she?

That was the trouble with Jilly. She came and went at will. Sometimes she left me hanging. And sometimes she'd be so annoyed with me, she'd disappear for days.

There was still no sign of her as I finished my breakfast, so I distracted myself by going out in search of things that would deal with my cough and restore my face.

The Boots I'd discovered the day before proved, once again, to be exceptionally helpful. I swigged down two doses of Benylin, then tucked the bottle into my jacket pocket and went up the road to the health care shop—which was, providentially, open on a Sunday.

"I know just what you need," said the earnest young woman in the white lab coat.

She placed a jar of extremely expensive skin cream in my hands. "Infused with *Helix Aspersa Muller.*"

"Which is…?"

"The naturally-produced slime from free-roaming snails which are humanely farmed under certified organic conditions."

I unscrewed the lid and gave it a sniff.

"Packed with nutrients like hyaluronic acid," she continued, "as well as glycoprotein enzymes, antimicrobial peptides, and proteoglycans. Also reported to alleviate warts, calluses, and acne.

Apply as needed."

#

Half an hour later, I emerged with three jars of male facial product.

I carried on up the road to have a look at the famous High Bridge.

I took some pictures.

I don't consider myself a great photographer. My daughter, Jennifer, can claim that skill—and she takes pictures for a living. Jenn would no doubt argue that the eye of the photographer is what's most important: capturing that one particular essence—however tiny—that elevates your picture above the ordinary and makes it absolutely unique and memorable.

Back in the old days, when you had to load film into a camera and you got negatives and prints back from the processing lab, your photo collection was something special. Pictures that you stuck into an album and showed off to captive friends and relations. Something you could look at later, to remind yourself of a holiday or a special event or a highlight in your otherwise ordinary life.

Nowadays, everyone's been everywhere you have. And if they haven't been there in person, they can go there virtually. I know it's not the same—you're missing the smells and the sounds, the tastes and just being immersed in it all—but the photo you've taken on your phone is exactly the same as the photo 6,000 other people have taken, with only minor variations: where the sun is (or isn't). Who else is (or isn't) in the picture. How much the passage of time has altered the subject in question.

I sometimes wonder why I bother. I suppose it's just human nature. A memory jog. A small way of reminding yourself that you were actually there. And that you experienced all those other things that happened around the time that you took that picture.

I found a timber-framed building which happened to house a handy coffee shop, and I went inside for some lunch.

I arranged my tuna mayonnaise sandwich, its salad garnish and its hand-chopped chips artistically on the plate, and snapped a piccie for my followers. I also shared some of my photos of the High Bridge.

I'd started out in rehearsals posting pictures of what I was eating. And then I'd expanded my food observations to include a few random thoughts about how the rehearsals were going and at least one exclusive tidbit about the band that my followers weren't likely to find anywhere else.

After we hit the road, I continued the postings, so that now, my thoughts were organized into a sort-of trip diary. I had a lot of fans reading about my day-to-day activities on the road. And I was enjoying it a lot.

I sat down to check my phone for messages.

At last.

Good afternoon, my love. Are you going to Lincoln Cathedral?

Why? I asked.

I feel you must pay the cathedral a visit. It has something to do with Keith.

Keith our ex-fiddler…? I don't understand.

Keith, your Mad Hatter, Jilly replied. *That is what you named him, isn't it?*

I didn't recall telling her that.

Yes, I said.

There's a grotesque in the cathedral. The Imp. He's quite famous.

Does the Imp know Keith? I asked.

Lemsip, Otrivine, oregano oil, zinc, Vitamin C, echinacea, green tea and Benylin had a lot to answer for. It was a good thing I hadn't applied the snail slime.

My love, are you doubting me?

No, no, Jilly. I'm sorry. You're my guardian angel. You have ways and means that mere mortals such as myself can only aspire to.

Now you're mocking me, Jason. Perhaps I'd better go.

No! I said. *No! I'm sorry! I'm not myself today…He's not going to topple onto my head, is he?*

Go and see him, Jilly replied.

CHAPTER FOUR

I love old churches. They have a certain smell…I've never been quite able to put my finger on what it is, but I've seen curious discussions online, and I've even discovered people who want to douse themselves in "old church scent" and have put out requests for suggestions. To the best of my nose-memory, I can only tell you that it's a mixture of ancient stone, musty air, the beeswax they use for candles, whatever they use to polish old wooden pews, and, if it's a Catholic church, centuries of burned resin incense: benzoin, frankincense and myrrh.

There's something really calming and comforting about the smell of an old church. There's something about the feeling you get when you first open the door and go inside.

Perhaps it's because this is where, over the centuries, people have come together to meditate and focus their thoughts—their prayers—in a mass gathering. I've always believed that when you centre that kind of intense thought inside a building, the energy stays. It dissipates into the walls and the vaults, the columns, the arches, the windows and floors.

The Imp at Lincoln Cathedral sits on top of a support pillar in the Angel Choir. You have to put 20p into a machine in order to see him properly. He's got a Mr. Bean haircut, six teeth, an upturned nose and outsized ears.

I inserted my money. A light snapped on, and there he was, leering down at me.

"Do you know the story?"

For a moment—only a brief moment—my Benylin-infused brain had me convinced the question was coming from Up There. But no. The voice was female, and, like a pantomime ghost, it was behind me. I turned around.

The owner of the voice was shorter than me, but I think she and I must have been about the same age. She was on the heavy side, and she had dark, chin-length hair cut into a sort-of bowl shape, with a fringe. She was wearing black trousers made out of stretchy material and a black windbreaker which was unzipped to reveal a t-shirt. I recognized the t-shirt. Freddie sold them at our merch table. They were printed with an updated version of the band's old fig-leaf logo, the same one Rolly had on his drum head.

I have a good memory for faces and I was pretty certain I'd seen her out in the foyer after some of our shows, though she'd never come forward to introduce herself.

"Which story?" I asked, wondering if she'd followed me or if it was by mere coincidence that she happened to visiting Lincoln Cathedral at the same time I was.

"The story of the Imp," she said. "Popular legend maintains that Satan sent a group of imps to cause havoc in the cathedral. And after they'd gone on a rampage breaking windows and damaging the choir and assaulting a priest, an angel appeared and ordered them to stop. One of the imps refused and was turned into stone."

"And there he is," I said, as my 20p ran out and the light blinked off.

"You're Jason."

"I am," I said. "But I wasn't with the other imps, I swear. And I had nothing to do with the smashed windows."

I'd made her laugh. "I'm following you on Instagram. I hope you're feeling better."

"Much better," I said. "Thanks."

"I've got tickets for all of your shows."

"*All* of them?" I said.

"Yes, all of them. I'm a huge fan. Always have been. When you announced the reunion tour I was over the moon."

This last bit came out in a sort-of gush, as if she'd been holding it inside her for ages and it was the most important thing in the world that she needed to tell me.

"I'm Lynn," she added.

"Hello Lynn," I said.

"It would be funny if that thing came crashing down here, wouldn't it?"

"Sorry…?" I said.

"I mean, after Leeds…"

"Leeds?" I said.

Lynn was looking decidedly uncomfortable.

"Yes…the stage door."

"How do you know about that?"

"My friend works in the ticket office. I'm sorry…I thought it was common knowledge…"

Now she was looking frightened. Mortified, actually. As if she'd offended me and I was going to hate her forever because of it.

"It's all right," I said. "It's just that management asked us not to say anything."

Lynn looked like she was going to cry.

"Truly," I said. "Don't worry. You haven't done anything wrong."

She seemed relieved.

"Thank you," she said, and her face lit up with a genuine smile. "See you tonight, then."

She backed away from me—as if I was royalty—and then she turned around and walked across to the other side of the Angel Choir, where I suspected she was going to keep an eye on me while she pretended to study the ceiling.

I returned my attention to the Imp, dropping another 20p into the slot and zooming him in through my phone. The Mad Hatter from the theatre in Leeds looked more like Keith than this one did. Why was Jilly so insistent that there was a connection?

I took a picture before the light snapped off again. I glanced back to see if Lynn was as intrigued as I was, but she'd evidently got bored with me and wandered away.

I bought a little pewter replica of the Imp in the cathedral's gift shop.

Do I believe in good luck charms? I suppose I do. When I was working aboard the *Sapphire* in Alaska, I always carried a tiny humpback whale tail with me for luck. It was one of those things that all the tourists bought (along with bear claw salad tongs, miniature totem poles, Tanzanite earrings and Lladro parrots). It was made out of white gold, and I kept it in the pocket of my trousers. It was with me when the *Sapphire* went down, and, after I was rescued, I swore I would never, ever lose sight of it.

I still have it. I had it with me on that day. If only it was half as good at cures for the common cold as it was for saving my life.

I popped the Imp into my jeans pocket and trudged back down the hill to the hotel.

#

I had an hour-and-a-half until our sound check.

Most sensible souls would have taken advantage of that and had a lie down. I thought about it, but the meds were doing their job, and there was something else I wanted to do. I checked Instagram to see if Jilly was around—she wasn't—so I sent her a message to let her know I'd found the Imp and asked her what I was supposed to have seen there and why it had something to do with Keith. I waited for a few minutes.

Nothing.

So I switched on my laptop and went over to Generations, the family tree research site I often use when I'm trying to work up profiles on missing people. You can discover a lot on Generations. Births, deaths, marriages, children. Voters lists. Addresses. Photos and certificates, passenger lists, visas and entry cards and newspaper clippings.

And not all of it's ancient. A lot of it is surprisingly current.

My daughter was the one who'd talked me into doing a Generations DNA test.

"Go on," Jenn said. "I'll do it too. It'll be fun."

"It" was one of those spit-into-a-plastic-tube things that you send off and then, magically, six weeks later, you discover you have 4,907 fifth-to-eighth cousins you've never heard of.

"I can tell you who we're related to," I said. "They all come out of the woodwork at Christmas. I have to buy them gifts."

"But are you sure?" Jenn said, her eyes sparking mischief. "Are you really really sure?"

I was pretty sure I knew who my ancestors were, but the idea that I'd possibly descended from Ragnar Lothbrok or Attila the Hun was, I had to admit, intriguing.

I'd had the results for a while, but I'd been too busy rehearsing to actually sit down and build a proper family tree.

Now that we were a couple of weeks into the tour, I had the spare time I needed to focus on it properly.

The trick to putting together a family tree is to start with what you know. So I'd entered myself, and my son Dom, and Jenn, and Emma, my late wife. And then I'd added my sister, Angie, and her husband, Tom. My parents. And mum's brother, Mitch, and dad's brother and sister and all of their families, including Rolly Black. And finally, my parents' parents.

I had quite a nice little chart, all neatly laid out. There were nudges that pointed me in the direction of documents that supported everyone's' existences—birth and marriage records, the occasional census. (The last one Generations supplied was from 1939, when the government had ordered the creation of a civilian wartime register.) And, of course, I had access to other peoples' family trees that contained the same—and more—information.

My mother's last name is Green. And, as she never actually got around to marrying my dad, it was never legally changed to Figgis. That ought to have made it easy to track her side of the family, but surprisingly, I'd hit a brick wall. I couldn't find any record of mum's birth.

Fair enough, I thought. There was probably a glitch somewhere in the spelling of her name. I'd run into that problem a few times when I was looking people up.

And the fact that her own parents hadn't got married until around the time her younger brother, Mitch, was conceived shouldn't have been an issue either.

But there was something else. And it had troubled me from the moment I'd logged on to see my list of DNA matches. I didn't seem to be closely related to anyone at all named Green.

I knew there could have been any number of reasons for that, including a lack of relatives who had actually submitted their vial of spit to the website.

I'd found a few of mum's relations—cousins, uncles and aunts—who'd joined Generations and built their own family trees, but when I clicked on their names, I was told that they either weren't a match or they hadn't done a DNA test.

I'd have accepted that—reluctantly—if I hadn't been in touch with Nick. Nick was four years older than me and his father was Ted Green, who was the brother of Frank Green, and Frank Green was my mum's father. Which made Nick my first cousin 1x removed. I knew Nick had done the DNA test because he'd told me. But he wasn't coming up as a match in my list—and I wasn't showing up as a match in his.

By the time we'd rolled into Leeds, I had a pretty good idea what it all meant. And it really wasn't something I could easily ask my mother about. For one thing, I wasn't sure if she was actually aware that Frank Green might not have been her dad. That was the likeliest explanation, although at first glance there was also the possibility that Danny was the product of an extra-marital affair and his father wasn't Ted Green at all. Which would have been one explanation—except that Nick's sisters, Audrey and Sylvia, had also done the DNA test, and they didn't come up as a match to me either, so unless their mum had been exceptionally promiscuous, it was looking very much like my first guess was correct.

So now, I was on a quest to find out who my grandfather really was. And until I could figure out a way to tactfully approach my mother with the question, I was going to have to apply my own research skills to sort it all out.

I got my Generations DNA match list up on the screen, and scanned down the names to see if anybody had been added since the last time I'd checked.

Nobody new. Just a whole raft of names that made no sense to me at all, who I assumed were related to whoever had deposited their DNA into my grandmother, Vera Patterson, in the middle of the Battle of Britain.

The most logical person to ask would, of course, have been Granny. But she was very elderly—ninety-five, in fact. And, sadly, not altogether there anymore. You could hold a conversation with her—just. But you could never be certain that what she was telling you was an actual memory, or something she'd imagined, or something that someone else had told her about something else which may or may not have been true at all.

Frank, her husband—the man my mum had always called Dad—was long dead.

The next most logical person to ask would have been Mitch. But I was as leery about approaching him as I was my mother. It was the sort of thing that could, in all honesty, shatter a person's world. And I really didn't want to be the one who was responsible for that. Especially while we were on tour.

CHAPTER FIVE

I had a sort-of day-of-routine that I followed on show days. I showered and shaved at the hotel, then I walked 'round to the sound check at the theatre (or took a taxi, if we were staying more than twenty minutes away). Dinner followed the sound check, and then there was a period of waiting around to perform—which, for me, usually involved a ciggie or two out back with Tejo, a packet of M&M's for that all-important additional sugar boost, a mug of coffee, some conversations on Instagram, and a personal tour of the venue.

I tried not to vary the routine too much. I wasn't superstitious. Oh all right, maybe I was.

I'd taken it easy during the sound check. Playing the guitar wasn't a problem. But singing was absolute torture, so I'd decided to preserve my voice and I'd got Bob to stand in for me while Tejo tested my mic levels.

An empty theatre before a show always gives me a sense of something privileged and exclusive. I used to feel the same way when I was at sea and wandering around the *Sapphire* at two in the morning, when all the passengers were asleep and the decks were deserted.

The Pantheon was gorgeous inside and its predominant colour—like the colour in a lot of those old nineteenth century theatres—was red. Rich red upholstery on the seats, flocked red wallpaper, a decorative scarlet curtain with gold tassels and fringes.

I hiked up the stairs to the gods and stood on my own at the very top, gazing down the steep pitch to the stage, where all our instruments had been set up by Kato, our equipment manager. Kato was an interesting addition to the crew—a female in a role that had always been traditionally male. She had short blonde hair and large teeth and she was gregariously friendly when she wasn't insulting me.

Old English music halls were designed by architects who weren't all that worried about health and safety. Their main concern was the audience's sight line, and because of that, the railings at the bottom front of the balcony were usually less than three feet high.

I was standing in Row A, acutely aware that all that was between me and a drop of about thirty feet into the stalls was that slim brass rail that didn't even reach my waist. Suddenly, I had the creepiest feeling that I was being watched.

And along with that came a sudden and dramatic paralytic fear. I'm not afraid of heights, but Mitch is. And I remember him explaining to me that his wasn't so much the fear of being so high up, as it was the fear of not being able to control himself if he was suddenly seized by an irrational desire to jump.

It was exactly that fear I was experiencing. I was terrified to move. Someone was behind me. I could feel their eyes burning into my back. And what overtook my imagination was my only means of escape—leaping over that railing.

It was, of course, utterly ridiculous. I shoved my phone into my jeans pocket and grabbed hold of the brass rail with both hands and gripped it, tight, focusing my attention on my Strat, propped up on its stand on the stage below.

I listened to my pounding heart and my breathing and the silence all around me. Whoever was behind me wasn't making a sound. And then…it was over. They left. I didn't hear them, didn't see them…but I sensed it. They'd gone.

I let go of the railing and backed up the stairs, gripping the arms of the seats. At the top, when I felt safe, I turned around. And I saw them: two grotesques, fixed to the back wall, laughing at me.

At first glance you'd have thought they were cherubs, fashioned out of white marble, the sort of thing you'd find decorating a chapel. But no, these were not in the least cherubic. In fact they reminded me of those drama masks, Comedy and Tragedy. Which was probably what they were intended to portray.

But both of them had completely twisted faces and they frightened the life out of me.

Perhaps it was just my state of mind.

Perhaps it was just the Benylin.

But I had the creepiest feeling they weren't the only ones who'd been in the balcony with me just then.

#

Our caterers were another luxury provided by my mother, who had less-than-enthusiastic recollections of tours, back in the day, fuelled by a never-ending menu of cold chicken sandwiches.

Roadworks wasn't a big outfit, but the two ladies who ran it—Mary and Janice—were event veterans. And they'd stepped in at the last minute when our original firm, Up the Hill, had to pull out of the tour due to a family emergency.

Mary and Janice drove their own truck and fitted everything into flight cases, which they rolled on and off at each of our venues. They came complete with their own portable chairs and tables and tablecloths, disposable stuff—napkins, tin foil, plastic wrap, paper towels—and compostables—our meals were all served on fabulous bamboo plates with matching knives, forks and spoons which were completely recyclable.

They were dab hands at doing the local scout for fresh food and then getting everything set up and cooked in time to feed our little entourage—and whoever else we might have had dropping in as special guests.

They served dinner backstage after our sound check on show nights, using whatever empty space could accommodate us. They provided handwritten menus and cuisine lovingly prepared with fresh ingredients from local markets.

That night, we had a crab starter, goat cheese ravioli and a raw spinach salad with honey Dijon dressing. And to finish, raspberry and almond tarts and a little bowls of custard topped with Devon cream and blueberries.

"You all right?" Rolly asked, as I helped myself to the ravioli.

"I've been better," I replied.

My experience in the theatre had rattled me. I suppose it showed.

"Cheer up," Rolly said, adding an extra serving of ravioli to his plate. "We've got a sellout crowd tonight."

"We've got a sellout crowd every night," I said, opting for two bowls of spinach salad to make sure I was staving off tour scurvy.

It wasn't until I was deciding between the raspberry and almond tart and the custard with Devon cream and blueberries, that my mother decided to tell me about the anonymous message someone had left on her phone that afternoon.

"On your mobile?" I said.

"On the phone in my hotel room," she replied. "While I was out shopping."

"What did they say?"

"They informed me that we were lucky not to have been killed by the gargoyle. Had a little rant about the state of the country. And told me to watch out."

"Sorry?" I said. "You've received a threat?"

"I suppose you might call it that," my mother replied, helping herself to the custard and blueberries. "It might just have been a nutter, blowing off steam. I haven't deleted it. Come back to my room after the show and have a listen."

#

I don't really get nervous before a performance. I used to, but I've done it so often now, especially at the Blue Devil, that it's second nature to me. What I do get is a little adrenaline kick just before I go on. And I don't mind admitting that I love the attention, the applause, the feeling of connecting with an audience that I know has come specifically to see us. I love their affection. I love the feeling I get knowing that they want to hear us—me—play. I suppose they feed my sense of accomplishment and my ego. I wouldn't go so far as to say I crave their validation. But I grew up in the spotlight. And because I had well-known musical parents, I was always going to be put under the microscope and comparisons were always going to be made.

I gave up trying to compete with their legacy a long time ago.

The Figs weren't—and never have been—a high-tech act. No lasers or *Live and Let Die* pyros, no huge screen up the rear with rolling cameras on tracks in the pit, no complex SFX and multi-level stages.

No multiple trucks filled with rigs and hundreds of rolling flight cases, either. We had a single van for all our equipment and it was driven by Kato, who also took care of moving our gear on and offstage and setting it all up.

Our stage was decorated simply, with a series of long curtains suspended from rods, and for lighting we used the permanent spots supplied by the venue, plus a couple of extras that we'd brought along to enhance the mood during some of our songs. We had wedgies in front of us and amps in the back and Tejo with his trusty mixing board to make us sound excellent.

I'd like to say that night's show went well and without incident. But that wouldn't be true.

Our gigs usually ran to about two and a half hours. Eight tunes in the first set list, a thirty minute interval, then another nine tunes and the two encores. Figgis Green's songs have never been long, drawn-out affairs. Quick and to the point for maximum radio play, relaxed a little for live shows. And we were sticking to the familiar versions of nearly everything.

We'd come back from our break and had played through the first three songs, "Viaggio Italiano" (which was a jaunty tale based on a nightmare vacation my dad's sister had taken with her husband in the 1970s, with rollicking riffs from the first movement of Mendelssohn's *Italian Symphony* thrown in for good measure); "Jay-Jay," which was a lazy, slow shuffle jazz piece that my dad had composed about me (and which was, secretly, my favourite tune in the show); and "Four Strong Winds," the Ian and Sylvia classic where I sang the lead vocal and mum joined me on the chorus.

Mum has always loved the loneliness and futility in the lyrics describing the end of a love affair—and though she's never been to Alberta, she believes wholeheartedly in Ian Tyson's claim that the weather's good there in the fall. (I *have* been to Northern Alberta and I can tell you, reliably and without any word of a lie, that it's very fucking cold in the middle of February, never mind the fall.)

We'd finished "Four Strong Winds" and I was beginning to swelter under the lights. I think I may have had *Helix Aspersa Muller* dripping off my face and onto my guitar. I really hoped Janice and Mary weren't planning on serving escargot anytime soon. I hated to think I might be chowing down on one of my humanely-farmed certified organic facial product's cousins.

We started "The Fog's Lament," which my parents had always claimed was an old English folk song, but in fact they'd made the whole thing up, cleverly creating lyrics that sounded like something a fair damsel stuck in a medieval turret would have dreamed about as she waited to be rescued by a lusty knight.

And, as I waited for a break in my fingering so I could wipe the sweat out of my eyes, there was a commotion down in the front row.

Our audiences were fond of getting up to dance during our more energetic songs, and "The Fog's Lament" was very definitely one of those.

You can't really make out a lot from the stage when the spots are on—they essentially blind you. You can see the general shapes of people but you can't really single out their faces. But we all saw someone keeling over and not moving.

We stopped the show and waited while the person was brought 'round and then helped up and taken out to the foyer by a couple of guys from Security. It looked like a woman, and, while she was able to walk, she was very unsteady on her feet.

After the show, in the foyer, we signed things and chatted and glad-handed and posed for pictures, but nobody had any news about the woman, whether she'd been able to leave on her own or had been taken to the hospital.

Afterwards, still buzzing and not nearly tired enough to sleep, we all walked back to the hotel and gathered in my mother's room to listen to her message.

"Well, hello, Mandy."

The voice was female.

"About that gargoyle. Weren't you the lucky ones, eh? You could have been killed. Or Jason."

She wasn't wrong.

"Accident waiting to happen, if you ask me. Shoddy workmanship. Bloody foreigners coming over here, taking all our jobs, lowering the standards."

There was a pause.

"Or maybe it was deliberate. There's a thought, eh? The perfect murder. You never know, do you? You'd best watch out."

Click.

I studied the phone. It had a little screen in it and lots of buttons you could press to see a record of who rang you and who left messages. The sort of phone that often confounded my mother, who grew up and lived a good portion of her life in an era when you just lifted the receiver when you heard the double-ring and you said hello and that was that.

I pressed the buttons and read the information. Mum had only received the one call. In fact, that was the only call she'd got all day—because anyone who knew my mother personally knew the best way to reach her was on her mobile.

The little screen on the phone didn't reveal the number of the caller and it didn't provide a name.

In the old days, hotels had switchboards and operators. These days it's all conference bridging and VOIP, virtual receptionists and in-room checkout.

"Don't you think we should report this to the police?" Beth asked, doubtfully.

"Not worth their time," mum replied. "I'm not even sure it's a crime. A crank call, yes. But it's not really a threat, is it?"

"It's an implied threat," I said.

"It's not," mum said. "I think we can safely delete the message and say goodnight."

I stopped her from erasing it until I'd played it again and recorded it on my phone.

Just in case.

CHAPTER SIX

In the morning, after I'd had my breakfast (poached eggs, Lemsip, Benylin and coffee) and before we checked out, I went down to Reception and asked how someone could get access to a hotel guest's phone.

My mother didn't want me to bother. But it seemed the prudent thing to do.

I was attended to by a Hospitality Assistant named Rowan.

"If the caller knows the full name of the guest, they'd be put straight through to the room."

"Without confirming the room number at all," I said.

"That's correct. And if the guest is not in their room, or chooses not to answer, the caller will then be prompted to leave a message."

"Fair enough," I said. "The little screen didn't tell me who'd rung. It was blank."

"Normally it would provide you with that information," said Rowan, with utmost concern. "Unless, of course, the caller has programmed their own phone not to reveal their identity. As many do these days."

"That's probably what happened," I said.

"And if, of course, the caller is actually staying in this hotel, and they knew which room they wished to call, they would simply dial 8 followed by the appropriate extension, and they would be put through directly."

"Thank you," I said.

I wasn't left with any great sense of satisfaction. Regardless of whether they were staying in the hotel or calling in from outside, whoever had left the message had made it pretty clear they didn't like my mother.

And I still wasn't sure how they knew about the Mad Hatter. We'd kept it quiet. It wasn't on the news. It wasn't anywhere on social media. Lynn knew...but only because she was friends with someone in the theatre's ticket office.

Or so she claimed.

#

Our next stop was Norwich, about two hours away. Freddie had arranged a late checkout, which meant we were having lunch aboard the bus: sandwiches and wraps and a nice assortment of little slices and cakes, along with fruit juices and freshly-made tea and coffee.

I grabbed a baguette and my three therapeutic orange juices and carried them back to where I was sharing a table with Mad Hatter Keith, who'd been permanently stuck back together with industrial-strength glue by Kato.

"I understand," said Bob, who was sitting across from me, with Beth and Mitch, "that *Helix Aspersa Muller* is now joining the band as our onboard beauty consultant."

"That's right," I said, "and I'll be offering complimentary dollops of slime to the first hundred people who can correctly answer the question: How the fuck do you even begin to understand how Ticket to Ride works on your phone?"

Earlier in the tour, Bob, Beth and Mitch had invited me to take part in their favourite train game. And I'd honestly given it a try. It had taken me an entire hour just to understand the bloody tutorial. In the end, I still had no idea of the difference between green, orange and blue tickets and why I needed to collect three of them—or two locomotives—in order to make any kind of progress.

I hated playing games on phones.

"Care to join us?" Mitch inquired, from across the aisle, for the 1,798th time.

"No," I said, for the 1,798th time.

He's a nice bloke, really. My favourite uncle.

"Scrabble?" he tried, holding up his phone so I could see the screen.

He was only doing it to annoy me.

I was rescued by Freddie. "Two things," she said, sliding Keith over to the wall and sitting down. "I've just got off the phone with the management at the Pantheon. The woman who passed out last night in the front row. Her name's Lynn Wayland. Quite a faithful follower, apparently."

"I wonder if that's the same Lynn I met at Lincoln Cathedral," I said.

"Well, if it is her—she's diabetic. She'd forgotten to eat and her blood sugar dropped. They took her to A&E as a precaution but she was well enough after a few hours to be released. She didn't need to be admitted. Just thought you'd like an update."

"Wayland," I said, repeating it so I'd remember it. "Thanks."

"The second thing. I had a chat with the theatre manager at the Duke of York in Leeds." She paused. "The police have been checking the remains of the gargoyle and they're wondering if it might have been tampered with."

"Oh, great," I said.

Mitch, Beth and Bob stopped playing Ticket to Ride and looked over with interest.

"There was apparently a small crack at its base that they'd known about for years. It wasn't deemed to be particularly dangerous—they'd had it inspected six months ago. But the police have been up on the parapet to have a look, and they seem to think that someone could have got hold of a hammer and chisel and had a go at it until it came away."

"That's a lot of work for a random vandal," Beth said.

"Someone with a grudge against the theatre?" Bob supposed.

"Someone with a grudge against Keith," Mitch replied, amused. "He is quite repulsive."

"Someone with a grudge against my mother," I said.

"Why do you say that?" Freddie asked.

"Yesterday's phone call."

I realized Freddie had been sorting out a problem with the merch when mum had mentioned her unfriendly voice message. Freddie hadn't heard the story.

I told her what had happened. I played her my recording of the message.

"That is concerning," Freddie said, with a frown. "I'll make sure Mandy's name's changed on all the hotel bookings."

She stood up.

"The West Yorkshire Police have only just opened their

investigation into the falling masonry, but I've given your mum their number. I really think she should mention that message to them. It might be nothing. Then again…"

"I'll make sure she does," I said.

"They may want to speak to you as well, Jason. Since you were a witness."

"I was very nearly a victim," I said, pointedly.

#

My mother was sitting on a sofa upstairs, mobile to her ear, providing the West Yorkshire Police with a very colourful description of what, exactly, had gone through her mind as the Mad Hatter had smashed into the pavement in front of her.

I spotted a sightseeing pamphlet from Cardiff on a side table. I grabbed it and scribbled on it: *Tell them about the woman who left the nasty message.* I waved it under her nose.

She nodded, animatedly, and I carried on past the bunks, where Tejo and Neil were catching up on some sleep, both snoring noisily on either side of the aisle. I went into the private bedroom and shut the door.

I pulled out a packet of Rowntree's Fruit Pastilles and popped one into my mouth to stave off my cigarette craving.

And then I made myself comfortable on the bed and got Instagram up on my phone.

There she was.

My love, Jilly said. *I'm very glad you met the Imp. He and I correspond frequently. He tells me about the people he's seen. I tell him what's going on in the world outside the cathedral. He has a somewhat limited perspective, as you might have guessed.*

Did he tell you he'd seen me? I inquired, humorously.

He did, in fact. He commented on your jacket—brown suede, if I'm not mistaken?

It is, I said.

And the woman you were speaking with. Her name is Lynn.

She's a fan, I said. *She's been on tour with us. She's got tickets for every show.*

I waited to see if Jilly was going to mention Lynn's medical emergency after the interval. But she didn't.

You must keep a close eye on her.

Shouldn't be difficult. Since she seems to be keeping a close eye on me.

I'm not sure why I feel you must watch her. But I believe it's important, and I believe there is more to come.

More what? I asked.

I don't know, my love.

You're as bad as Kezia Heron, I said.

I'll forgive you for not trusting me, Jason. After all, you're very nearly a proper private investigator. You must, of course, always double-check the facts for yourself.

I smiled. It was true. I'd written and passed the Level 3 Award exam and I'd qualified for my license. The only thing stopping me was the actual application.

I wanted to tell you about something that happened to me yesterday in Lincoln, Jilly. After our sound check. I went up into the balcony and as I was looking down at the stage I had the oddest feeling someone was behind me. And then I had a sort-of...panic attack.

Which theatre, my love?

The Pantheon.

You were afraid you were going fall over the railing.

That's it! How did you know?

There was a tragic accident there in 1891. A woman called Betty Humphrey was attending a play with her beloved. She was sitting in the front row of the balcony and, when the play finished, she stood up and either fell—or was pushed—over the railing, whereupon she plummeted to her death. Her fiancé was arrested for her murder but he was acquitted due to a lack of evidence. Betty's spirit is occasionally seen—or felt—in the balcony, and those few who have witnessed it always report the same thing: they're seized by a fear that they're going to fall over the edge and be killed.

I shivered.

I do firmly believe in ghosts. I've encountered several in my lifetime. And no, I'm not afraid of them. I think they're the essence of souls that can't find respite in death and the unresolvedness of their circumstances is so powerful that their spirits and all that energy manages to cross over into our side of the world.

I don't know why there are so few of these instances instead of a teeming multitude. But think about the times that you've entered a place where you've actually felt the presence of so many centuries of thought and habitation—churches are very good examples—and it doesn't seem so far-fetched.

I think all our souls go somewhere else when we die. I'm just not convinced it's anywhere the traditional theologists would have us believe.

And nobody had warned me the Pantheon was haunted.

You are slowly returning to awareness, Jilly said.

Awareness of what?

Your intuition, my love. Do you remember when you were aboard the ship?

I do remember, Jilly. I learned a lot from you.

I had hoped you would continue to listen to what your feelings were telling you.

I was busy travelling, I said. *And then when I came back to London…I was busy looking for work.*

Your intuitive skills never leave you, lovely. You simply shut the window. And now, you must find a way to open it again.

To be honest, I wasn't sure I wanted to.

Something else, I said.

Yes, my love?

My mother got a message on her phone yesterday. It was a woman. Her accent was…I don't know…South London? I'll send it to you.

I uploaded it to one of the remote servers I often use, sent her the link and waited while she listened.

This message is driven by anger, Jilly said.

Yes, that's obvious from her rant. But I don't understand what my mother's done to make her so upset.

Leave it with me, my love, and I'll see what I can discover.

Thank you, I said.

How's your cold?

It's getting better, I lied.

Please look after yourself, Jason. I'm terribly concerned about your health.

Am I going to come down with something worse than this?

Jilly didn't answer me. Instead, she asked: *Where are you playing next?*

Norwich, I said.

Will you visit the cathedral? You must see the bosses.

More friends of yours? I inquired.

Remember to look up, Jilly replied.

CHAPTER SEVEN

The Royal Lionheart in Norwich was another one of those Grade II listed buildings that my mother had insisted Freddie book for us. You know the sort of hotel I'm talking about. Renovated and refurbished so they merit a four-star listing—but constantly undergoing restoration, usually while you're trying to sleep in the morning after a late night. And their restaurants close before you've finished your show. And they're still closed when you have an early start.

I was prepared for the worst…but my room actually turned out to be a pleasant surprise. The WiFi was working. There was an old-fashioned clawfoot bathtub as well as a shower, and the hot water was definitely flowing through the pipes (I checked). And the windows could be unlatched and opened so I could blow my ciggie smoke outside instead of down the sink drain and therefore avoid setting off the hard-wired alarm over the door.

The room also had rather a lot of antique furniture in it, a very nice parquet wood floor and a marble-framed fireplace beside the bed.

I set up my laptop and logged onto Generations. I'd looked for my mother's birth record using the last name Green, but that hadn't worked. I'd tried with just her birth year—1941—and her first names—Amanda Susan. That had come up empty as well.

I knew that if someone had been born out of wedlock, there was a legal process for the registration of their birth. If the father was absent when the birth was registered and he didn't otherwise take responsibility, the child was registered under its mother's surname, and the maiden name was left blank.

So I did a search for Patterson, my Granny's last name.

I found a handful of Pattersons within a five-year window, 1940 to 1945, where the mother's surname was the same as the child's. Two were boys. Three were girls. None of them were Amanda Susan. And none of them were from Hampshire, where my mother always maintained she was born.

But those three girls seemed to be my only options.

Their mothers' first names weren't supplied. The only way I was going to be able to find out who they were, was to order their actual birth certificates.

I went over to the GRO—the General Register Office—and put in a request for all three, paid the Priority fee to have each of them dispatched by Royal Mail on the next working day, and then really had to think about where I wanted them sent.

Having them delivered to a hotel was not ideal.

I reckoned my best bet was my girlfriend, Katey, who was coming to see us in Cambridge, on Wednesday.

I gave her a call.

"Of course you can have them posted to me," she said. "I love a good mystery. Do you think your mum's the illegitimate daughter of some World War Two fighting hero? That would be fun. I've always thought she looks a bit like Winston Churchill when she scowls. 'We shall fight them on the beaches…'"

I laughed. "More likely she's the daughter of some lonely American soldier who found solace in the arms of my Granny," I said. "It happened a lot back then."

"And for Cambridge, shall I pack my special see-through black nightie…?"

"That," I said, "would be excellent."

"And the purple thingy that vibrates and has three different settings…?"

A new toy. Katey was always full of surprises. One of the reasons I loved her so much.

"Yes please," I said.

#

At about half-past four that afternoon, Constable Hutton from the West Yorkshire Police turned up to chat with my mum and me. He looked younger than my son, Dom, who was studying film at college.

"You're a bit far from home," I said. "We're in Norfolk Constabulary territory now."

"We all collaborate, in one way or another, as required," Constable Hutton replied.

"And he's a fan," my mother added, pouring out cups of Earl Grey tea that she'd ordered from Room Service.

"'The Gypsy Rover,'" said Constable Hutton, gracing us with his slightly out-of-key rendition of my whistled intro. "A personal favourite."

The song had been the Figs' first release, in October 1965, and it had leaped unexpectedly into the charts at a time when record sales were dominated by the Beatles, Manfred Mann and the Rolling Stones. We opened all our shows with it.

"Constable Hutton was just telling me about the workmen who were repairing a window above the parapet at The Duke of York in Leeds last week," mum said, when he'd finished.

She offered me (and Constable Hutton) a chocolate Hobnob from her personal stockpile.

"It seems," she continued, "that one of them might have accidentally given our Mad Hatter a whack with his ladder."

"I didn't see any workmen," I said.

"They'd gone home by then," said Constable Hutton. "But that accidental bump may have contributed to the crack widening and the object falling."

"So you don't think it was a deliberate act," I said.

"My son," said my mother, "thinks someone's got it in for me."

"Our investigation is ongoing," said Constable Hutton. "But we're not excluding the possibility that it could have been the workmen and their ladder."

"My mother received a threatening phone call," I said.

"Yes...that's why I'm here, actually. Following up. Since it doesn't seem to have been reported to the Lincolnshire Police."

"I wouldn't really call it threatening," said my mother. "More a xenophobic rant with unfriendly overtones."

"I would call it threatening," I said.

"You didn't save the call, I suppose...?"

"I did," I said, and I played it for Constable Hutton on my

mobile.

He listened with interest, then took out his notebook and pencilled in some comments.

"Can you send that to me?" he asked, giving me his card.

"You may as well know about Jason's psychic woman, too," my mother said, sipping her tea as I sent the constable the same cloud link I'd shared with Jilly.

"She's not my psychic woman," I replied. "But she was right, wasn't she? Something 'dropping'?"

"Anybody can predict things," said my mother. "And if they don't come true, we shrug it off and say, oh well, better luck next time. If they do come to pass, we overlook the law of probabilities of it *not* happening and leap to the conclusion that the person must have been somehow gifted to have seen it coming."

I was never going to get her to change her mind.

"Her name is Kezia Heron," I said.

Constable Hutton wrote it down.

"And she did strike me as being very genuine," I added.

"Other than being completely unsure about anything other than the word 'dropping'," mum replied humorously, offering me the packet of Hobnobs. "Another biccie…?"

"And what, exactly, did this Kezia Heron say?" Constable Hutton inquired.

I told him.

"And this was…" He checked his notes. "Two days before the event in Leeds."

"Yes," I said. "In Sheffield."

"And you didn't notice anything unusual or anyone lurking above you as you were going into the theatre in Leeds?"

"I didn't see anyone," I repeated.

"I wasn't looking up," my mother replied. "I was hunting through my bag for my tag."

We were all accounted for on the tour. Backstage, we all wore security tags on lanyards. If you weren't a part of the show or an invited guest, you were escorted out.

"And I was tying my shoelace," I said.

"Can either of you think of anyone who might want to cause you harm?" Constable Hutton asked. "Any recent disagreements? Ill will?"

"Keith Reader," I supposed, after I'd thought about it for a moment. "Our fiddler. He walked out during rehearsals and we had to scramble to replace him. He'd always been at odds with my dad and quite a bit of that anger came back while we were rehearsing."

"I'm not sure he'd resort to violence, though, Jason." Mum wasn't impressed with my suggestion. "And he's far too ancient to be scrambling up onto parapets and lintels and whacking away at the masonry. He's eighty, for God's sake." She paused. "And the voice was female."

"Anybody else?" Constable Hutton asked.

"Nobody at all," my mother replied.

"So, no other disagreements or arguments with the band…?"

"I can't honestly imagine anyone in the Figs wanting to smash our heads in," I said.

"Could you give me a list of everyone connected to the tour anyway? We may want to interview them in order to eliminate them from our inquiries."

I hunted for some paper. I found a couple of pieces of hotel stationery in the top drawer of the dressing table and a pen hiding underneath the phone. Nobody writes anything by hand anymore.

I scribbled down all of our names and what we did in the band, and then I added the crew—Tejo, Neil, Kato, Janice and Mary, Freddie and our bus driver, Beaky, and what all their jobs were.

"The West Yorkshire Police expects the highest standards from its officers and staff," Constable Hutton assured us, as I handed over the list. "We cannot guarantee we'll be able to resolve all crimes that have been reported to us...however we are committed to providing a service that responds professionally and appropriately. We will continue to investigate."

He seemed to be satisfied that he'd appropriately conveyed his force's testament of Customer Service.

"Thank you very much," said my mother.

"It was very nice meeting you both," said Constable Hutton, finishing his tea. "And, on a completely personal note…" He withdrew something from his pocket. "I wonder if I might prevail upon you to sign my Figgis Green tea towel…"

#

The fireplace in my room was bothering me. You know when you pick up a certain awareness, an overwhelming *something* that worms its way into your imagination and you can't make it go away.

I kept looking at the black and white marble surround and the black metal grate, and I couldn't shake that feeling.

It was so strong I actually rang down to Reception to see if there was another room available. But there was a convention in the hotel the following day, and they were fully booked.

I checked to see if Jilly was around.

She wasn't, of course.

I sent her a message anyway.

What do you know about the Royal Lionheart Hotel, Jilly? I've tried looking up its history but I can't seem to find the kind of information I'm looking for. I've got this fireplace in my room...

Then, I distracted myself with laundry.

Freddie took excellent care of our stage clothes. We had two of everything, and because we were always staying for a couple of days wherever we were performing, getting those cleaned was easy.

But, for anyone who's curious, yes, our regular clothes—including socks and underwear—were our own responsibility.

I had a clever solution for on-the-road laundry. I freely admit I borrowed the idea from a fellow musician, who wrote about it in one of his tour diaries. I owe you one, Ken.

1. Run warm water into the bath.
2. Throw in your clothes.
3. Add soap.
4. Strip down, climb in, and walk all over everything until it's clean.
5. Rinse and hang on a portable line to dry (the clothes, not yourself, unless you're into kinky things like that).

Don't ever let anyone ever tell you that I'm not domestically self-sufficient.

Also I have very clean feet.

#

I knew that bloody fireplace was going to give me bad dreams.

In the middle of the night, I was woken up by an apparition.

I was lying on my back, and I opened my eyes. It—he—was standing beside my bed, looking down at me. I saw him very clearly. He was wearing a cap with a badge on it—with wings—and a thick white crewneck sweater, a grey flying jacket, grey trousers, a yellow inflatable lifejacket and fleece-lined boots. And he was smoking.

I waited for him to say something, and when he didn't, I sat up. Whereupon he vanished.

You know that moment when you're somewhere between asleep and awake. And you're never quite sure which it is, because your sleeping brain is switching off and your waking-up brain hasn't quite engaged yet.

My eyes were open. A street light outside my window was shining into the room and I was staring at the fireplace, where the airman had been standing.

And I could still smell his burning cigarette.

CHAPTER EIGHT

"A guest in one of the other rooms," my mother said, sensibly, in the morning, when I joined her for breakfast in the hotel's restaurant. "There are gaps underneath the doors."

"Except," I said, "the rooms are all non-smoking, and the alarm would have gone off."

"Someone on the pavement outside, then," mum shrugged, pouring herself a cup of tea.

"And yet," I said, drinking my coffee, "Biggin Hill."

When I was eight, my mother and Granny Vera had taken me to Biggin Hill, the former RAF base in Bromley, Kent, which was famous for its squadrons which helped win the Battle of Britain. It was 1976 and a few of the buildings were still standing, though they were empty and in danger of falling into disrepair. They had a lovely little chapel which had been built in the 1950s, under the auspices of Winston Churchill himself, and that appeared to be the main purpose of our visit—though I'm ashamed to say that I wasn't particularly interested in it, in spite of my Granny's attempts to instill some sense of World War Two history into my childhood.

It was a blazing hot day when we walked up the path, past the two "guardians"—which, in 1976, were a real WW2 Hurricane and Spitfire and not the replicas which later replaced them. We went inside and even at age eight, I was immediately struck by the sense of peace and serenity that embraced us. I felt it. I know my mum did too. And the look on my Granny's face was heavenly. I mean that.

She was a young woman during the war—a WAAF—and I knew she'd been posted to Biggin Hill, though I wasn't sure what her job had been.

So going to visit St. George's Chapel on that particular day in August 1976 was like a visit to my Granny's past.

I walked around the chapel with mum and Granny, looking at the Book of Remembrance and the panels containing the names of fallen airmen. To be honest, I was more interested in having a look at the two airplanes outside, but I understood that this visit was important to Granny, so I did my best to be patient.

The chapel was fairly austere—simple red brick, all straight lines and a distinct lack of ornamentation, typical of post-war Britain—but I remember being impressed by the floor, which was parquet and which had been constructed from wooden blocks fashioned from the propellers of decommissioned aircraft.

We sat for a few moments in one of the pews, and Granny told me about the day in 1940 when Biggin Hill had been particularly badly bombed and the room where she and her colleagues were working was destroyed, necessitating their relocation to an empty butcher's shop down the road.

As I was digesting Granny's story, there was a noise. All three of us heard it. It sounded not unlike a coin dropping to the floor and then rolling away from us, under another pew. It was very distinct. We listened, then looked at each other. Then mum got up to look for the coin.

She couldn't find it.

And it seemed it was just me who noticed the faint smell of a freshly-lit cigarette.

We were the only people in the chapel at the time.

And the smell hadn't been there when we'd come in. I'd have sworn to it.

I was convinced it was the ghost of a dead airman, letting us know how much he appreciated that we'd come to visit.

Hello, I thought, my heart and imagination filled with newfound respect. *I'm pleased to meet you, too.*

As far as I could recall, that incident at Biggin Hill was the only time my mother had accepted the idea that ghosts existed and were able to manifest themselves in extraordinary ways.

"Biggin Hill was different," said my mother, as the waiter brought her eggs (soft boiled—apparently very tricky to get right in this hotel—she'd had to send the previous ones—rock hard—back to the kitchen). "Your grandmother had a sweetheart who was killed in action, and every year she visited the chapel to remember him. I always went with her. That year—1976—we took you with us because Granny felt you were old enough to understand."

"But you never took me again."

"There was no need," my mother replied, applying HP Sauce to her eggs, and a liberal sprinkling of black pepper. "That coin was for you. The connection was made."

I felt a shiver. I'd not been told this before.

"That was the only time you heard it?" I asked.

"It was," mum confirmed.

"What was his name?"

"Flying Officer Lee Merrifield," my mother replied, buttering her toast. "He was with 72 Squadron. They moved around a lot but they were based at Biggin Hill several times, and he was killed in action when his Spitfire was shot down by enemy aircraft over Dungeness."

"Did he smoke?" I asked.

"No idea. You'll have to ask your Granny."

"When was he shot down?"

"August 31, 1940."

I know what you're thinking. I was trying to work it out in my head as well. My mother's birthday was July 13, 1941.

But F/O Lee Merrifield had been dead for at least two months by the time my mum was conceived.

#

After breakfast, my mum and I went to see the cathedral.

Norwich has over 1,500 historic buildings inside its city walls, including thirty-three medieval churches, more than any other city in northern Europe. Mum pointed this out to me as we set out. She's big on touristy details. She and Katey once met up over lunch and spent nearly three hours comparing notes about a mountain in Switzerland which, when Katey had last visited, boasted cable cars and a cliff walk and an unparalleled view. But when mum was there (with me and my sister and my dad in the late 1970s) the cable car ride to the top had been undertaken entirely in dense cloud. Since it was a sightseeing package that had been booked weeks in advance, there were no refunds due to the weather. All we could see were the cable car lines, stretching down behind us, and if we craned our necks, the cables rising ahead of us and disappearing into white fog. At the top, we had lunch and watched a video about how stunning the view would have been if it hadn't been so foggy.

"Points for mitigation, decent sandwiches and an excellent cup of coffee," Katey had suggested, ever the travel agent.

"I shan't be going back," my mother had replied.

It was a good thing the internet didn't exist in 1979 or she'd have also made her point on one of those websites that collects comments from disgruntled travellers. Even though the weather was beyond anyone's control.

"We ought to have been given a refund," she added.

"You," I'd said, later, "are exactly the sort of client Katey had in mind when she abandoned vacation travel for the mundane safety of corporate accounts."

"This cathedral," said my mother now, consulting one of the touristy sites where she might have posted her complaints about Switzerland, if it had existed at the time, "is one of the finest examples of Romanesque architecture in Europe. It also boasts the second tallest spire in the country—bested only by Salisbury—and the largest cloisters in England. Its restaurant is also an excellent place for refreshments."

"No videos of the view in the event of fog…?" I inquired.

Mum gave me one of her looks.

"I've been instructed to seek out the bosses," I said.

Mum checked her phone. "The large cloister features over a thousand of them," she said. "Each decorated with a theological image. I'll leave you to it while I explore the gift shop."

#

When the venerable builders of England's Gothic churches were constructing their vaulted roofs, keystones were essential to secure the places where the supporting ribs intersected. The undersides of these keystones were often decorated with elaborate carvings of birds, animals and humans.

Jilly's instruction to me was clear: *You must see the bosses.*

Which was easier said than done. They were all very high up, and they were all extremely difficult to pick out.

I hunted for an app on my phone that provided descriptions and pictures.

There.

Better.

I sent Jilly a message. *Which bosses am I meant to be looking at??*

I waited, but her angelic presence was obviously required elsewhere.

There were a couple of musical carvings which struck me as highly amusing…and then I discovered the Green Man.

His face leaped out at me from my phone. I peered up at the cloister roof.

He had long fair hair and what looked like four stalks of green and gold kale growing out of his forehead and cheeks. He looked rather pleased to be where he was—he was most definitely smiling down at me—although the expression on his face, and particularly in his eyes, was verging on slightly demented.

He'd been placed there in the fourteenth century.

And the most bizarre thing about him was that his face was almost exactly the face I'd seen on the spirit of the airman who'd come to visit me in the night.

I stood underneath him, looking up, focusing my phone's camera lens and zooming in.

"He's my favourite, too."

The female voice was directly behind me and was most definitely terrestrial. I turned around.

Lynn.

"He looks so real and so contemporary," I said. "He could be someone pouring drinks down at the pub."

I could see my mother, returning from the gift shop, laden with shopping bags. I hoped she hadn't bought me socks. Or a Black Death tea towel. Although a tin of Norwich Cathedral Assorted Biscuits wouldn't have been refused.

"I come and say hello to him every time I visit Norwich," Lynn said.

"Does he say anything back?" I asked.

"Oh yes, every time," she replied, which did actually worry me somewhat.

Only Jilly was allowed to have conversations with stone carvings in churches.

"This is Lynn Wayland," I said, to mum. And then I added: "The woman who collapsed in Lincoln."

"How are you?" my mother asked, and I knew it was genuine concern. "When we saw you fall over, we stopped the show for a few minutes while you were taken out."

Lynn looked embarrassed. "I'm so sorry. I'm never going to live that down. I take insulin, but when your metabolism's regulated like that, you have to remember to eat. My lunch was rushed and not very good, and I didn't have a snack and I forgot completely about dinner, so of course my blood sugar plummeted and I nearly passed out. They gave me some glucose at the A&E and I was quite all right in an hour or so. But I'm so cross with myself for interrupting your show."

"Never mind," mum said. "We like a bit of variety every now and then to liven up the routine of touring, don't we, Jason?"

"Like that Mad Hatter in Leeds," I replied.

"Preferably less heart-stopping," said my mother. She looked at Lynn. "You must come to the foyer after the show and meet the rest of the band. I'll introduce you to everyone."

Lynn was beaming. "I will," she promised. "See you tonight, then!"

#

We had lunch in the cathedral's Refectory.

I went for a three-cheese quiche with beetroot and roasted red pepper and my mother decided on two sausage rolls and a salad with crisps.

I took a quick picture and sent it over to Instagram.

"She seems a nice person," mum mused. "Are you sure she's not your guardian angel?"

"Positive," I said. "Lynn's all about the band. And six years ago, when Jilly saved my life aboard the *Sapphire*, I had nothing to do with Figgis Green."

"Other than being my son. Some might consider that a fairly important connection."

"Jilly rang you to tell you I was all right after the ship went down," I reminded her. "It was two in the afternoon where you were, and five in the morning where I was, in a life raft drifting off the *Sapphire's* starboard bow. How did Jilly know where I was? How did she get your telephone number? It's ex-directory. And how do you explain the door that wasn't there on the ship, and the WiFi signal that didn't exist?"

"You'd inhaled a lot of smoke," my mother replied, taking a bite out of her sausage roll. "And the door was cut into the hold as part of the backstage area in the ship's theatre. Not a lot of people knew about it but perhaps you did. Unconsciously. You used to perform on that stage. You did that thing with the big scissors."

It was true. Thursday evenings, after Sailaway from Ketchikan, we put on a crew talent show. The opening act was a number called *If I Were Not Upon the Sea*—a longstanding tradition on cruise ships. I was a Sergeant Major in a scarlet tunic and fake bearskin cap. The cast also included a busty Blackjack Dealer; a Tennis Player whose successive layers of shorts ended up down around his ankles; a Nurse in a Very Sexy Uniform armed with a hugely frightening hypodermic needle; a Taxi Driver; a bad-tempered Seamstress brandishing the aforementioned pair of scissors; and a Ballerina, always a male in a tutu.

The lyrics were filled with predictably ribald seaside humour, as were the actions, which generally involved the gents getting their lower anatomy whacked and the ladies having their upper anatomy tweaked and the ballerina at the far end exposing his arabesque.

I came out of it the least traumatized. I did a great gruff Queen's Guard. My dignity remained intact. I didn't lose my trousers.

Sometimes mum's logical explanations could be infuriating. But I had to admit she was right. I knew that stage—and what was behind it—pretty well. Perhaps it really had only been my subconscious reminding me of something I'd forgotten.

That still didn't explain the messages on my phone when there was no WiFi and no power to generate a signal, because the *Sapphire's* entire crew had abandoned the ship and the engine room was flooded.

And it didn't explain how Jilly knew that I was safe, and how she'd got hold of mum to tell her.

I was digging into my quiche and my mother was cutting up her second sausage roll when her phone bleeped.

"Bloody hell," she said, reading the message.

"What?" I asked.

"Text from Freddie. Flat tires on the bus."

"Tires? I said. "Plural? How many?"

"Six."

"Six?" I said, incredulously.

Our bus had ten wheels: two singles at the front, and four pairs at the back.

Mum turned her phone around so I could see the photo Beaky had sent.

There was our grey and aqua conveyance, listing forward at a very drunk angle. The two front tires were completely flat, as were the four outside ones at the back.

"That," I said, "is no accident."

Mum was composing her answer to Freddie when a friendly-looking fellow wearing a white collar that identified him as a man of the cloth approached our table.

"I'm terribly sorry to disturb you," he said, to my mother, "but I've been asked to give you this note."

He held the piece of paper out. Mum took it, assuming, I suppose, that it was a request for an autograph or a selfie.

But it wasn't that at all.

The note was typewritten. *Good thing those tires didn't go flat while you were on the road. That would have been very nasty. And dangerous. Best make sure nothing else goes wrong with your bus, Mandy. Wouldn't want you—or Jason—to meet with any serious accidents, would we?*

"Who asked you to give this to us?" I said.

The priest turned around and nodded at a table beside the door. "Oh dear," he said. "She's gone now. She was sitting just behind me, over there."

"What did she look like?" I asked, getting up.

"She was quite…rotund," the priest replied. "About your age, I should think. Long dark hair. Wearing a knitted cardigan—red—but then, of course, she had on a long black coat…"

I ran out of the Refectory and down the stairs, past the lift, and outside. To my right was the parking lot. To my immediate left, the open archway of the entrance to the Reading Room. Around the corner from that, the long paved lane leading up to the cathedral. I bolted around to the lane, but it was impossible. Whoever she was, she'd had too much of a head start.

CHAPTER NINE

Beaky, our driver, was a band-tour veteran aged about sixty, with a very long and distinguished nose—hence his nickname. His uniform was a flat tweed workmen's cap that wouldn't have looked out of place in London's docklands in the 1920s, a white collarless button-up shirt with rolled sleeves that revealed matching blue anchor tattoos on his forearms, a black waistcoat, and very battered jeans.

When he wasn't driving the bus, he played in a Dire Straits tribute band—The Sultans of Knebworth—and he hired bikes in all the places we visited and cycled to all the sightseeing spots.

He was a grandfather six times over.

"I do a walk-around inspection every day," he said.

Mum and I had taken a taxi from the cathedral to the long-stay car park where Beaky had left the bus, due to the inconvenient lack of a suitable lot in the immediate vicinity of the Royal Lionheart Hotel.

"And I personally check those tires once a week," he added, as I lit up a ciggie. "They were new when we started this tour. In top condition. One flat would be all right, though very unexpected, I have to say. Two would make me suspicious. Six is downright vandalism."

"It is downright vandalism," I confirmed, showing Freddie and Beaky the letter the priest had handed my mother at Norwich Cathedral.

"Oh hell," Freddie said, reading it.

"Isn't it difficult to flatten big tires like that?" mum asked.

Beaky shook his head. "All you need's something solid and thin to push the valve stem aside."

"Is there any CCTV?" I asked, looking around.

"Over there," Beaky said.

I could see some cameras mounted high up on poles. One was aimed at the parking lot's entrance and exit. Others were strategically placed around the perimeter of the lot, which wasn't very large.

"I'll see if we can access the footage," Freddie said. "And I'll ring the Norfolk Constabulary. Not that they'll do much other than log it. But, you know, insurance. Just in case."

"Tell them to get in touch with Constable Hutton from West Yorkshire," I said, digging out his business card.

Freddie took a picture of it, and one of mum's letter.

"The tires weren't slashed…?" I checked.

"Not slashed," said Beaky. "And it would be bloody difficult to cut through all that rubber anyway."

"When do you think it happened?"

Beaky had his mobile out and was arranging for a truck to come with some pneumatic air and a hose and a service person to make sure there wasn't any damage to the tires' stems.

"No idea," he said. "I parked here yesterday after I dropped you off at the hotel. I did my walk-around and everything was fine. This is the first time I've been back since."

#

By the time the bus was fixed, it was too late to go back to the hotel. We were due at the McInnis Playhouse for our sound check. And we actually needed Beaky to be there.

We'd arranged to do a private charity fundraiser the following week at Oakden Manor, an estate near Tunbridge Wells. The estate was owned by Giles Jessop, a very old and dear musical friend of my mother's. Oakden was also where Colin Beresford, our manager, had arranged for our show to be recorded for an album and a video.

I was glad we'd decided to do the recording later on in the tour, instead of right at the start. There's that old saying about every piece of music having to be learned twice—once in rehearsals and then a second time out in front of an audience. And then once you're playing in front of audiences, it takes a while before you've "settled in" and got to know your voice and your instruments and the band dynamics as a whole.

By that point in the tour, we had literally got our act together.

And Giles had got in touch with us to float an idea.

He'd seen The Sultans of Knebworth in concert, and had realized that our driver, Beaky, was a pretty damned good picker—just like his hero, Mark Knopfler.

One of Giles's favourite tunes happened to be "Sultans of Swing," and he wondered whether Beaky might join forces with us to play that particular piece at our upcoming Oakden gig. No vocals, he stressed, just five acoustic guitars coming together in an exclusive one-off.

"Five?" I said.

"Yes, five, with me."

We couldn't really say no. We were being paid extremely well to indulge two hundred and fifty of his closest friends in his newly refurbished Coach House, all proceeds going to charity.

And the entire show was, after all, being filmed with a view towards monetizing the event to everyone's mutual benefit.

Giles did actually have a solid musical background. His band, Brighton Peer, was a big part of the British Invasion in the 1960s. His dad, Gilbert, was a titled chap—the 17th Earl of Brighthelmstone—hence the play on words.

We had no idea about his current musical skills. But with four pro's backing him, even if he was a bit rusty, we didn't think it would matter much. We could always ask Tejo to mute his mic if he turned out to be dreadful.

"Licensing rights?" I'd checked.

"Leave it with me," Giles had replied.

And that was that.

Beaky, Bob, Mitch and I rehearsed the song, in between shows, until we'd got it nearly perfect.

And that afternoon, during our sound check, we were going to play it through, for the first time, with Brighton Peer's esteemed front man.

#

Giles Jessop was a bit younger than my mother, with a shock of white hair which had once been bright red, according to mum's memory and a photo I'd seen from the 1960s, featuring him and his twin sister, Arabella, sitting in a field of daisies.

And he still had the cheeky look that had made the girls scream when his band was climbing the pop charts with songs about unrequited love and the heartache of summer goodbyes.

"How are you all?" he shouted, jovially, walking up the main aisle of the theatre with his guitar as if he owned the place (although given his income, and his status in *Burke's Peerage*, I wouldn't have been at all surprised if turned out he did).

"We're well, Giles," my mother replied, into her mic. "You know the band, of course."

He did. We'd prepped for our tour at another one of his family's properties, Stoneford Manor, on the south coast, near Bournemouth. He'd shown up a couple of times to see us while we were rehearsing.

"Hello Figs," he said.

There were some stairs up to the stage off to the right, which he ran up, nimbly.

"You're new."

He said this to Beth. The last time Giles had seen us, we'd still had Keith on our payroll.

"Beth Homewood," Beth said. "Pleased to meet you. My grandfather loved Brighton Peer."

"Good God, woman, you make me feel ancient. Never mind. Happy to meet you, too. And your Mark Knopfler disciple. Hello Beaky."

He stuck out his hand, and Beaky shook it, warmly.

"He's invited to our event, by the way."

"Beaky?" I said.

"Mark Knopfler," Giles replied. "Confirmed yesterday. He won't be performing, of course, but he expressed delight in knowing that you lot would be, and he can't wait to see what we do with 'Sultans.' If that doesn't put the fear of God into you, I don't know what will. Still, you know what they say. Imagine him with nothing on—that'll get you through the evening. Where would you like me to stand?"

#

It turned out Giles was a tad rusty. Even after five run-throughs, he was still having what Mitch diplomatically referred to as "challenging moments."

"Never mind," Giles said. "I shall go home and practice, and I promise you I'll be up to scratch on the day."

"Perfect," I said, vacating the stage to have a quiet word with Tejo before we carried on with our sound check.

#

I reconnected with Jilly before dinner, as I was sitting outside the theatre, chuffing with Tejo. I told her what had happened with the bus, and the note that we'd been given in the cathedral's Refectory.

This is serious, Jilly replied. *The writer of that note seems to be singling you out.*

I'd just assumed it was my mother who was the target.

I feel it has more to do with you, my love. You must be very careful. And it's connected somehow to the original band."

What makes you say that?

Go right back to the beginning.

All right, I said, doubtfully. *By the way, I saw the bosses.*

And I told her about the Green Man, with his long fair hair and the green and gold kale growing out of his face, his subtle smile and the slightly demented look in his eyes.

I'm very pleased you met him, Jilly said.

Is he another friend of yours?

He is, but we've only very recently become acquainted. His name is Lee.

I stared at my phone. That shivery feeling again. And it wasn't because I had a cold.

Last name…? I asked.

He doesn't have a last name, my love. None that he's mentioned, anyway. Why do you ask?

I told her about the airman standing over my bed, and the ghost at Biggin Hill when I was eight, whose name was Lee Merrifield.

And the bizarre thing was, Jilly, my airman's face was almost exactly the same face as the Green Man at the cathedral. But that Green Man's been up in the eaves since the 1300s.

What day were you at Biggin Hill, my love? Can you recall?

It was August 31, 1976, I said. My Granny went there every year on the same day. Her sweetheart was killed on August 31, 1940. He's commemorated in their big book. And on their chapel wall, too, I think. We were convinced it was him dropping the coin—and welcoming me.

And his name was Lee?

Flying Officer Lee Merrifield, I said. *Do you know him?*

I don't, my love. But I shall look into it. And you must visit your grandmother and ask her about her sweetheart. She's very elderly and her memories are fragile.

I will as soon as the tour's over, I promised.

#

That night's show went smoothly. No hitches, no hangups. We all hit our cues, nobody was out of tune, we didn't forget our lines and I didn't break any strings.

And nobody in the audience had to be carried out by Security.

Glad-handing with the fans around the merch table in the foyer, I was glad to see Lynn finally plucking up her courage and coming forward to introduce herself. She'd bought half a dozen posters—which we all duly signed with our black Sharpies and, true to her word, my mother introduced her to Mitch, Rolly, Beth and Bob.

Afterwards, walking back to our dressing rooms to change into our street clothes, Mitch said: "She looks familiar. I can't think why."

"She's been to every show," mum replied.

"And she's the one we had to stop for in Lincoln," I added.

"It's not that," Mitch said. "I feel like I've met her before. A very long time ago. Can't think why. Or where."

#

Back at the hotel, I made myself a cup of tea and ordered a grilled cheese sandwich from Room Service, to which I planned on adding a generous dollop of Branston pickle from my personal hoard.

Have you ever been desperate for a spoonful of Branston pickle with your cheese sandwich, only to be confronted by a brand new glass jar with a tight lid that won't budge? Even worse, you're on tour with a band, the jar of pickle is in your hotel room and nothing, nothing, will make it budge? Not even the steam coming out of your emergency tea kettle?

Fear not, gentle readers. I had the solution. I was travelling with an old-school manual tin opener—a "church key"—that had a pointy tip at one end for puncturing lids. But that wasn't what I used it for. I used the pointy tip to slide underneath the rim of the metal lid of the glass jar, and with a simple twist of the wrist and a slight "pop," I'd broken the vacuum seal and the lid could be easily unscrewed.

The trick is to have a pointy tip which is thin enough to get under the rim of the lid. It may take some initial hunting to find a suitable tool…but once you've discovered this amazing time-saver, I guarantee you'll never let it out of your sight.

You're welcome.

#

Cheese and pickle sandwich duly consumed, I opened a fresh packet of Riesen, my latest confectionery obsession—bite-sized pieces of dark chocolate and chewy caramel.

I enjoyed a late night ciggie, blowing the smoke out through the window, which I was able to crank open partway.

And then I logged onto my laptop and did a search for Kezia Heron.

There are plenty of ways to track people down these days, and they're all publicly accessible, sometimes for a fee, sometimes free. Private investigators use them a lot—as do the police.

I logged into 192.com, which provides you with a goldmine of information about individuals, including their Electoral Roll entries over multiple years and a background report that tells you, among other things, their age, whether or not they've ever owned property and the identities of co-occupants where they've been living.

Nothing. Even if I tried various variations in the spelling of Kezia's first and last names.

A general Google search brought back similar results.

I went over to my account at Generations and had a look there for anything recent that 192.com might have missed. I estimated she was young…early twenties. There were a few Kezia Heron's…but they were all listed in census records and probates and death indexes from more than a century earlier.

And then I tried social media. It's a rare thing nowadays for someone not to have some kind of online presence on at least one of the popular platforms…and there were one or two that were close—with similar spellings—but a quick look at their profile pictures informed me that they were very definitely not the woman in the flowing gypsy skirt who'd come to see us in Sheffield.

I abandoned the search, and went to look for Merrifields, instead.

I knew it was impossible that Lee Merrifield could have been my mum's father. He'd been dead for almost a year by the time she was born.

But why, then, had Granny wanted me to go to Biggin Hill with her, all those years ago? And why had I been visited by the spirit of a dead airman whose face resembled almost perfectly the face of a Green Man in Norwich Cathedral, and whose name—according to Jilly—was Lee?

I typed "Merrifield" into the search field in my DNA results.

The system hesitated for a couple of seconds, and then gave me its answer: exactly three matches, all very distant fifth-to-eighth cousins, and none of them with more than ten cM in common with me.

So there was a connection, but it was so far back, it wasn't even considered reliable.

The three distant cousins all seemed to have descended from one Jacob Merrifield, born in 1321 in the parish of Taverham, Norfolk—about five miles north-west of where I was currently sitting, on my bed, in central Norwich, with my laptop.

In order for anyone named Merrifield to be my grandfather, I needed to find someone who shared between 1,450 and 2,050 cM with me.

And nobody with that kind of DNA result was present in any of my Generations results.

CHAPTER TEN

The tires on the bus had been re-inflated and certified free of further damage. Our luggage was loaded. Our room dockets had been settled, and Freddie had checked us out. We were on our way to Cambridge.

One of the nice things about having the bus was that we didn't have to drive ourselves around the country. Dealing with traffic jams, road works, useless sign posts, detours and awful weather can be more stressful than any performance. You seriously can't play at a hundred percent after spending a day getting lost, encountering one-way streets going in all the wrong directions, and trying to find your hotel.

And having two onboard toilets was absolutely an added—and completely necessary—luxury.

I'd like to say that my cold was showing signs of improvement, but that wouldn't have been true. It wasn't any worse…but it wasn't getting any better, either. I was still congested, still trying to conserve what was left of my voice, and, if I didn't regularly apply liberal squirts of Otrivine, I'm convinced I wouldn't have been able to breathe at all.

As we made our way out of Norwich on the A11, Freddie came back to sit with me and our resin mascot, Keith. Someone—I suspected Beth—had bought him a Norwich Canaries peak cap, which she'd popped on top of his "mad hatter" chapeau, and a pair of matching green and yellow sunglasses. He looked quite intimidating with his lopsided grin and missing teeth. I wondered if there was a bar scarf in the offing.

"I've spoken with Norfolk Constabulary about the flat tires and the note you were given at the cathedral," Freddie said. "They maintain it can't really be construed as a direct threat. As such."

"I'd say that very much depends on the context," I replied. "If you add it to the voice message and the Mad Hatter in Leeds…I'd maintain there might be a pattern."

"I don't disagree," said Freddie. "But their attitude is, two unrelated incidents, which may or may not have something in common, do not constitute a major crime. In spite of you having a fan at the West Yorkshire Police who's very diligently filed his report into their system. And especially when you're in a band that might count any number of nutters among its followers."

"But," I said, "the note was typed. It wasn't an off-the-cuff thought scrawled in a hurry in the Refectory. Whoever wrote it came prepared. The woman who delivered the note knew the tires were flat, and she knew, exactly, when Beaky would discover that. And when you were going let mum know about it. Everything was planned. She was watching us and waiting."

"I can only do so much," said Freddie. "I'll give you a name and a number and you can take it up with them."

She wrote the Norfolk police contact information down for me.

"And I've asked for the CCTV from the parking lot," she said. "But they're taking their time replying."

"Thanks," I said.

"What was that fan's name? Lynn?"

"It wasn't her," I said.

"You don't know that. If she's travelling by car and following the bus, she knows where we're staying. And after we unloaded, it would have been easy for her to trail Beaky to where he parked."

"I have a hard time accepting that she'd wish any harm to anyone. Especially me."

"Funny thing about obsessed fans," Freddie said, getting up.

I waited for a further comment, but she didn't provide one, and instead went to the back of the bus to play Ticket to Ride with Bob, Beth and Mitch.

My mother joined me at the table with two cups of tea.

"I was thinking about Cornelia," she said.

Cornelia Caskey was a fifty-three-year-old hairdresser who'd developed an unnatural attachment to my father—to the point where she was convinced he wanted to marry her, and the only thing holding him back was his living arrangements with my mum. Throughout most of the 1980s, she bombarded dad with love letters and gifts—at one point even an engagement ring. She was in and out of court three dozen times, and was finally diagnosed as suffering from something called erotic paranoia. Dad's failure to respond to her constant overtures had Cornelia convinced that they were simply an ongoing test of her love.

She steadfastly refused to accept any psychiatric help and, after ringing mum and dad's phone two hundred and thirty-nine times over a six month period and then turning up at their house in Hertfordshire and setting fire to mum's car, she was finally sent to prison, where, ironically, she died of a heart attack, unrepentant to the end.

"Cornelia's dead," I replied. "And anyway, she was in love with dad and was convinced you were standing in her way. This is a completely different situation, isn't it?"

"Whoever it is," said my mother, "she seems to be at odds with you, as well. You were mentioned in the phone call. And in the note. I was reminded of Cornelia because she professed to be filled with love, yet everything she did was ultimately prompted by some serious anger directed towards me."

"Jilly thinks it's all motivated by anger, as well," I replied. "And that it has something to do with the Figs' beginnings."

"I can't imagine why. The original band was Mitch, Rolly, me, your father, Keith and Rick Redding."

"Keith again," I said.

"Much as he liked to disagree and as bad tempered as he was, Keith's not a vindictive person. I really can't see it. What about Rick?"

Rick had left the group before I was born, but I'd bumped into him in 2012, when he and his wife were passengers aboard the *Sapphire*.

"Fifty years is a long time to carry a grudge," I said. "He was with me and Katey when the ship went down. I honestly don't think he could be behind all this."

"Then perhaps you might give him a ring," my mother replied. "If your guardian angel's pointing you in his direction, perhaps she has a clearer head about it all than you do."

#

Rick had booked the cruise to Alaska as a surprise first wedding anniversary gift for his wife, Carly.

Carly had been less than impressed, and had spent the majority of the voyage complaining about it to anyone who would listen.

Part of the problem was a distinct lack of attention from Rick, who, every time I saw him, seemed to be on the phone dealing with Shag Pile, the band he was managing, who were bogged down in Bognor Regis, due to a blown gasket on their bus, affectionately known as The Pile Driver.

You really couldn't make it up.

"Jason, mate! How are you?"

Rick was my mother's age. He sounded a lot younger. And it hadn't been hard to find him—he still had the same mobile number.

"I'm good," I replied. "On tour. With the Figs."

I immediately regretted saying that, considering he hadn't been asked back by mum and his place had been taken by Bob.

But Rick didn't seem to mind.

"Bygones," he said, surprising me. "I'd pop in to say hello…but we're not very handy. I've retired to a nice little property in the Portuguese countryside. To what do I owe the honour of your call?"

"Actually, Rick, we're having a bit of trouble with some…incidents. Minor incidents, but still concerning. And someone mentioned that they thought it might have something to do with the original band's lineup. Possibly long-standing resentments. I thought you might be able to shed some light."

"No long-standing resentments on my part, mate. I let those go years ago. As you know."

I did know. Rick had harboured some bitterness when we'd first met…but in the week that he was aboard the *Sapphire*, we'd become friends, and whatever had been bothering him was, quite honestly, sent to the bottom of the Gulf of Alaska with the ship.

Rick was one of two people whose lives I'd saved that night.

"Can you think of anyone else?" I asked.

"Keith," he said, making me smile. "But that's a given, isn't it?"

"Keith walked out during rehearsals."

Rick laughed. "Bloody typical. Tell you what, though, mate. It's not the original Figs lineup you want to look into if you're thinking about long-standing resentments. You want to look into the group your mum and dad were in before that."

"Paisley Ascot?" I said. "What kind of long-standing resentments?"

"Ask your mum," Rick replied, a touch of amusement in his voice. "I'm not going near that one."

#

I knew very little about Paisley Ascot. They'd never really been on my radar—I'd spent most of my life being the *defacto* curator of Figgis Green's history. I had to go online to refresh my memory.

Someone had created a Wikipedia entry but it really didn't contain a lot of information. A trio of friends—Annie Hobbs, Tony Figgis and Mandy Green—had formed the band in 1963, the idea being they'd cash in on the folk music movement making its way across from America.

They'd played coffee bars and art schools, church halls and youth clubs, and were sometimes referred to as "the English Peter, Paul and Mary"—except that they were two women and one man, and they never really did achieve the recognition—or the chart-climbing glory—that "Puff, the Magic Dragon" had brought the group they were trying so hard to emulate.

They'd broken up the following year.

I knew that mum and dad had played as a duo for a little while in 1964, and then in 1965 they'd put the Figs together, recruiting Mitch, because he owned a bass guitar, and dad's cousin Rolly, because he had his own drum kit, and their mate Keith Reader, whose parents had sent him to classical violin lessons. They put adverts in *NME* and *Melody Maker* for someone to play rhythm guitar and Rick Redding turned up. And the rest, as they say, is history.

I really couldn't find much else online about either Paisley Ascot or Annie Hobbs. Other than the fact that they all wore paisley-patterned scarves when they were onstage, mum was a demon on the zither, dad played an amazing banjo when he wasn't on guitar, and Annie's main musical contribution was banging a tambourine.

Rick's suggestion that I ask mum about resentments in the band was certainly intriguing. And I would have popped upstairs to ask her—but we'd arrived in Cambridge.

#

The Eagle and Lion Hotel had started life as a coaching inn and drinking establishment in 1879. It was three storeys high and had an early check-in and my room, on the third floor, overlooked a lovely green park. There was also little fridge, and a coffee-maker, and the WiFi was working flawlessly.

Best of all, the hotel had a surface parking lot immediately adjacent to the premises and there was enough room for the bus and the equipment and catering vans, which made Beaky, Kato, Janice and Mary very happy.

I arranged all of my cold medicines and supplemental cures in a neat row on the little table beside the bed, and then checked my phone for messages from Jilly.

Hello, my love, she'd written. *I have done some research regarding your hotel room in Norwich.*

And what did you find out? I wrote back.

She replied a few minutes later.

It seems that in 1793, two men got into an argument in your very room, after a drink-fuelled evening in the downstairs bar. One of them was killed, and the killer tried to cover it up by dragging the victim to the fireplace, lighting a fire, and claiming that the poor fellow had, in an alcoholic stupor, stumbled into it, hit his head, and summarily expired, burning half his face off in the process.

Gruesome, I said. *My apparition didn't have a burned face, though.* I paused. *Was my ghost the murderer?*

I don't believe so, my love. But there is a connection. The fellow who was killed was named John Merrifield.

Merrifield, I said. *The same last name as my Granny's airman.*

Yes, my love. They are all descended from someone who lived very near to Norwich.

Jacob Merrifield, I said. *I've looked him up. But I have very little DNA in common with that side of my family. They're all very, very distant cousins.*

Have you found out about the band's beginnings?

I have, I confirmed. *I spoke to Rick Redding. And he thought I should look into the first group mum belonged to, Paisley Ascot.*

Yes, said Jilly. *Of course. Before Figgis Green. Who else was in the group, besides your mother?*

My father and a woman named Annie Hobbs. They were a trio.

It is Annie Hobbs who you should pay particular attention to, Jilly replied. And now you must go downstairs, because your lovely Katey is waiting for you.

On cue, a new text ding-dinged my phone.

I'm here, Rockstar! Come and collect me at Reception.
How the hell did you know that, Jilly? I asked.
But she'd gone.

#

I went downstairs to the Eagle and Lion's timber-panelled, marble-floored lobby. With its antique furniture and huge glass windows, it really was a beautiful hotel—I hadn't really had time to appreciate its grand entrance hall when Freddie had checked us all in earlier.

"Welcome to Number Eleven," I said, to Katey. "I've planned a fabulous surprise."

She kissed me—a rather extravagant display of openness, since she vastly prefers to bestow her affections in private. "I love your surprises," she said. "And I've missed you."

She held up a brown envelope.

"Your family secrets."

#

I think Katey's joining me on tour would have been much more memorable if she'd walked into our sound check, the way Jeanine did at Shank Hall in *Spinal Tap.*

But Katey knows how to pronounce "Dolby" and she'd never make me wear a jumper featuring my astrological sign (it's Taurus).

I'd met her aboard the *Sapphire*. She was with a group of travel agents, and desperately wanted to leave the business. She was also desperately ending an eighteen-year marriage. We'd fallen astoundingly in love. Katey was the other person who'd jumped off the ship with me the night the *Sapphire* sank.

Back in London, she decided not to leave the travel business after all, and simply switched from holidays and honeymoons to businesses and corporate conventions.

Our relationship is now what we both like to think of as "independently-faithful."

While we were waiting for lunch, I opened the envelope from the General Registry Office.

Inside were copies of the three birth certificates I'd ordered: the three females who'd come into the world between 1940 and 1945, where the mother's maiden name and the baby's surname were the same: Patterson.

The first was born on April 13, 1945. Her name was Brenda May Patterson. Her mother was Harriet Patterson and her birth was registered in Kingston, Surrey.

The second was born on July 2, 1943. Her name was Bernadette Margaret Patterson. Her mother was Lucy Patterson and her birth was registered in Manchester.

The third was born on July 13, 1941. Her name was Merrilee Susan Patterson. And her mother's name was Vera, and her birth had been registered in Hastings, Sussex.

CHAPTER ELEVEN

Katey was looking at me.

"Are you ok?"

"I just need a minute," I said.

It's difficult to explain how I was feeling. Stunned would be a good word. I'd just discovered something nobody else knew about my mother. I'd been digging and hunting and wondering, and now, all of a sudden, there it was.

The truth about her birth.

Well, almost the truth. I still didn't know who her father was. And her first names were confounding. I'd always thought she was Amanda Susan. But no…her first name was actually Merrilee. Not even close to Mandy.

I gave Katey the certificate and she studied it with interest.

"It could have been Lee Merrifield," she said.

"No," I replied. "It couldn't. He died on August 31, 1940. That's more than a year before my mother was born."

"Well, your Granny was a brave woman, anyway. She wasn't married and she had a baby. Which wasn't terribly respectable back then, though I'm sure it happened quite a lot."

"And it was wartime," I added. "Everything was different in the war."

#

After lunch, we went up to my room, where Katey left her

overnight bag and I collected my jacket. And then, it was time for my surprise. I walked Katey over to Coleridge's Punting Station at Mill Lane.

"Are you sure?" she said, doubtfully. "It's nearly October."

"It's Cambridge," I replied. "And it's what everyone does."

It was actually quite a warm day for the end of September—and a bonus, it was sunny. I checked us in and paid our deposit.

The attendant helped Katey into one of the little mahogany flat-bottomed boats tied up at the dock.

I took my place on the till at its stern.

The attendant gave us a quick briefing, then handed me the pole.

"Now's not the time to inquire whether you've ever done this before, is it," Katey said, struggling—unsuccessfully—to hide the look of alarm on her face.

I suppose the realization that I'd arranged what was essentially a self-hire punting adventure, minus an experienced chauffeur, did come as a bit of a shock to her.

"Oh ye of little faith," I replied, plunging the pole into the deep mud at the bottom of the river. I gave it a push, and we were off.

"Let me guess." She was sitting with her back to the bow, facing me, a folded tartan blanket clutched tightly in her hands. "You worked as a punter in between your bouts as a busker when you came back from your world travels after the *Sapphire* sank."

"Correct," I said. "Please pay attention to the Safety Talk. Keep your hands inside the boat at all times in case we bump into anything. There will be no demonstration of the correct way to abandon ship."

Katey smiled, remembering my halfway-comic performance aboard the *Sapphire*, where, during the drill, I had to show a lounge filled with passengers how to put on their lifejackets.

"The water's really shallow," I assured her. "Nothing like the Gulf of Alaska."

She smiled again.

"There's a bit of a drop in the riverbed on the way to Quayside, near where we turn around. But for the most part, it's only about three feet deep."

"It's bloody cold, though," Katey said, deliberately ignoring my safety warning and reaching over the side to dip her fingers into the water.

I navigated us out of the old mill pool, which was crowded with empty punting boats tied up to their moorings. We had a lovely duck for company, its glossy green head glinting in the afternoon sun.

"It's not too busy at this time of year," I continued. "It's worse at the height of summer. Choc-a-block. Like rush hour on the M4."

I planted my pole to steer us under the first bridge—Silver Street. The pole landed with a resounding clank.

"Gravel bottom," I said, as I managed to bump us up against an empty boat moored under the bridge. "It's like riding a bike. You never forget where the overhanging trees whack you in the face and where the river bends around the corner and the wind nearly blows you into the opposite bank. And, of course, the location of the submerged tow path the horses had to navigate with water up to their chests because they weren't allowed to trespass on the college lawns."

Katey dipped her fingers into the water again. "Merrilee's an interesting name, isn't it? Nothing like Mandy."

"I think it might be an amalgamation," I said. "Merrifield and Lee. Merrilee."

I navigated us all the way under the Bridge of Sighs, which was built in 1831 to link the old buildings of St. Johns College on the east side of the river to the new accommodations on the west side. The Cam narrows just after that, and I had to duck down to avoid getting my head lost in an overhanging willow.

As we floated past Magdalene College, the riverbanks changed from open green fields to high brick walls.

"This is the deepest part," I said, thrusting the ten-foot pole down into the mud, which left me with about twelve inches to work with. The pole was soaking wet as I guided it out, and the cold water trickled down my arm and onto my jeans. "I know you can swim."

"With and without a lifejacket," Katey laughed, a little nervously. "And I know you can launch an inflatable raft."

I was looking ahead to Magdalene Bridge and estimating where would be a good point to turn around after we'd gone under it, when something suddenly whacked my pole—*crack!*—and it flew out of my hands and crashed into the water.

And then that something whacked me. My legs. Both legs. Behind my knees. It hurt like hell and I knew I was falling. I remember everything that went through my mind in an instant: *I've lost my balance. I'm going over. I can't stop myself. Fuck.*

I plunged into the river. I sank down, waterlogged by my jeans and shoes and shirt and jacket. I had the presence of mind to hold my breath and the further presence of mind to kick hard once my feet hit the mud and gravel on the bottom, so that I shot back up to the surface. But I still inhaled water. I was coughing. And wheezing. I had a horrible flashback to the *Sapphire*. And something I hadn't thought about in six years—a recurring nightmare where I dreamed I was drowning.

Fighting for breath, I looked for Katey. *There*. I swam over and grabbed onto the edge of the boat.

"What happened?" I gasped.

"Two people in a canoe," Katey said, looking down the river.

There they were—a flash of colour—a blue hoodie and someone—larger—in a black coat. Paddling away rapidly.

"Did you see their faces? Anything?"

Katey shook her head. She leaned over the other side of the punt and retrieved my pole.

A bit further to the south of us was a flat grassy area that, if I'd been in better shape, I could have swum to. But my knees weren't working properly and the water was really really cold. I could feel my arms and legs starting to go numb.

I manoeuvred my way around to the bow, hand over hand, and managed to haul myself back aboard without capsizing the boat. I half-fell, half-clambered into the front seat. I wrapped myself up in Katey's tartan blanket to try and stop myself from shivering.

"There's a paddle by one of the seats," I said. "Can you get us over to the Coleridge station at Quayside? It's on the other side of Magdalene Bridge."

#

I've no doubt the young lady who tied up our punt had seen numerous customers give up halfway through their rental and return their boat there instead of going back to where they started. I'm not sure she'd seen quite as many people report that they'd been attacked by two people in a canoe who'd subsequently scarpered.

"Will you be all right?" she asked, wide-eyed and full of concern, as I handed over the soaking tartan blanket and the pole.

"Cold and wet," I said. "And I very nearly drowned…but otherwise…" I assessed my condition. "Alive."

"Ought we to ring the police?"

That was a very good question. This was no random act of

violence. Someone very definitely had it in for me.

"I'll take care of it," I said.

My legs hurt like hell. I imagined some colourful bruises were busy developing under my jeans.

"And there wasn't any property damage," I added, in case Coleridge was concerned about their boat.

"Still," said the young lady, "we don't often have things like that happen here. Cambridge is very quiet. Filled with students. Studying. Not attacking people minding their own business on the river."

"Your Kezia Heron's predictions are certainly proving to be accurate," Katey mused, as I limped around the corner with her to the taxi stand. "All those 'droppings'. The pole falling into the water—followed by you. And before that, the air pressure in all of your bus tires and your Mad Hatter in Leeds."

She looked up and scanned the sky.

"Just checking for seagulls," she said, humorously.

I tipped the taxi driver well to take us the short distance back to the Eagle and Lion Hotel. Plus, he was going to have to dry out his back seat before he picked up his next fare.

I squelched into the lobby and dripped into the lift and we went straight upstairs.

In my room, Katey got me a towel from the loo and then I emptied my wallet onto the desk, laying out all my cards and money and bits and pieces of paper.

My phone was soaked. But at least I hadn't lost it.

I had a few other things in my jeans pockets.

My little pewter talisman Imp from Lincoln Cathedral. My whale tail. My cigarettes and lighter.

Katey propped my Imp and my whale tail up beside my Amex card. "I'll go and see if I can find some rice."

"And a packet of Benson and Hedges Gold and a new lighter…?" I asked.

"If I must."

I called my mother on the hotel's land line to tell her what had happened, and then I rang Freddie.

"Oh for fuck's sake," Freddie said. "Right. That's the Cambridgeshire Constabulary, then. We might as well be doing a tour of regional police forces. I imagine they'll want a word with you."

"I'll be in the bath," I replied.

#

I sank down into the steaming water. I was right about my legs. The cretins had got a really good hit in—one solid red mark across the backs of both calves, just below my knees. The red weals were developing into quite amazing black and purple bruises.

Katey was back fifteen minutes later. "Convenience shop 'round the corner," she said, putting the plug into the bathroom sink and pouring in the rice from a very large bag. She fetched my phone and buried it deep. "Care for some company?"

The bath was one of those wonderful old deep cast iron vintage tubs with room for two.

"Wouldn't mind," I replied, watching her undress. "I like those knickers."

"New just for you," she said, sliding them off and climbing in. "I'd imagined a slightly different scenario, of course."

She sat with her back to the taps and played with my toes.

"I'm sorry about the disappointing afternoon," I said. "That wasn't how it was supposed to end."

"I hope you weren't going to ask me to marry you," Katey said. "I know those romantic Proposal Punts are very popular."

I laughed. "Not on your life," I replied.

"Thank God. I had enough of that the first time 'round."

"I don't think I'll ever get married again," I said, though I may have sounded a bit more wistful than I intended.

"You know what I fancy," Katey said, tickling the bottoms of my feet.

I waited.

"Rock star sex."

"I'm not altogether certain I'm capable of obliging at the moment," I replied. "Aging-folky-pop sex with dodgy legs, possibly."

"On your bus," Katey continued. "I've never been on a band's tour bus. A romantic dinner followed by a sexy interlude. It has a dining area, hasn't it? And bunks?"

"Bunks and a posh private bedroom at the back. With all the mod cons."

"Well then," Katey said.

"Wear your new sexy knickers?"

"And that special black see-through item that I packed especially."

"I'll have a word with our driver."

"I can tell you're extremely interested in my suggestion," Katey said, with a smile. "Thunderfingers."

CHAPTER TWELVE

Freddie had given all of us—artists and crew—a confidential handout at the start of the tour which listed everyone's mobile numbers. It had come in handy more than a few times. And it was about to make itself even handier now.

I rang Beaky, hoping that he hadn't taken himself off to the pictures or buried himself in a dark pub with half a dozen new friends and plans which would take up most of the evening.

"Nah mate," he said, when he returned my call, ten minutes later. "I've rented a bike and I'm doing a tour of the city. Keeping fit for the grandkids. What can I do for you?"

I relayed Katey's rock-star-sex request, using slightly less salacious words.

"Tell you what," Beaky said, "I'll be back by six. That'll give you time to order up your romantic dinner and whatever else you've got planned. I'll bring the keys to your room. Fair enough?"

"Fair enough," I said. "It's not an unusual request…is it?"

"Far more common than you think, mate. And you're not the first one on this tour to avail themselves of the upstairs accommodations for an extra-curricular romp."

That did surprise me.

"Not the roadies…?" I guessed. I knew Tejo, Neil and Kato hated that term. They were much happier being known as "crew." Especially Kato.

"You call me that again, mate," she'd said, giving me one of her broad, toothy grins, "and I'll make sure the next time you plug in, you get the shock of your bleedin' life."

"Not the roadies," Beaky confirmed.

"Catering…? Freddie?"

"Nope."

"Bob and Beth," I guessed.

"Nope," Beaky said, again.

Part of me didn't want to know any more. The only people left were my relations. Mitch had been happily married to Auntie Jo since 1964. My cousin Rolly was also very content in that department, as far as I knew. And both were senior citizens—albeit very active ones, and in very fine shape. And being married's never stopped anyone before.

I really wasn't sure what I would think if it turned out to be my mother.

And why would any of them request the use of the bus anyway, when we all had our own very decent hotel rooms, which were probably twice as comfortable and far more convenient?

Private fantasies, I supposed.

What goes on tour stays on tour.

#

The Cambridgeshire Constabulary did indeed want a word with me. But they took their time getting there.

Eventually two very nice officers showed up—Constable Tucker (the female half of the duo, rather attractively blonde, with deceptively—I thought, anyway—delicate-looking features) and Constable Fingal, who was very tall and Scottish, and reminded me of Danny in *Local Hero,* who had a facility with languages and fell in love with Marina, the mermaid with the webbed toes.

Constables Tucker and Fingal came up to my room and occupied the two available chairs. I sat on the bed with Katey, and provided them with a statement about what had happened to me on the river. And then Katey told them the same thing, from her point of view.

They, too, didn't really consider it a major crime.

"Still," said Constable Tucker, "it was an assault. And the consequences might have been a lot worse if you'd been knocked unconscious."

"Or weren't able to swim," Constable Fingal added.

"We'll make some inquiries," said Constable Tucker, getting up.

"Hang on," I said, also getting up. "This isn't an isolated incident."

Constable Tucker sat down again.

"It started in Sheffield," I said. And then I told her about Kezia Heron's prediction. The Mad Hatter in Leeds and my mother's unfriendly phone call in Lincoln. The flat tires in Norwich and then the threatening note in the cathedral. And I gave them Constable Hutton's contact information at West Yorkshire Police.

"Your tour does seem to be somewhat jinxed," Constable Tucker mused, writing it all down in her notebook. "Have there been any follow-up communications regarding your plunge into the River Cam?"

"Not yet," I said. "But I'm sure there will be."

"You'll let us know…?"

"I will," I promised.

#

Beaky turned up, as promised, at ten past six, with the bus keys and the Owner's Manual.

"When was that extra-curricular romp?" I asked. I really wanted to discard the information he'd given me earlier. But I couldn't.

"Cardiff," Beaky replied, opening the tech specs to the pages where all of the switches on the dashboard in the driver's compartment were explained.

We'd played Cardiff on September 13. The first week of the tour.

I tried to remember. We'd been joined backstage by the widower of an old school friend of my mum's. A dapper gentleman with white hair and impeccable taste when it came to shirts and ties…and he'd brought her a bouquet of roses…

"That's it," I said. "I don't want to know any more. Thanks."

Beaky grinned. "Here's how you get the electrics and the water going," he said. "Best lock the bus while you're inside and especially while you're upstairs. And don't forget to tidy up when you're finished. Leave it as you found it. Lock it up securely. You can return the keys at breakfast tomorrow."

#

Our dinner that night was delivered by an efficient member of the Room Service staff. I tipped him £20 and, with an amused look on his face, he helped us smuggle it out to the bus.

There was smoked salmon to start, served with crème fresh and an assortment of accompanying herbs, followed by roasted beef with truffle mashed potatoes, wild mushrooms and a Bordelaise sauce, and, for afters, a fabulous tart with candied citrus, brown sugar and clotted cream.

I'd asked for a bottle of sparkling rose wine for Katey, and several bottles of posh fizzy water for me. And a tiny romantic box of selected chocolates, which I'd talked the Room Service people into pilfering from their Honeymoon Package.

We set it all up on the little table on the main floor of the bus.

I adjusted the lights.

"Isn't Keith going to serenade us?" Katey inquired, humorously, as I moved his resin head to the sofa and buried it under a pillow.

"There will be no witnesses to our indiscretions," I replied, adding a second pillow to make sure.

"Can we have some music anyway?"

I checked what we had on the player by the kitchen. "If you're after AC/DC or Aerosmith I suspect you'll be out of luck," I said.

"Any drug-addled sleep-deprived groupie-magnet noise will do."

"Cliff Richard and the Shadows," I replied. "Steeleye Span. I think Mitch has been at the programming. Dusty Springfield."

"Dusty would be nice."

I set it up—*The Very Best of…* One of my contributions to our on-board entertainment.

And to the driving beat of "I Only Want to Be With You" we toasted the bus, the tour, and the damned River Cam.

#

My phone was back in my hotel room, drying out in the rice in the bathroom sink. I was half-expecting Katey to get a text from Freddie or mum, interrupting our dinner to inform us that a missive had arrived with more dire predictions of danger.

But—nothing.

After finishing off the fabulous candied citrus and clotted cream tart, we repaired upstairs to the Artist's Bedroom, where Katey surprised me another new pair of knickers, and the black see-through nightie she'd been promising me.

I dimmed the lights and Katey switched off her phone. And then I pretended I was an outrageously wild rock star with a huge cock and an entourage that was bankrupting me, and she pretended she was a free spirit named Rainbow, rebelling from everything her parents held sacred, and we did our best to emulate what they might have got up to in 1979, minus the drugs, the booze and the legendary plaster cast trophy.

After which we fell into a genuinely exhausted sleep, wrapped in each other's arms, and we stayed that way until about 2 a.m., when I was woken by a persistent bell and the ear-piercing scream of approaching sirens.

"Bloody hell," I said, sitting up.

Beside me, Katey stirred. "What?" she said, sleepily.

"I think it's the fire alarm in the hotel."

I clambered out of bed. Katey took a little longer.

I got dressed quickly and ran downstairs and outside. By then, Katey was right behind me.

It was a chilly night—we could see our breaths. Everyone who was staying at the hotel had gathered in the parking lot, very near to where the bus was, and they were milling about in whatever they'd gone to bed in.

It reminded me of that scene in *Lost in Translation* where Bill Murray and Scarlett Johansson join all the hotel guests in the street in their nightclothes. In the film it turns out to be a false alarm.

It turned out to be a false alarm in this case, too. We found mum, Bob, Beth, Mitch and Rolly standing in a tight huddle with their autumn jackets thrown over their night things.

Bob had bare legs under a dressing gown. Beth was in leopard-print leggings.

Mitch was wearing what looked like a frock coat over his blue and white striped pyjamas.

Rolly was in fleecy orange sleep pants.

And my mother was wearing a proper long nightgown and, displaying complete clarity of mind in the face of a dire emergency, was clutching her handbag and another one containing her laptop.

In another huddle, nearby, were Tejo, Kato, Neil, Beaky and our two catering ladies. They were all fully dressed and looked like they hadn't been to bed at all—which wouldn't have surprised me in the least.

And in between the two groups was Freddie, wearing fuzzy bear claw slippers and baggy tie-dyed Aladdin pants, her wild black hair falling all over the place. She was, of course, talking animatedly into her phone.

"Oh yes," my mother said, eyeing me and Katey. "And where have you two materialized from? Certainly not the hotel—I banged on your door on the way out."

"They were on the bus," Mitch said, much amused. "I only wish I still had their kind of energy."

"Or pull," Rolly added, as I dug into my pocket for my fresh packet of ciggies, and lit up.

It took the fire brigade half an hour to determine there was no fire, to reset the alarms and put the lift back in working order.

In *Lost in Translation*, Bill and Scarlett repair to the hotel's bar to share a few intimate drinks. We contemplated it, but decided not to—mostly because the bar was closed. And even if it had been open, this was Scholarly England, and I wasn't sure Cambridge decorum would allow us to troop in wearing our PJ's. Three-quarters of the band was over the age of seventy, anyway, and I suspect they'd have much preferred to be back in their beds than downing a pint.

And I really wasn't feeling all that well.

Katey and I collected the detritus of our dinner and tidied the bus, locked up and went back to my room. I wrote a note to remind myself to return the keys to Beaky. I checked my phone—there were still a few droplets of water behind the glass screen—best to leave it alone 'til morning—and reburied it in the rice in the sink.

I had developed a sore throat. I'd tried to ignore it for most of the evening, but now I could feel my sinuses beginning to block up as well. And that zappy feeling was back—the one I got when my immune system was gearing up for another fight.

I sprayed some Otrivine up my nose and sucked on some zinc lozenges.

And I would have happily collapsed into bed with Katey and fallen asleep until noon, but it was not to be. Just as I switched off the light, I heard a loud pounding on my door.

"Jason! I need you!"

It was my mother. And she didn't sound happy.

I pulled on the white dressing gown the hotel had thoughtfully provided for my personal use, and unlocked the door.

"Someone's been in my room. They've taken my clock."

"Are you sure?"

"Of course I'm sure," my mother said, as if I was daft.

Katey was looking at me questioningly from the bed.

"Hang on," I said. "I'll get dressed."

CHAPTER THIRTEEN

"It's a special alarm clock," I said to Katey, pulling on my jeans and t-shirt. "Dad gave it to her for her birthday. She always took it along on tour when he was alive. And after he died…"

I stopped.

"What?" said Katey.

I laced up my trainers. No socks.

"The clock's hands are set permanently to the exact time that he died," I said, kissing her. "Back soon."

#

My mother's room was just down the hallway from mine, and it featured a balcony that overlooked the same tidily-manicured grassy park. The balcony had a glass door made up of small square window panels separated by wooden cross-pieces. The glass in the window panel next to the door handle had been smashed in.

"Don't touch that," I advised.

"Yes, Chief Inspector," my mother replied. "Fingerprints. Hairs. Body fluids. I know you've passed the course."

"I was more concerned about you cutting yourself," I said, because most of the sharp shards of glass had fallen on the floor beside the bed. "And mind your feet."

"I'm not sure which upsets me more. The absolute gall of someone helping themselves to my clock, or the fact that they managed to get into my room at all, while I wasn't here."

"I'm glad you weren't here," I said.

"I'd have given them a good bollocking and sent them swiftly on their way," mum said.

"That's what I mean. I'd have feared for their safety. Have you reported it to Reception?"

"I have. While I was waiting for you. The Night Manager is on his way up."

"And Freddie?"

"Not yet."

I fired off a text, using mum's phone.

Two minutes later, there was a knock on the door.

Freddie was still wearing her baggy Aladdin pants and bear claw slippers, and her wild black hair was still attempting to emulate weightlessness in space. "What's happened now?"

I showed her the damage to the balcony door. "And they've taken mum's clock."

Freddie knew how important the clock was to my mother, as did everyone in the band and the crew. Even our fans knew about it. But there was something more that absolutely nobody else was aware of. Marking the exact time of his passing wasn't my mother's only memorial to my dad. Inside the clock were his ashes. Not all of them—she'd scattered most of him elsewhere, including the flower garden behind their house in Hertfordshire. But she'd kept back a tiny amount which she'd sealed up inside the clock, after she'd removed all of its workings.

The thief had made off with something more valuable than they actually knew.

Freddie let the Night Manager into the room.

His name tag said Albert and he looked like someone who would rather have been a Day Manager. His blazer seemed very temporary. Sleeves too long and shoulders too wide. He obviously hadn't bothered to have them altered since he wasn't planning on making Night Manager a permanent career choice.

And he really wasn't very good at sorting out what he ought to be doing next.

"Perhaps you should ring the police," Freddie suggested. "Your insurance people will want a report."

"Especially if we sue," mum added.

Albert looked extremely alarmed.

"I'll come with you," said Freddie. "Thanks to these two, I seem to be on a first name basis with most of England's constabulary."

She escorted him back downstairs.

"Did they take anything else?" I asked, looking around the room. Nothing seemed disturbed. No pulled-out drawers, no cast-aside objects. Not that mum had anything else worth stealing with her—years on the road had taught her to leave anything valuable at home and to be permanently prepared for lost luggage.

"Only the clock," mum said.

There was a Room Service card lying on her bed, the thing you leave on the outside of your door to pre-order breakfast. My mother had hung hers on the handle before she'd gone to sleep. It was still there—I'd seen it when I'd come in.

It seemed odd that there was a second one.

I picked it up.

Something was stuck to the other side.

#

The Cambridge Constabulary were on their way. And another manager—who seemed to be more senior—had taken over from Albert. His name was Robert Sharpe.

"My utmost apologies," he said. "Albert's a trainee. Perhaps you'd be more comfortable waiting downstairs in the lounge? I've arranged for some tea and biscuits."

Freddie was already down there, tucking into a pot of Earl Grey and an assortment of Bourbons, Chocolate Digestives and Jammy Dodgers.

I showed her the breakfast card, making sure I held it by its edges. I'd already committed the cardinal sin of handling evidence from a crime scene. I probably shouldn't even have removed it from the room.

What had been pasted to the other side was a piece of paper with a typed message.

Freddie read it aloud. "'Hope Jason enjoyed his plunge. Tick. Tock. Counting down.'"

She looked at me.

"Counting down to what?"

"God knows," I said. "But again—meticulous advance planning. Whoever broke into the room left it as their calling card. And they knew what they were going to steal. It's an inside job."

I took a photo of the note and then carefully put it to one side for the police.

"When Kezia Heron approached us after the show in Sheffield," I said, "she wanted to speak to both of us, not just mum. I was walking beside mum when the Mad Hatter came down in Leeds. The message on mum's phone mentioned me. The flat tires on the bus would have impacted all of us if they'd caused an accident but the note the priest delivered mentioned my name, again. And then yesterday, I was attacked on the river. I think I've been the target all along. And not mum at all."

#

I was very surprised—but extremely pleased—to discover that the Cambridge Constabulary had sent along Constables Tucker and Fingal to investigate the stolen alarm clock.

"Shift work," Constable Fingal explained. "We were doing our late turns the other day."

"And now we're on nights," said Constable Tucker.

It was about 5 a.m. by then. Freddie had gone back to bed. My mother was on her third pot of tea, but I could tell she was fading. I'd resorted to my cold meds—the ones that promised to be "non-drowsy."

"Biccie?" mum said, offering the plate.

"Thank you," said Constable Tucker. I felt like we were old friends.

"Three for three," I said, showing her the note on the flip side of the breakfast card.

After we gave our respective statements—and Constable Fingal had sealed the breakfast card into a plastic evidence bag—Robert accompanied us back upstairs to mum's room.

Both police officers examined the broken glass in the balcony door, and then opened the door and stepped outside.

I followed them out.

"Your thief looks to have been quite agile," Constable Fingal remarked, squinting up at the roof.

I didn't disagree. But then, our thief might well have been the same person who'd managed to climb onto the parapet over the stage door in Leeds and shoved the Mad Hatter earthward. And the same person who'd crawled under our bus in Norwich to let the air out of the tires. And paddled away swiftly after whacking me behind the knees with their oar on the River Cam.

"We'll have someone come down to assess the room for forensic opportunities," Constable Tucker said, to mum. "It would obviously be better if you could move to different accommodations for the duration of your stay."

"I'll see to it," Robert replied.

"Do you mind if I take my frocks with me?" my mother inquired. "I'd love to leave them behind for your forensics chaps. But I'm touring with my band and I'm living out of two suitcases and I've got a show to put on tonight."

#

With mum safely transferred to a different room, I went downstairs with Robert, Constable Tucker and Constable Fingal to have a look at the hotel's CCTV.

I probably shouldn't have been there. But they didn't ask me to leave.

And we didn't see anything—or anyone—unusual on the top floor hallway cams.

We did see the mass exodus of guests when the fire alarm went off. Including everyone in the band—Bob and Beth, Mitch, Rolly and mum—making a bee-line for the nearest stairs.

We ran through the footage that covered the next hour. Nobody else came out of my mother's room. And then, after the fire brigade left, everyone trooped back in and disappeared behind their respective doors.

"In and out by way of the roof and the balcony," I said. "A very fit individual, indeed. Do you know which alarm was pulled?"

"I can tell you," said Robert, consulting his computer. "Yes. It was the one on the second floor."

We had a look, focusing in on the exact time that the alarm was activated. There were two cameras. The first caught the back of someone in baggy trousers and a blue hoodie, wearing a backpack, walking along the empty hallway to the fire alarm, pulling it, and then opening the door to the adjacent stairwell and disappearing.

The other camera was mounted at the other end of the hallway, facing in the other direction. We saw the same person, this time full-on, emerging from the stairwell at that end and walking towards the fire alarm, then pulling it. But their hood was up and their head was deliberately lowered—as if they knew they were being watched.

I couldn't tell if it was a man or a woman—and I didn't think Constables Tucker and Fingal knew either—though I was prepared to guess it was probably a female. Women have a lower centre of balance than men, and wider hips. When they walk, they have a slight horizontal swaying motion. It's unconscious. They also have shorter strides.

"I don't suppose there's CCTV in the stairwells," I said.

"Sorry," said Robert. "No. Some areas aren't covered. The roof. The cellar. The stairs."

"Where did she come from?" I wondered. "One of the guest rooms?"

We examined all of the footage from all of the hotel's hallway cameras on all three floors. We went back to midnight, two hours before the alarm was pulled.

Nobody bearing any kind of resemblance to the woman in the blue hoodie showed up. The hotel was about fifty percent occupied, but it was late at night, and most of the guests were already in their beds.

Again, I spotted everyone from the Figs on the third floor, and, down on the second floor, the crew: Beaky, Freddie, Kato, Neil, Tejo, Janice and Mary. They all appeared to be having a party in Kato's room. There was a lot of coming and going.

"So we don't know where she came from," I said. "She pulls the alarm. She goes back into the stairwell—I'm assuming the stairs go up to the roof?"

I could tell I was becoming a bit of an irritant.

"They do," Robert said, patiently. "Both sets of stairs go up into the hotel's attic and from there, you can access the roof through a single door."

"Is that door locked?"

"It's locked from the outside," Robert said, "but the inside's got a standard panic bar. The same as the stairwell fire exit doors on the ground floor."

"So after she pulls the alarm, she knows there are cams on each floor, so she runs up to the roof…across to where she knows my mother's room is, climbs down, breaks the window, steal the clock, leaves the note…then goes out the same way she came in. How does she get back inside if the roof door from the attic locks automatically?"

"She propped it open," Constable Tucker said, with a shrug. "Knapsack."

We ran the footage again from each of the floors, this time looking for someone exiting the stairs. But nobody in a blue hoodie and baggy trousers emerged from any of the stairwell doors.

There were cameras outside the hotel, though, and, providentially, two of them were aimed in the general direction of the fire exits.

"There she is," I said.

Again, she seemed to know where those cameras were. She'd come out of the exit with the last of the hotel's guests. But instead of following them to the hotel's muster point in the parking lot, she'd abruptly turned and walked away in the opposite direction.

The only new thing I could tell from her appearance was that she was carrying something in her hand—no doubt my mother's alarm clock.

"Can we run these exterior camera feeds backwards?" I asked.

We did.

"There," I said. "Look."

Ten minutes before the fire alarm was pulled, the camera showed the woman in the blue hoodie walking up to the exit door. The door was pushed open from the inside. All we could see was the helpful hand. Which might have belonged to a female too, as the hand seemed smaller than a man's, and the fingers were definitely shorter and more slender. The camera's resolution and the lighting wasn't good enough for me to be able to tell if the back of the hand had any hair. But it seemed to me there was an absence of varnish on the nails, and there were no telltale rings or other items of jewellery.

The woman in the blue hoodie slipped inside. And the door slammed shut.

"She definitely had an accomplice inside the hotel," said Constable Tucker. "An employee. Possibly someone who cleaned the rooms and would have known about the clock."

"Except," I said, "we only got here yesterday afternoon."

"Bed turndown service?" Constable Fingal supposed.

"I think it's someone who knew about mum's clock well before now," I said. "Someone who's staying in the same hotels we are. I think it's one of the fans."

CHAPTER FOURTEEN

I'd wanted to go over all of the CCTV footage again, from all of the hotel's cameras, but both Robert Sharpe and Constable Tucker reminded me that we'd already been over the floor and exit cams twice, and we'd seen no one—other than the woman in the blue hoodie—who looked remotely suspicious.

"What about fingerprints?" I said. "That hand on the fire door's panic bar."

"A long shot at best," said Constable Tucker. "You know as well as I do how many people touched that on their way out of the hotel tonight."

She was right, and I was grasping at straws.

"It is fairly late," said Constable Fingal, adopting a slightly more conciliatory tone. "And I'm sure you're missing your sleep, Jason. Leave it with us. We'll go over it all again later and let you know if we spot this woman—or whoever was helping her— anywhere else in the hotel."

"And we will have a look for fingerprints on the second floor stairwell doors, as well as the roof exit," Constable Tucker promised.

It was nearly 5 a.m. I went back to my room reluctantly. I really didn't think, in the grand scheme of things, that this investigation was going to end up being high on their list of priorities. Aside from the note, which had convinced me beyond doubt that this was all part of a larger plan, the truth was, this was a simple break and enter. And the only thing of questionable value that had been taken was my mother's alarm clock.

It wasn't as if anyone had been murdered.

#

I woke up eight hours later to full-on congestion, a cough, a spinning head, and lungs that hurt whenever I breathed in.

This was not a good sign.

When I was fourteen, I'd had a bad cold and a temperature, and I'd insisted on going to school. It was winter and there was snow on the ground, and I'd run part of the way to catch up with some mates, and that had been my downfall.

The bad cold quickly developed into pneumonia and I ended up in the hospital.

"I don't suppose you have a thermometer," Katey said, feeling my forehead.

"Not part of my touring kit," I replied.

"I'll pop out and buy you one. You really ought to stay put until you're needed for your sound check."

I knew I ought to listen to her advice. The health of band members was something you always had to keep on top of—especially with half the group being of a "certain age." We really didn't want to let our audience down. Some of them would be travelling hours to get there—and a lot of them, I knew, were long-term fans, going right back to the start of the Figs. This might be their last opportunity to see the band, ever.

I waited 'til Katey had left and then I rang Room Service and mum, in that order.

My mother arrived first.

I staggered out of bed, wrapping myself up in my white dressing gown so that I was decently attired when I let her in.

"You look dreadful," she observed, and it wasn't a comment on my fashion sense.

"I feel dreadful," I said.

Mum dragged a chair over to my bedside as I crawled back between the sheets. "Neil should have a look at you."

She was already texting him.

"I spoke to Rick Redding," I said.

"And…?"

"He's in Portugal. He hasn't got any long-standing resentments against the Figs. Or me. Or you. But he did suggest I talk to you about Paisley Ascot."

"Good God." Mum was surprised. "I haven't thought about them in years."

"There isn't much information online. I've looked. Why did you and dad split from Annie Hobbs?"

"We didn't. Annie walked out on us."

"Why?"

Mum placed both of her hands on her lap and interlaced her fingers. She looked at me. "Because your father turned out to be far more interested in me than he was in her."

"Ah," I said. "Fair enough."

"They were a couple long before I was invited to join."

"Who invited you?"

"Your father. I was a bit like Cilla Black—I was working in one of the music clubs—I was the coat-check girl—and once a week the resident band invited people to come onstage and show off their talent. So I got up and sang. Tony was in the audience that night and afterwards he approached me with his idea."

"His idea that he hadn't bothered to discuss with Annie," I guessed.

"Of course not. Annie was perfectly happy to keep Paisley Ascot as a duo. She had lofty ambitions. The trouble was, she was otherwise singularly untalented. She could bang a tambourine and she looked good onstage, but that was it. Tony was her ticket to ride. And Tony knew that if they were ever going to get anywhere, they needed to add a third person who could actually do something useful."

"Which was you."

"Which was me."

My lunch arrived: macaroni and cheese with a green leaf salad and toasted focaccia, and a pot of Earl Grey tea. My mother tucked the pillows up behind me. I felt like I was fourteen again.

"And was Annie happy with the arrangement?"

"No, she was not. But your father convinced her."

"And then the inevitable happened."

"Of course it did," my mother replied.

"What happened to Annie after the split? I tried a general search but her name didn't come up anywhere."

"No idea. She did come to see us after we'd put the Figs together. We invited her backstage and introduced her around. She sent me a few letters after that. And we had some conversations on the phone. But we eventually fell out of touch."

"How old would she be now?" I asked.

"She's a couple of years younger than me. But certainly not in any state to be clambering across rooftops and onto hotel balconies."

I smiled.

"We're looking for a much younger woman," I said.

I poured myself a cup of tea and added milk and sugar. Delicious. How can anyone drink tea without milk and sugar? It's barbaric.

"Did Annie know about your clock?"

"She was there," said my mother. "We were celebrating my birthday in a restaurant—just the three of us. Tony gave it to me, all gift-wrapped, pretty paper, huge bow, and a beautiful card. That was the last straw for Annie. That was the night she walked out."

#

Katey's trek to the nearest Boots resulted in a high-tech digital thermometer that informed me my temperature was 39.6°C—and Neil showed up about ten minutes after that to confirm my diagnosis.

"Your pneumonia could have been caused by any number of things," he said.

"Notwithstanding the accidental inhalation of half of the River Cam," I replied.

"Including that. And based on your history it could be a virus rather than something bacterial. In which case a course of antibiotics won't help at all. I shouldn't do it, but I'll prescribe them anyway—just to cover all the bases. And the pineapple cure for your congestion."

Every musician knows what the pineapple cure is. It involves ten pineapples (preferably organic), thoroughly blended into ten pints of pure juice. The active ingredient's bromelain and it's famous for breaking down mucus. Singers often ask for it in their riders.

I hoped Janice and Mary were up for a pineapple hunt and that the food markets of Cambridge were going to be able to oblige.

"Stay in bed," Neil said. "Drink plenty of fluids. Cut out the smokes. And with any luck we'll see you this evening."

Katey made herself useful once again by taking Neil's

prescription for antibiotics back to Boots and waiting for it to be filled.

I retrieved my phone out of the rice mound in the bathroom sink and called Kato.

"And what do *you* want?" she said.

"Would you mind setting out a stool for me onstage tonight? Aside from the fact that my head's in a fog, both of my legs are killing me. I don't think I'll make it through the show if I have to be on my feet the entire time.

"If I must," she said, bad-temperedly.

"No sabotaging my leads," I added.

"You're bloody wireless, mate. Fat chance."

I logged onto Instagram and answered a couple of public postings from followers who'd been concerned that they hadn't seen anything new from me for more than twenty-four hours.

Where are you, Jason? You have us all worried!

It's not like you to be AWOL like this. We've missed your food updates! What did you have for dinner last night?

My sister lives in Cambridge and she heard about a fire alarm at one of the hotels. Hope that's not where you're staying…

I posted a picture of the view from my bed—my feet under the covers, my laptop bag, the window and the curtains.

Slightly under the weather, I wrote, *and saving my energy for tonight's show.*

And then I switched over to my private messages.

Jilly, I wrote. *I'm not well. It seems I've developed pneumonia.*

My love, she wrote back, almost immediately. *I wasn't wrong to be concerned about the state of your health!*

You weren't wrong, I agreed.

And then I told her about punting on the river with Katey, and about the two people in the canoe. And the fire alarm and mum's clock being stolen and the note they'd left behind. The footage we'd viewed from the hotel's CCTV. And Rick Redding. And Paisley Ascot. And Annie.

At the end of it all, my fingers were quite worn out.

My goodness, said Jilly. *You have been busy.*

Who knew that Cambridge would be so eventful? I replied.

You must ask Lynn about the canoe, Jilly said.

Why?

Because she was there.

In the canoe??

No, Jilly said. *But nearby.*
How do you know that?
I was watching, my love.
Some guardian angel you are.
There was a brief moment of silence.
And then:
I'll forgive your irritation. I know you're ill.
If you were there you could have done something, I replied.
I did, Jilly said.
What did you do?
I waited.
Silence.

#

Katey came back with my antibiotics, which I dutifully downed.

"I've got another mission for you," I said. "Those two people in the canoe came at us from the opposite direction. They had to have got their boat from a place on the other side of Magdalene Bridge. Coleridge rents out canoes from their station there, but so do two other firms."

"And you want me to do some sleuthing to try and find out who they rented from."

"I have no faith whatsoever in the Cambridge Constabulary," I replied.

"I think I can manage it," Katey said, giving me a kiss. "One person in a blue hoodie, the other wearing black. Their names should be on the rental agreement. Piece of cake."

#

I woke up a couple of hours later, feeling better. The antibiotics were doing the trick, I thought. Bacterial pneumonia, then. Not viral.

I rang Neil to confirm his diagnosis. I promised I wouldn't smoke. And then I phoned my mother.

"Stay in bed until we actually need you onstage," she said. "Beaky can stand in for you at the sound check."

#

I went back to sleep and stayed that way until half-past six, when Katey woke me up with pan fried chicken and wild mushrooms in a white wine cream sauce from a little bistro down the road, and the details of what she'd discovered about the canoe rental.

"It wasn't Coleridge," she said, dragging a chair over to the bed and consulting the notes she'd typed into her phone. "There's another firm that only does canoes, no punts. Balfour Boats. Ninety minutes for £35. Students and seniors welcome, Rugby Club members…YHA…" She paused to help herself to a forkful of my chicken. "Balfour was the last of the three that I checked, but one of the attendants remembered renting the canoe out to a woman in a blue hoodie yesterday because they'd only had three bookings all afternoon."

"Well done," I said. "You're wonderful."

"Thank you. If I ever get tired of putting bums in airline seats I might turn up as your assistant. If you ever get your license."

"Did they give you a name?"

"They did," Katey said. "Jacqueline Bolton. Does that sound familiar?"

"Not at all. Were they able to give you a description?"

"Oh yes," Katey said, her eyes positively lighting up. "Blonde hair. Mid-twenties, they thought. A bit older than your average student."

"Agile?" I guessed. "Fit? Able to leap small buildings in a single bound?"

"Sporty," Katey agreed.

"And the other person?"

"Also a woman. Not in the least athletic-looking, rather heavy, in fact, with long, dark hair."

"That's the same description the priest at Norwich gave me when I asked about the woman who'd handed him the note. My age?"

"Possibly," Katey said. "They guessed she'd be in her fifties."

"And did Jacqueline Bolton pay with a credit card?" I was hoping, if she had, I could use it to try and track down an address—amongst other things.

"Cash," said Katey. "Balfour Boats usually only accepts debit and credit cards but it was a slow day and I suppose they didn't want to turn away the business. Here's a copy of the receipt."

She held up her phone so I could see.

"Payment in full and a security deposit," I said. "Rare these days to be carrying that amount of real money around with you."

"That's what I thought. But if you really don't want to leave a paper trail…Oh…and one last thing. They didn't return the canoe. It was found abandoned about an hour later at The Mill, where you and I started out."

#

"You haven't died, then," Mitch mused, in our dressing room at the Newnham Theatre.

I'd showered and shaved and applied snail slime to my face. I'd drunk a gallon of pineapple juice. I'd eaten an entire packet of Fruit Pastilles.

Katey and I had shared a taxi from the hotel and Katey had gone off to have a pre-show drink at a little pub around the corner because the main doors to the theatre hadn't opened yet.

"Ask me again at the interval," I said.

The Newnham Theatre had undergone a complete refurb since the last time the Figs had played there. Apparently, they'd improved the sound. Rolly'd told us that, previously, there'd always been a slap-back from the back of the hall, which meant he'd heard his snare drum half a second after he'd played it, which he'd found extremely off-putting.

My own observation was that, like a lot of theatres that spend a lot of money on front of house, they never seem to do much with the dressing rooms backstage.

Ours was dingy and under-lit and it smelled of mildew.

I found the hangers where Freddie had left my stage clothes.

"You missed a very tasty lobster bisque at dinner," Mitch said.

I pulled on my freshly-washed shirt and jeans. I really hoped the stool that I'd asked Kato to set up for me was in the right place. There wasn't a lot of time for last-minute adjustments once we were onstage.

Back in the day, the Figs had begun their gigs in total darkness. Five-minute warning…mum and dad standing in the wings with the rest of the band…a pitch-black stage…house lights out. Ten seconds to adjust their eyes, and then each of the Figs had walked on and picked up their instruments and, as the lights had come up, they'd started playing.

But when you're travelling with a group of elderlies, and your tour insurance has all kinds of waivers and exclusions regarding safety, liability and risk factors, you'd best not tempt fate. Neil had therefore designed some very effective subdued lighting for our entrance, which grew in intensity as we took our places, and then the full effects cut in as we launched straight into "The Gypsy Rover."

I was lacing up my shoes—I'd chosen brown Mephisto Trevors for the tour—they have good ankle support and they're wonderful when you have to do a lot of standing and you factor in the weight of a solid body electric guitar hanging off your shoulder—when I heard a frantic hammering on the dressing room door.

"Guys!" Beth shouted. "Are you decent?"

I was decent. Bob was shirtless. Mitch was in his dressing gown and Rolly, always one to cut things fine, was still in the shower.

I opened the door.

"You'd better come to our dressing room," Beth said. "Mandy's really really sick."

#

I'm not good with people vomiting. My years on the *Sapphire* gave me some tolerance, but never enough. You can't avoid passengers getting seasick, and most of the time they have the presence of mind—and the time—to find a toilet. But accidents still happened. Sometimes right in front of me, when I was in the middle of my show in the TopDeck Lounge. And it was a struggle for me to carry on without getting sick myself.

The door to the dressing room loo was open. I heard groans and violent retching. I couldn't look.

"You ok, mum?"

"No, in all the whoreson drudges of bacon-fed knaves, I bloody well am not."

I knew things were bad if my mother was quoting Shakespeare.

She flushed the toilet and I peeked around the corner.

Mum was kneeling on the floor on a folded-up towel. She was hunched over the bowl, her forehead resting on her arm, which was braced across the seat.

I didn't dare go in. Even if it was my own mother, and she'd held my head more times than I can remember when I was a child and throwing up the remnants of something particularly gruesome like cheesy pizza with tomato sauce and chunks of mushroom and pepperoni.

"Could it have been something you ate?" Beth asked, sympathetically.

"I bloody well know it's something I ate," mum said, with a groan.

Her body was wracked by another series of spasms. I looked away.

"Bring me water. I need water."

Mary and Janice had left a flat of water bottles on the counter beside a jar of M&Ms. I tossed one of them to Beth, who had more courage than me and went in to give it to mum.

She downed a third of it in one long gulp.

I heard banging on the dressing room door.

It was Neil. "Beth texted a medical emergency," he said. "What's up?"

"Mandy can't stop being sick," Beth said, from the bathroom.

"I know these symptoms," mum said. She let out another groan. The water she'd just drunk was coming back up.

I looked away.

Beth flushed the toilet.

"Mussels," mum said, trying to catch her breath. "Allergic."

"Does she have an epi-pen?" Neil asked, his voice taking on a professional urgency.

"It's not that kind of allergy," I said, realizing what mum was referring to. "It's a sensitivity in her gut. I have the same thing. It doesn't cause anaphylactic shock. Mussels have a toxin that most people can deal with. Our bodies treat it like poison."

I was surprised that was what mum was suffering from. But we both knew the symptoms. And neither one of us would go anywhere near the offending bivalves. Not deliberately, anyway.

"Try to keep drinking the water," Neil said, quickly checking mum over. "The vomiting will stop once you're rid of the toxins—but we don't want you to rupture your esophagus in the meantime. Or pass out from dehydration."

"I really don't think I'm going to be able to go on tonight," my mother said, as I handed two more water bottles to Beth.

CHAPTER FIFTEEN

I've said this before, but on the grand scale of things that can go wrong when you're on tour with a band, having to cancel a show is right up at the top. Eleven on a scale of one to ten.

Nobody wants it to happen, whether it's for illness or technical issues or something else. Especially when it's extremely last-minute and you don't have time to reschedule the gig before you announce the bad news to your audience, most of whom are already in their seats and waiting for the lights to go down.

I know from personal experience that if you're ill, you'll do everything in your power to deal with your symptoms—including ignoring them and hoping they'll go away—until the last possible moment. And even if you're hovering on death's doorstep, you'll struggle to go on—like I was—stuffed with meds and pineapple juice and subjected to so much steam my hair was beginning to look like one of Katey's shower scrunchies.

But, with my mother and her food poisoning, it just wasn't possible.

Freddie had now joined us in the dressing room.

"Are you certain?" she said. "Are you absolutely certain?"

"Absolutely certain," I replied.

"Lecherous obscene and greasy tallow-catch certain," mum echoed, from the toilet.

"Doctor's orders," Neil added.

"I'll ring Colin," Freddie said.

It wasn't just a simple case of calling off the show. Our manager would have to get in touch with our promoter, and they'd have to sort out the financial hit the theatre was going to take from our cancellation. With any luck they'd only charge us their out-of-pocket costs for the night, especially if we could work out a date when we could come back and do a make-up.

And there was always that insurance that we'd all had to have medical examinations for. I would argue that unintended mussels ingestion was very definitely an unforeseen circumstance.

Freddie went to break the bad news to the rest of the crew while I walked back to our dressing room to let Mitch, Bob and Rolly know.

After which, I texted Katey.

And then, someone had to go out and tell the audience.

"I think it should be all of us," Mitch said.

We agreed, so at 8:30 p.m., Rolly, Beth, Bob, Mitch and I walked out onto the stage to make the announcement.

There was a huge round of applause from the sell-out crowd, who were obviously expecting "The Gypsy Rover."

But the house lights stayed on.

I lifted my mic out of its clip on the stand.

"We're terribly sorry," I said, aware of just how rough my own voice sounded. "But it seems Mandy—my mum—has come down with a serious case of food poisoning."

There were gasps from the audience. I could see their faces for a change—Neil wasn't at his desk, blinding me with his spots.

"She'll be all right," I said. "We're travelling with a medic."

"At our age it's written into the contract," Mitch quipped, to laughter.

"Unfortunately," I said, "she's not well enough to perform, and since she's more or less an integral part of the Figs…I'm afraid we're going to have to cancel tonight's show."

There were disappointed groans. Some more sympathetic gasps followed by scattered applause and a few people shouting, "Get well soon, Mandy!"

"If you hang onto your tickets," I said, "I'm almost certain we'll be back in a couple of weeks, after we've had a chance to reschedule. As long as…" I stopped. My brain had gone blank. I couldn't, for the life of me, remember the name of the venue. Hello Cleveland. "As long as the theatre's available," I said, quickly.

All in all, they took it well.

But then, we weren't the Sex Pistols or The Clash and our followers weren't a mob of angry yobs yelling for Maggie Thatcher's head.

Everyone filed out of the theatre in an orderly fashion. And there was absolutely no spitting.

#

Back in the dressing room, Freddie'd arranged for a taxi and Neil was getting ready to go along to make sure my mother was safely put to bed.

Mum had made her way from the toilet to a chair, where she now slumped, wrapped in a blanket, waiting to be helped outside. I knew her head had to be pounding. That was the worst of the symptoms after the stomach spasms and the vomiting stopped: a headache on par with the worst migraine you could ever imagine.

"I'm so sorry," she whispered. "How were they?"

"Very sympathetic," I replied. "And they wish you well."

"They're lovely people, our fans."

"Newnham Theatre," Mitch said, humorously, giving me a poke.

"Cambridge," Rolly added.

At least we hadn't got lost backstage.

"Can you remember what you had for dinner?" I asked mum.

"Spinach salad," she said, hazily. "There were some green beans…I had those…and the lobster bisque."

The handwritten menu for that evening's meal was sitting next to the jar of M&M's. I scanned over the offerings.

A spinach salad with dried figs, ricotta cheese and a bacon vinaigrette dressing. Green beans sautéed with lemon, parsley, butter and almonds.

Janice and Mary hadn't included a rundown of all of the ingredients in the lobster bisque…but I was willing to bet that was the simmering gun.

Freddie's phone played a few seconds of "Roving Minstrel"—her ring-tone for texts. "Taxi's here," she said.

Neil looked at me. "Did you want to come along too, Jason? An early night wouldn't do you any harm."

"I've got a few things I need to sort out," I replied. "But I promise I'll go straight to bed after that."

#

The original catering firm that we'd hired for the tour was called Up the Hill. The two principals were a couple of ladies, Jack and Jill, and they'd joined us towards the end of our rehearsals in Stoneford. But they'd had to pull out at the last minute because of a family emergency.

They'd scrambled and found us a replacement—Mary and Janice from Roadworks Catering—and we couldn't have been happier. They were every bit as good as Up the Hill. Actually they were probably a bit better—and they didn't charge as much.

By the time I located Mary and Janice in the big common room where they'd served dinner that evening, I'd been joined by Katey.

"Lovely speech," she said. "But your security bloke didn't want to let me backstage. I was apparently lacking the requisite lanyard."

"Sorry," I said. "They should have messaged me—we're supposed to escort all our guests. How did you get past them?"

"I said I was Rainbow, your favourite groupie," she said, "and I described the inside of your tour bus, the colour of your toothbrush and how big your cock was."

"They still shouldn't have let you in," I said.

Roadworks' collapsible tables and chairs had all been neatly folded and stacked. Tablecloths in bags, ready to be washed and pressed. Disposable stuff consigned to the rubbish and the compostables appropriately collected.

Mary and Janice were sharing a sofa, chowing down on their own dinner, waiting for their pots, pans and utensils to cycle through the little portable dishwasher they'd hooked up to a sink in the corner.

"Mussels!" said Janice, after I'd told her what had caused my mother's gastric distress. "There's no way on earth that lobster bisque had mussels in it. We'd never have put them in—we know you're allergic to them. And your mum. It's in the notes."

"We made that bisque ourselves from absolute scratch this afternoon," Mary added.

"Do you work from a recipe?" I asked.

"Yes, of course." Mary got up to find the laminated sheet of paper she kept in a three-ring binder. "Here you are."

It seemed pretty standard. Lobster bisque for twenty—to accommodate guests and second helpings. Stock made out of the tails, the usual stuff that went into the soup itself—garlic, flour, cream, tomato paste, spices, carrots, onions, celery…

"And you didn't add any other seafood?"

"Absolutely not," Janice assured me.

"Have you got any left?" I asked.

Mary held up her bowl. "Just this."

"Mind if I take a few spoonfuls?"

Mary went hunting for a suitable container and came back with a paper cup, into which she poured a tiny portion of the soup from her bowl.

She handed the cup to me, and I drank it down.

"Quicker and cheaper than a forensics lab," I said.

#

A little group of fans had congregated outside the theatre's stage door.

"Jason!" It was Lynn, with a very worried look on her face. "Is your mum all right? We saw her being helped into a taxi. She looked awful."

"Just a touch of food poisoning," I said, repeating the official line. "She'll be OK tomorrow. Oxford's still a go."

"Please give her my best wishes."

"I will," I promised.

Lynn hesitated, as if she wanted to tell me something else. I remembered what Jilly had said.

"I wonder," I said, carefully, "if you might know anything about what happened to me yesterday on the river."

Lynn looked distinctly uncomfortable. Her eyes darted to the other fans, who were lingering nearby.

"Let's go over there," I suggested, nodding at a corner of the little alleyway, next to an adjacent building. "It's quieter."

Lynn followed Katey and me to the darkened doorway. A street light shone down on us, making the area look like the cover of a noir crime novel. I half-expected a mysterious woman in a fedora, raincoat and fishnet stockings to step out of the night with an unlit cigarette, asking for a match.

"You went punting," Lynn said.

I knew I'd put her on the spot.

"Did you see us?" I asked.

Lynn nodded.

"Where were you?"

"I was on the bridge."

"Which one? Magdalene?"

Lynn nodded again.

"And did you see what happened just before we got to the bridge?"

That look of unease again. "You fell into the river."

"Actually, I was attacked. By two women in a canoe."

"Yes," Lynn said, after a moment.

"So you saw them hit me."

Lynn nodded a third time. Reluctantly.

"Do you know who they were?"

Lynn shook her head.

"I have a name. Jacqueline Bolton."

A moment's hesitation. Then: "I don't know who she is. I'm so sorry."

I didn't believe her.

"I'm really sorry, Jason—I must go. I'm really glad you're all right. All the best to your mum."

#

"She's embarrassed you caught her stalking you," Katey said, as we walked around the corner in search of a taxi.

"You're not wrong. But the name Jacqueline Bolton did mean something to her."

I stopped. My insides were beginning to cramp up. First signs.

"Are you all right?" Katey asked.

There was no mistaking the absolute knowledge that my stomach was getting ready to expel everything it contained. I was starting to sweat. And my mouth was filling with saliva. And that was definitely a headache beginning behind my eyes.

I couldn't prevent the spasm. I panicked, pressing my hand over my mouth, but projectile vomit's one of those things you really can't hold back. It seeks another path. And I really didn't want it coming out of my nose.

I staggered over to the gutter, thankful it was dark and the street lights right there weren't overly bright and nobody, as far as I could see, had their phones out, ready to sell my picture to the highest bidder with a lurid headline: *Stewed Figs Frontman Spews All.*

#

The taxi got us back to the hotel in under five minutes. I bolted upstairs to my room while Katey paid the driver. I landed in the loo just in time to make another contribution to the sewers of Cambridge.

"I'd hate to have seen what would have happened if you'd had an entire bowlful of the stuff," Katey said, closing the door to our room.

My head was killing me. I was shivering and shaky. I swished some peppermint mouthwash around and found some ibuprofen. I grabbed a bottle of water from the bedside table.

"Somebody knew both me and my mother were allergic to mussels," I said.

"And they deliberately added it to the stock? It's not looking good for Mary and Janice."

"I don't think they had any idea. You saw them—they were shocked. And adamant they hadn't added anything that wasn't in the recipe. On top of which, mussels aren't something you can just pop incongruously into a pot. They're very distinctive. Even without their shells. My mother would have noticed them immediately."

"Not if they were put into a blender and processed into a liquid," Katey said, making me feel even more ill.

I looked up Janice's number.

We were a small enough group that Mary and Janice could usually handle the shopping, the prep, the cooking and the cleanup themselves. But when we'd played Birmingham, we'd hosted a group of music students who'd been studying Celtic influences on modern pop. Bob had invited them—he'd been a guest lecturer on their course before he'd joined our tour.

And because of the additional guests, our caterers had needed to called in a couple of locals to help out with the extra work.

"Just out of interest," I asked, after Janice had answered, "did you have anyone else helping you out tonight?"

I put my phone on speaker so that Katey could listen in.

"No," Janice said, "but Jackie from Up the Hill popped in to say hello. We had no idea she was coming…she obviously talked her way past Security."

"Jackie from Up the Hill," I repeated, looking at Katey.

"Jacqueline."

"That's her, yes."

"Her last name's not Bolton, by any chance…?"

"It is, yes," Janice said. "Jackie Bolton. Why?"

CHAPTER SIXTEEN

"How long have you known Jackie Bolton?" I asked.

"Not a long time," Janice replied. "And not very well either, if I'm honest. I'm friends with Gillian…Jill. We met at catering school."

I was lying on the bed, swigging water as if my life depended on it. The ibuprofen hadn't cut in yet. My head was splitting. My insides felt like they'd been twisted in two. But at least I'd stopped being sick.

"And when you replaced Up the Hill on our tour…they gave you handover notes?"

"Yes. Because we came on board at the last minute, we didn't actually have time to do our own prep—so we took everything over from them. Planned menus for the entire itinerary, the lot."

"I don't suppose you'd know whether Bolton is Jackie's birth name or a married name."

"I don't, Jason, I'm really sorry."

"Have you got her phone number?"

"Hang on two ticks." Janice was looking something up. "I don't have Jackie's, but this is Gillian's."

#

Most of the firms that cater music tours are big. And well-established. They've been around for decades and have a wealth of hard-boiled experience under their belts.

Up the Hill was small and relatively new. My mother was the one who'd suggested them to Freddie. And Freddie was the one who'd actually booked them.

I propped myself up with pillows and went online to look for some background before I actually called Gillian.

I started with Companies House, which is the government website that lists all of the pertinent details about every firm that incorporates itself legally in the UK. For absolutely no upfront money, you can get the registered address and date of incorporation (although most of the time the address belongs to a chartered accountant), current and resigned officers, insolvency information, the lot.

So, there they were, Up the Hill. Incorporated in 2016. Only one officer, Gillian Clyde. Filed all of their accounts on time. No issues with any of their finances.

And no mention of Jackie Bolton.

I located Up the Hill's website. I clicked on tabs and scrolled through the usual preambles about inspired and healthy food options, understanding the rigours of the road, skills in cooking styles and dealing with dietary preferences and riders (*six pounds of stemless carrots for juicing, three cases of melon-flavour Gatorade, absolutely no furry fruits…*). I finally found a page that included a write-up and a headshot of Gillian.

I vaguely remembered her from Stoneford. She and her partner had joined us during the last few days of our rehearsals, but I didn't recall seeing Jackie at all.

Gillian looked about thirty. She had brown hair and a nice smile. She had Professional Chef diplomas from Westminster Kingsway College and had got a couple of years' experience with two other catering firms before deciding to set up on her own.

"I like this," Katey said, leaning over the bed so she could see the screen. "Gillian is an enthusiastic lifelong learner who decided to embrace catering because 'food is fundamental to our very existence and the creation of a sublime eating experience is the sensory glue that binds us together in perfect love.' I bet she didn't write that herself."

"Do you find yourself drawn to my sensory glue when I cook us a spag bol?" I asked.

"Depends how much red wine you put into it," Katey replied, as I dialled up Gillian on my phone and put her on the speaker.

She answered immediately. "Is this the same Jason who's currently on tour with Figgis Green?"

"It is," I confirmed.

"I was so upset when we couldn't go with you. Though, of course, my family had to come first. How's the tour?"

"Actually," I said, "we had to cancel tonight's show. My mother ate something she shouldn't have."

"No!" Gillian's reaction sounded genuine enough. "What happened?"

"It seems some mussels found their way into the lobster bisque."

"But mussels were in the notes, Jason. For both of you. I remember because it was such an unusual allergy. And so specific. Shellfish, yes, that's really common. But you're OK with shrimp and lobster and even clams and scallops. It's only the mussels that make you ill."

"Yes, Janice and Mary confirmed they knew all about it. I'm not blaming them. Someone else came by to visit them this afternoon while they were doing the prep. It looks like it was Jackie Bolton."

There was silence.

And then: "I don't understand, Jason."

"Jackie knew about our allergy to mussels."

"Yes, of course. We reviewed the notes together just before we started working for you."

"I don't think it could have been anyone else."

"I'm so sorry, Jason. I don't know what to say. This makes no sense at all."

"How well do you know her?"

"Not well enough, evidently."

"But she does work for you…?"

"Not technically. She's freelance. She had a little bit of experience in the field and no education to speak of when we first met, but she was very keen to learn and I liked her attitude. Plus she'd learned about the Figs getting back together and touring, well before it was officially announced, and she told me about it, and I owed her for that."

"Really," I said. "How did that work, then?"

"I was with another firm. A Fine Mess. We catered that show you and your mum did near Swindon a couple of years ago. Crafty Knaves and Dodgy Wenches."

I remembered it well—a weekend festival featuring an amazing collection of British folk revival singers and bands. I'd agreed to accompany mum when she'd taken to the stage in a very special guest appearance.

"Jackie was also working for A Fine Mess. She was clearing up in the VIP tent when she overheard your mother discussing a possible Figs reunion with someone."

"Yeah," I said. "Me."

Conversations like that are hard-wired into your memory. The VIP area had been set up for all the performers, with tables and chairs and abundant food and drink. Mitch had got in touch with mum a few weeks earlier about doing the tour, and when we came offstage that afternoon, mum was full of ideas. She did all the talking and I listened and, that night, she rang Mitch and they started to put the plans in place.

"Well, it was providential, anyway," Gillian said. "I told Jackie I was on the verge of leaving A Fine Mess to set up my own firm, and that was just the impetus I needed. I knew your mother was impressed with my cooking at the festival and so I approached her when I created Up the Hill. And that's how we ended up with your contract."

"Did Jackie ever strike you as being angry with us?" I asked. "Does she have some kind of grudge against my mother? Or me?"

"Nothing she's ever mentioned," Gillian said, after a moment.

"Do you have her phone number? A physical address?"

"A mobile," Gillian said.

Katey wrote it down.

"She wouldn't give me her address," Gillian said. "She told me she was getting divorced and her soon-to-be ex was violent and she wasn't keen to let him know where she was."

"How did you pay her?"

"Cash. She insisted."

"And correspondence?"

"Text and phone." Gillian paused. "I hope your mother's going to be all right."

"She'll be OK," I said. "Fortunately it's not the kind of allergy where you swell up and can't breathe. However much Jackie may have mistakenly believed it was."

"What could she have been thinking?"

"That's what I'd like to know," I said. "Is Bolton her real last name?"

"Actually," Gillian said, "it isn't. She told me it was something she made up, to protect herself."

"Do you know what her real last name is?"

Gillian laughed, a little uncomfortably, I thought. "You're going to think me a complete idiot, Jason…but I honestly don't. That's the only name she ever went by."

"How about a photo?"

"Let me think. Yes. She was very leery of having her picture taken, obviously. But I do have one that the drummer of Tragic Fountain took when we catered their tour last year. They had to promise they wouldn't share it online."

Gillian found the photo on her phone, and texted it to me.

Jackie Bolton looked like she was in her mid-twenties, with long blonde hair parted in the middle and hanging straight down. Her eyebrows had been encouraged by a lot of artistic brown pencil. She had the kind of mouth some people would describe as "a rosebud."

"Please let me know what you find out about the mussels," Gillian said. "I'm definitely going to have to rethink working with her again if it turns out she's responsible. And please tell your mum I was asking after her."

"I will," I promised.

"So," Katey said, as I disconnected, "two years ago, in 2016, Jackie's working a music festival when she overhears there's a Figs reunion in the works. She convinces Gillian to take her on when she sets up her own catering firm, and they end up being booked to cater the tour. Very convenient."

"Very well-planned," I agreed. "Right down to her false ID."

I saved Jackie's picture to my laptop, then logged into an image search app to see if I could find a match online.

The app responded with quite a lot of photos from the 1970s of Mary Hopkin and Sally Thomsett. But nothing that really resembled the woman in Gillian's picture.

Jackie Bolton was as invisible as Kezia Heron.

"She got derailed when Gillian had to cancel at the last minute," Katey said. "But she knew about your allergies, and she knew what the menu plans were."

"And she saw her opportunity when the Figs rolled into Cambridge," I said. "She knew what the menu was for tonight…she knew it was lobster bisque. She paid Janice and Mary a friendly visit and added Magic Bullet Mussels to the pot."

"The million pound question is, of course, why? What does she have against you?"

"Or my mother," I said.

I keyed Jackie's number into my phone.

It went immediately to voice mail.

Of course.

"Jackie," I said. "It's Jason Figgis. I'd like to have a chat with you. Please give me a call back as soon as you can."

"Bet she doesn't," Katey said.

She was wrong.

Jackie did ring back, almost immediately.

"This is Jason," I said.

But Jackie didn't speak. Instead, I heard music.

It sounded vaguely familiar. The tune was reminiscent of "Dancing in the Castle," which was the seventh song in our first set list. It had been one of the Figs' biggest tunes in the mid-1960s. Our version was jiggy and jovial, but the lyrics were somewhat darker, relating the tale of a young woman, Esme, and her jealous sister, Gertrude, who thwarted every potential suitor who came Esme's way.

This version was entirely instrumental, and it was being played on a keyboard. And not very well.

The song ended.

And so did the call.

Almost immediately I received a text.

Gillian must have given you my number, Jason. Congrats on your sleuthing. I was in the audience tonight when you cancelled the show. I was surprised you were well enough to walk out onstage but perhaps you deal with mussels better than your mother. Or perhaps you didn't actually partake of my favourite lobster bisque. More's the pity. Think about the song. Blocking you now. Bye bye.

"What does she mean?" Katey asked. "Think about the song."

"I've got no idea," I said.

I tried sending a quick answer to her text, but my message just hung there, in the ether.

Not delivered.

Not read.

Blocked.

I didn't bother trying to phone her back.

CHAPTER SEVENTEEN

I texted Jilly and brought her up to date. Katey's investigation into the two people who'd rented the canoe. The lobster bisque and the cancelled show and what I'd found out from the caterers. And Jackie Bolton.

I'm so terribly sorry to hear about the mussels, Jilly said, a few minutes later. *And that unfortunate Jackie Bolton person. She sounds like a truly troubled soul.*

I don't suppose you happen to know who she really is…?

Not at all, lovely, I'm sorry.

I sent her Jackie's photo.

And I've spoken to Lynn, I said. *She did see the two women in the canoe. But she claims not to know who they were. And she says the name Jackie Bolton isn't familiar to her.*

Do you believe her, my love?

I don't, I replied.

Then you must trust your instincts, Jason. And remember that Lynn is essentially a good person. She's in love with you. And she truly doesn't want anyone to harm you. Or your mother.

If you say so, I said.

#

I felt marginally better in the morning.

Katey had remembered to put a breakfast card out, and while we waited for Room Service, I called the Cambridge Constabulary and asked for Constable Tucker.

"I'm afraid she's not currently available. Would you care to use our Web Chat service?"

I switched on my laptop and for the next five minutes had an online text conversation with a specialist police operator. I told her about the lobster bisque and suggested very strongly that the episode was likely related to both the incident on the river and the theft of my mother's alarm clock, and that the guilty party was very likely one Jacqueline not-her-real-last-name Bolton.

I think I must have sounded like a first-class head case.

At the other end of the chat, Specialist Police Operator 8011 displayed patient diligence.

And is there anything else you'd like to pass along?

I provided Jackie's phone number.

Constable Tucker might like to follow that lead if she wants a starting point, I said. *And, failing that, Gillian Clyde.*

I typed in her number as well.

Many thanks, Jason. And will you be available later in case Constable Tucker wishes to speak with you?

I believe I'll be on my way to Oxford, I said.

Ah yes, Morse territory.

I laughed.

Tell Constable Tucker she can call or text me anytime, I said.

If we can help in any other way, please do get in touch, said Specialist Police Operator 8011. *And I'm sorry you had to cancel your show last night. I had tickets.*

I laughed again.

Hang onto them, I typed. *We'll be back.*

I fired off a text to Freddie, updating her with much the same information.

She responded with a hot-headed, red-faced emoji that had a black strip of swearing where its mouth should have been.

My third call was to my mother.

"How are you feeling?" I asked.

"Surprisingly well," mum replied. "Aside from a ridiculously painful tummy from all that vomiting. I shall be spending today's journey in bed upstairs. How are you?"

I updated her on my state of health.

"And it was very definitely mussels that had been added to the lobster bisque," I said. "I've tracked the source down to Jackie

Bolton. One half of the original catering duo you hired in Stoneford."

I sent her Jackie's photo.

"Does she look familiar?"

"Not at all," mum said. "But I wasn't actually paying much attention. It was Gillian who I'd been in touch with. I do recall seeing her, several times. And you say this Jackie person added the mussels deliberately?"

"She came to see Mary and Janice backstage while they were prepping last night's food."

"And she's how old?"

"Mid-twenties." I paused. "Are you wondering about our break-in artist?"

"That, and whoever knocked you into the river."

"It's occurred to me that she might have some kind of connection to Annie Hobbs. Do you think that could be possible?"

My mother didn't say anything for a moment or two.

"Annie's the only person I can honestly say might—*might*—be carrying that kind of a grudge against me," she replied, finally. "But I don't see how that could possibly include you as well. Come upstairs when we're on the bus and I'll tell you everything."

#

Our plan had been for me to travel to Oxford with Katey, in her car. She'd never actually seen us perform—Cambridge would have been her first time. She was planning to stay on for our show on Saturday night and then, on Sunday, drive herself back to London.

"I'm sorry I won't be going with you," I said. "But I need to talk to my mother."

"Your show had better be worth all these damnable inconveniences," Katey replied.

"Or what?" I said, humorously. "You'll demand your money back?"

"I'll complain about you on Twitter," Katey said. "Comp ticket not worth the paper it was printed on. Stay home and watch *The Great British Bake Off* instead. Far more entertaining."

"See you in Oxford," I said, with a smile, kissing her goodbye.

I made sure my luggage was on the bus and all my instruments were safely stowed in Kato's equipment van—I've experienced enough misplaced bags and cases on the road to make this a mandatory step in my checkout procedure.

I made sure I had another bag of Fruit Pastilles in my pocket.

And then I joined mum upstairs in the artist's bedroom.

There wasn't room for an extra chair—and we didn't have any portable ones on board anyway—they were all with Kato—so I sat on the bed with my back against the padded headboard. My mother made herself comfortable beside me, and then she told me everything she could remember about Annie Hobbs.

"It wasn't so much the fact that your father chose me over her, although that was, quite obviously, a good part of it. Annie also strongly believed that if I hadn't come along, she'd have enjoyed a lucrative musical career. Instead of which, after Paisley Ascot, the world very quickly forgot who she was."

"Did she try?" I said, asking the obvious question.

"I'm sure she did. The trouble being, of course, that she really didn't have a lot to offer by way of talent."

"Odd that she blamed you instead of dad," I said.

"I'm convinced she was still in love with your father. And that's why she transferred all of her anger and resentment onto me. It was my fault for working in that club, my fault for getting up to sing, my fault that Tony noticed me. And then, of course, once we'd got the Figs going, my fault for us being hugely successful while she was reduced to living off benefits and never getting another stab at fame and fortune."

"Did she send you a lot of letters?" I asked.

"Enough. And there were phone calls. And backstage visits. The last time we had anything to do with one another was…" Mum had to think. "Christmas. 1970. We were in Wimbledon, doing panto. *Dick Whittington.*"

"I'd have been two-and-a-half," I said, also thinking. "I have a vague recollection of you in a costume…"

"Yes, you were there. Your Granny brought you backstage. Annie was there, too. Heavily pregnant and abandoned by the child's father and living in a rundown council flat. She made a point of telling me that. Mitch and Tony felt sorry for her, and gave her some money. I introduced you to her. And then she left. I don't think she knew I'd had a child. We never heard from her again."

"Annie," I said. "Variation of Anne?"

"Annabelle," said my mother. "She always hated that name."

#

Downstairs, at Keith's table, I set up my laptop and logged onto Generations.

I knew Annie was a few years younger than my mother.

But the only trouble with searching for Annabelle Hobbs, born within five years of 1941 (Generations wouldn't let me search exclusively forward—it had to be on either side), was that there wasn't actually anyone with that first name registered in that time period.

There were, however sixty-two results where the child's second name started with an "A." After I'd eliminated all the males, I was down to forty-one. And of those forty-one, twenty-six had been born before 1942, so I could safely discard them. That left me with fifteen females born between 1943 and 1946. Fifteen females I'd have to thoroughly research—middle names, electoral registers, marriages, divorces, deaths and other peoples' trees, the lot.

It wasn't a hugely daunting task. I knew where to look. But it was going to take some time.

And we'd just arrived in Oxford.

#

I had to hand it to Beaky for successfully negotiating the one-way road system in Oxford's town centre. All of us on the bus could see our hotel—each time we went around a corner, it only seemed to be a block or two away. We consulted Google Maps on our phones and took turns transmitting directions to the driver's compartment. "Left!" "First right!" "Second left after the traffic signals!"

"We're in the news," Freddie said, as we circled the town centre on our third attempt to find a way in to our hotel.

"For our record number of illegal turns?" Mitch inquired.

"For cancelling in Cambridge," Freddie replied, holding up her phone so we could see the headline. "It's a fairly accurate report. But there's a companion piece that lists all the mishaps that have 'plagued' the tour. Including your unexpected plunge into the river, Jason. Though they claim it was an accident and the story makes you out to be a clumsy amateur when it comes to punting."

"Fuckwits," I said. "And no mention of my two assailants

paddling away in their canoe, I suppose."

"Not a word," said Freddie. "But the theft of Mandy's alarm clock's in there. Which does cause me some concern as we haven't released that information at all."

I pulled the story up on my phone. It had been written by a reporter named Rose Saker. Her photo on the paper's website made her look about sixteen years old. She had a gold ring through her left nostril and a lot of short, messy blonde hair that reminded me of Paula Yates.

"Hello, Jason," she said, after I'd rung her and told her who I was, though I refrained from letting her know what I thought about her reporting skills. "What a good thing you can swim! Your band does seem to have encountered its share of problems, hasn't it?"

"A few of which haven't been mentioned publicly until now," I said. "Would you mind me asking who told you about my mother's missing alarm clock?"

"Nobody," Rose said, with a laugh. "It's common knowledge. Are you familiar with The Greenhouse?"

"The chat group," I said.

"That's the one. Have a look over there. It's the talk of the tour."

CHAPTER EIGHTEEN

I had to save my investigation of The Greenhouse—which was dedicated to all things Figgis Green—until later.

With the help of a bus lane or two, and at least one "No Access" road, Beaky had found a way in to our hotel.

The only trouble was, I think we'd misplaced Kato in the process.

The last we saw of her, she was on the other side of the road, driving our equipment van in the opposite direction.

We all waved.

#

Apparently there'd been a coaching inn on the grounds of the Radcliffe Hotel since the early 1600s, although the original was long gone and had been replaced by the current building in the middle of the nineteenth century.

It was in the centre of the city, and it was all bay windows and attics and tall chimneys, and it had absolutely no van or bus parking nearby.

Katey (who was obviously far more familiar with Oxford's roads than Beaky was) had arrived about three quarters of an hour ahead of the rest of us, and joined me in the hotel's lobby as Freddie was distributing our keys.

We went upstairs.

I'll always remember a 1996 interview with *Rolling Stone* magazine where Charlie Watts said he'd sketched every bed he'd ever slept in when he was touring.

I understood that completely. After a while, it does become a blur. Your hotel room turns out to be the one thing you can rely on for a little bit of variety. For me, anyway.

I remembered, during rehearsals, an overwhelming feeling of being stuck forever in the room where I was sleeping, because it wasn't my bedroom at home. The fact that I had to remind myself what day it was when I woke up, because I'd completely lost track of the calendar. The steady diet of breakfast, lunch and dinner from restaurants and coffee shops—I was really looking forward to getting on the road, if only because the meals before each gig were going to be catered to our specifications.

It was worse in the old days, before the internet. You'd be stuck on the bus or in the van, travelling from A to B, desperate for news from the "outside." You were insulated—relying on your tour manager to buy up all the papers from the next hotel's newsstand—then devouring them from front to back in your room and tuning into the radio or the TV to catch up on the football or the tennis or the cricket or whatever else had been going on while you were rattling down the M1.

It's not like that anymore. We're always connected to what's going on outside, in one way or another.

My room at the Radcliffe (Number Twelve, for those keeping track) was surprisingly unremarkable. Which was a shame, because I'd expected it to have at least a little bit of character, given its history. But no. It was very small, and rather plainly furnished in varying shades of culinary brown: mushroom walls, chocolate chairs, coffee curtains, Bisto bedspread. And a carpet on the floor with stripes that incorporated all of those ingredients—along with a touch of butter, just to stick it all together.

About the only thing that really impressed me was that the hotel's owners had almost-astoundingly managed to work a full ensuite bathroom into the layout, and it included a luxurious rainfall shower.

I sat down on one of the KitKat chairs, dragged over a tiny After Eight Chocolate Mint table, plugged in my laptop, and navigated over to The Greenhouse.

"I suppose you've been lurking there for years," Katey said, reading over my shoulder.

"I rarely post anything," I replied. "And if I do, it's mostly just to correct mistakes. The mods know who I am but I'm fairly certain no one else does. The last time I had a look in was when we were rehearsing."

"Cold Fingers," Katey said, amused. "Same handle you were using on Twitter when I first met you on the *Sapphire*."

"It's served me well," I replied, scrolling down through the topics. There were conversations about every day of our itinerary, and every show. Even the ones we hadn't done yet.

And Rose was right. My mother's missing clock was the talk of the tour. But nobody seemed to know what it actually looked like, so there were dozens of guesses with accompanying pictures which claimed to reflect mum's supposed taste in chronometry.

All wrong, of course.

I followed the thread back to see who'd started it. Someone called Castledancer.

Got an inside scoop, people. Mandy's room at the Eagle and Lion in Cambridge was broken into last night during the fire alarm. Quite a few things were stolen, including her treasured clock.

Castledancer was incorrect, obviously, about "quite a few things." But right about the clock.

I looked to see if there was any mention of my dad's ashes, but their insider knowledge obviously didn't extend that far.

Whoever Castledancer was, they seemed to be very active in the group. They also had a thread going about our hotels, and had correctly identified every place we'd stayed in. Though they hadn't quite twigged to Freddie's trick of booking mum in under a fictitious name.

And then there was the most recent topic…the cancellation of our gig in Cambridge. With absolutely no mention of the lobster bisque.

"If Castledancer's Jackie Bolton," Katey said, "she's playing her cards close to her chest."

"I have a pretty good idea who Castledancer is," I said, "and it's not Jackie."

"You could ask the mods."

She was right.

I sent off a message.

And then I read Castledancer's thread about the punting accident in Cambridge.

"Not a word about the two women in the canoe," I said. "Which explains why it wasn't in Rose's story."

"If Castledancer is Lynn," Katey reasoned, "why wouldn't she mention it? She saw the whole thing from the bridge."

"She knows who they are and she's protecting them?" I supposed.

"Or she's afraid of them," said Katey.

One of the Greenhouse mods—Dan—was obviously on duty.

Sorry, Jason. Not allowed to reveal true identities. Even to you.

Thanks anyway, I said. *Thought I'd try.*

I put my laptop to sleep, picked up my jacket and made sure I had my little pewter Lincoln Imp and my whale tail safely stowed in my jeans pocket.

"Where are we going?" Katey inquired.

"Hunting for gargoyles," I replied.

#

Oxford's New College was a quick walk from our hotel, along the High Street and then up Queen's Lane, a narrow little road populated on either side with parked bicycles and tall stone walls that protected secret gardens and historical hideaways.

"Wouldn't like to be caught here alone on a dark winter's night," Katey remarked.

It did strike me as being a very solitary and isolated sort of place—with a distinct lack of illumination, though there was quite a nice old-fashioned street light at the corner of the lane as it bent to the west and ran along the back of New College's Quadrangle.

The little road took us past a traffic barrier and underneath a covered walkway and out onto New College Lane, where a group of Japanese tourists had neatly assembled themselves in front of New College's tourist entrance, an old porter's lodge.

We tagged onto the end of the line and paid our £5 entry fee. We were handed a visitor map and guide, and admitted.

I had a quick scan around the Front Quadrangle—a grassy oval framed by a gravel pathway—to get my bearings.

"No gargoyles here," Katey said, consulting the guide.

"Give it a few minutes," I replied.

We walked through an arched doorway which opened onto a passage that took us into the Cloisters.

Amused—and obviously having no faith in my powers of prediction—Katey wandered off to explore the enclosed stone square with its intricately cut-out windows overlooking the lawn.

I waited.

I popped a Fruit Pastille into my mouth.

And there she was.

Lynn.

She'd been following us all the way from the hotel.

She wouldn't have made a very good spy.

"Hello again," I said.

"Hello!" she replied. "Have you come to look at the grotesques on the Bell Tower?" She held up a small pair of binoculars. "You'll need these."

I could see Katey, beating a hasty path back to us from the opposite side of the square.

"This is one of the two places where you can actually get a good view of them," Lynn added. "The other's down that way and around the corner, in St Helens Passage."

She indicated the direction with her head.

"Are you a Harry Potter fan?" she asked.

"I am," Katey said, saving me.

"Oh good!" Lynn exclaimed. "If you look through there—" She nodded at the grassy area visible through the open cloister arches. "—you can see the very famous nineteenth-century evergreen Holm-oak in the northwest corner, which, of course, was featured in *The Goblet of Fire*."

I think I must have appeared unimpressed.

"Where Draco Malfoy's turned into a ferret by Mad Eye Moody," Katey said, patiently, to me. And then, to Lynn: "He hasn't seen any of the films. Or read any of the books."

"Traitor," I said.

"I don't know what we see in him," Lynn said, with a sigh.

"More trouble than he's worth," Katey agreed, clearly enjoying herself.

"If you go onto the grass and look up at the Bell Tower," Lynn continued, helpfully, "you'll be able to see the gargoyles representing the seven virtues. Patience, generosity, charity, prayerfulness, innocent love, enthusiastic joy, and justice. All on this side, as opposed to the much gloomier north side, which is home to the seven deadly sins."

"The Philosopher's Stone," Katey said, humorously, to me. *"The Chamber of Secrets, The Prisoner of Azkaban, The Goblet of Fire, The Order*

of the Phoenix, The Half-Blood Prince and The Deathly Hallows."

"You," I said, as I followed them out onto the rectangle of lawn, "are a menace."

Lynn handed me her binoculars so I could observe the seven virtues in all their stony glory. "There you are. Don't say I never do you any favours."

Enough.

"I read a news story today about all the mishaps plaguing our tour," I said. "And when I spoke to the reporter about her sources, she suggested I have a look at The Greenhouse."

I gave the binoculars back.

"The chat group," Lynn said.

"The chat group," I confirmed. "Are you Castledancer?"

Lynn shook her head emphatically. "No way. Some of the things she posts…I wouldn't. I have got some sense of loyalty, you know. Even to you."

So—Castledancer was a woman. I didn't think Lynn realized she'd let that slip.

"Do you know who Castledancer is?" Katey asked, much more sympathetically than I would have.

Lynn shook her head again. "She won't tell anyone. She's as much a mystery to me as she is to you."

"How did she know about my mother's alarm clock being stolen?" I asked. "We didn't release that information to anyone."

"Perhaps she was staying at your hotel. A few fans have been doing that…the ones that have to travel. I can't afford it. Bed and breakfast, me. Perhaps Castledancer overheard you talking about it to the police."

"I don't recall seeing anyone else in the general vicinity while we were doing that," I said.

"Then I really don't know," Lynn said. "I'm so sorry, Jason. I wish I could help. But I can't."

"It's just that yesterday," I said, "outside the stage door, you really gave me the impression you knew who the two women in the canoe were. And the name Jackie Bolton seemed to mean something to you. So you can see why I'm a little sceptical."

"I'm not Castledancer," Lynn said, again.

"But you do know something about her," Katey said, "don't you?"

"And Jackie Bolton," I added.

Lynn was beginning to look nervous. She glanced around, and then, assured that we were alone in the Cloisters, she lowered her voice to just above a whisper.

"Have a look in The Greenhouse," she said. "Spicy Pickled Figs."

CHAPTER NINETEEN

I'd felt reasonably OK on the way over to New College, but the walk back to the Radcliffe Hotel exhausted me. I had to stop twice and rest. Neil's antibiotic pneumonia cure obviously wasn't as potent as advertised.

"I'll get us some tea," Katey said, consulting the Room Service menu when we finally got back to my room. "And lunch."

I desperately needed to lie down. "See if they have any Spicy Pickled Figs," I said.

"Nothing wrong with your sense of humour, then. You'll have to make do with Cheese and Ham Toasties, I'm afraid."

I must have fallen into a dozing half-sleep, because when I woke up an hour later, Katey had eaten her toasties and all of the chips that had come with them, and half of mine.

"I've looked up Spicy Pickled Figs," she said, showing me her phone as I rescued what was left of my lunch.

It was, of course, the title of a thread in The Greenhouse chat forum.

I am absolutely thrilled to bits to announce the arrival of a brand new Figgis Green website. Click on the link to read all about it.

And the author was—of course—Castledancer.

And the date of the announcement happened to be, more than coincidentally, the first day of our tour.

I've followed Figs' fans over the years. Before we'd ever heard of the internet, there were clubs and newsletters, typewritten song lyrics circulated with blurry black and white pictures, photocopies of magazine stories and coveted tidbits of news, savoured and shared as if they were nuggets of earth-shattering importance.

When the internet arrived in the mid-1990s, everyone who'd been off-limits socially was suddenly within reach. Mitch had a Myspace page. So did my mother, but she didn't really understand how it worked and got me to do her updates whenever I was adding things to mine. There were newsgroups and chat forums and then fan sites and Facebook and Twitter…and everyone was on those, even mum.

I thought I knew all the Figgis Green fan sites. But Spicy Pickled Figs was new, and it was behind a lock—you had to request membership and provide a birthdate in order to get access.

I sent in my query, using a pseudonym that had come in handy a few times before: Paula McIntyre—a fifty-seven year old grandmother with a legitimate-looking Facebook profile that had pictures and postings and connections to old friends at a prestigious girls' school in the English countryside that no longer existed.

My request was dealt with quickly—I barely had time to finish my chips. I was admitted. I went in to have a look around. And I very soon wished I hadn't.

"You seem concerned," Katey said.

"Unsettled," I replied.

I'm used to being under scrutiny. My sister and I grew up in the glare of publicity and we weren't overly bothered by the constant presence of reporters and photographers in our lives. We were often featured in magazine spreads documenting Tony and Mandy's "at home" domestic arrangements.

By and large it was respectful. My parents led relatively uncomplicated lives, bereft of controversy (much to the dismay of many an editor, I'm sure). Journo's weren't the ruthless door-steppers you see these days. And snappers had to haul heavy cameras and lenses around and pack flashbulbs and spare rolls of film (which they then had to get developed) and there just weren't as many opportunities—or markets—for their shotgun photos as there are today.

I would classify the Spicy Pickled Figs site as neither respectful nor particularly kind.

There was a section that contained fan fiction. I had a look through it. Some fanfic can be really good. Sometimes it transcends really good and is actually well-written and tells a fascinating story.

This wasn't that.

I'm not sure what it is about fans that they want to imagine personal relationships that have no basis in reality. Why, for instance, did the author of one story want to pair my dad with Ben Quigley in a BMD master/slave scenario that ended up with both of them consummating their relationship, slathered in cooking oil, on the floor of a recording studio? And why did they want to include me in a bizarre relationship with Spock from *Star Trek's* hitherto unknown sister?

"What," Katey said, with a highly amused look, "are you reading?"

I showed her my screen.

Katey could barely contain her laughter.

"It's all very well for you," I said, turning my laptop around again. "You're not in bed with a pointy-eared half-Vulcan struggling with a sex drive muddled by intrusive human DNA."

"Hers or yours?" Katey mused, glancing over the Room Service menu. "Two Rocky Road Sundaes for dessert with a side of *pon farr*?"

"Chocolate sauce will do," I said, soldiering on.

Midway through the collection I discovered a series of stories I can only describe as self-indulgent drivel.

And a lot of it was really nasty. Not nasty in the sense that it was badly-written—although that was a big part of it. Nasty in that it seemed mean-spirited and filled with a lot of anger.

There's a well-known area in fanfic that deals with hurt and comfort. A lot of fans (many of them female) enjoy reading about (or seeing, in the case of a TV show or a film) their hero being injured, accidentally or on purpose. That then leads to that hero having to be looked after by another character, often a love interest, and the relationship can then carry on to something verging on erotica. Though when you've been beaten to within an inch of your life and your tenderly applied bandages are covering wounds that, in a hospital, would have you hooked up to drips and drains and monitors and O_2 lines, I'm not sure a romping fuck would be the most pressing thing on your mind.

A lot of the stories were about my dad. And me.

A number of others were about fictitious characters...but it was pretty obvious who they were based on.

And they all made me feel extremely creeped out.

Our Rocky Road sundaes arrived. I fled the fanfic and went to have a look at the Picture Gallery, which offered a showcase of drawings, some of them brilliant and others very badly informed by the cooking oil incident in the recording studio.

"Is that position actually possible…?" Katey said, squinting at the screen.

"Not unless you're missing a leg and most of your right arm," I replied. "And you've got a guitar with a bendy neck."

"What's in that section called Real Life?"

I was curious too. I clicked onto the link.

I'm familiar with most of the pics that have made their way into the public domain over the years. But Castledancer had two I'd never seen before. They were shot in black and white and showed my parents, in their twenties, having dinner at what looked like a table in a posh restaurant. The other one looked like it was taken around the same time—mum and dad again, standing by a ship's railing, their long hair tossed by the wind, the sea foaming behind them.

I saved them to my phone and texted them over to my mother.

Where have you been hiding these? I asked.

I had my answer in less than thirty seconds.

They were taken on board the Queen Mary in August 1967. Southampton to New York. The prints went missing when we had that break-in.

I knew about the robbery. It was in Stoneford, in April 1968, a month before I was born. One evening, while mum and dad were out at the pub, a person (or persons) unknown entered their house by way of a downstairs window and helped themselves to a variety of things, including a posh-looking box that they probably thought contained valuables, but which turned out to hold only photos and memorabilia from that *Queen Mary* crossing the year before.

The break-in freaked my mother out enough that their previously planned move to London was hurried-up, and I was born there instead of Stoneford. And although a few of the stolen items were eventually recovered, the photos and *Queen Mary* souvenirs had never resurfaced.

Until now.

Where did you find them? my mother asked.

I forwarded her the link and my login and password.

She sent a message back to me about ten minutes later.

Lots more of the stolen photos there, she said. *The entire collection, I'd say. Shall I ring for Chief Inspector Morse?*

#

Like the star influencers on YouTube and Instagram and TikTok, Castledancer was obviously revelling in the attention her website was bringing her. Her posts on The Greenhouse were attracting lots of *kudo's* and *wow's* and exclamation points and emoji's with impressed faces. She'd commented on, and put hearts beside, every single response.

I found Castledancer's profile and clicked on her PM option to see if there was any way to engage her in a private conversation.

Nope.

Disabled.

I went back to Spicy Pickled Figs to look for Contact information.

None provided.

I then did a quick check of Whois to see if they'd listed the name of the website's registered owner, but it looked like Spicy Pickled Figs was cleverly housed on a huge server that specialized in protecting its customers' identities.

The public face of Spicy Pickled Figs was obviously very private.

Just like Jackie Bolton.

"All that fanfic and all those hand-drawn pencil sketches couldn't have come solely from Castledancer," Katey said. "How do they get their work to her?"

"Let's see what else Lynn knows," I said.

I went back to my Instagram page and posted up a photo of the remnants of my Rocky Road sundae, along with an appropriate comment about my state of health.

It took Lynn two minutes to respond, reacting with a *Yum-Yum* emoji.

I sent her a private message. *I don't suppose you know any way to contact Castledancer?*

I'm so sorry, Jason, no. She's the one who does the contacting.

How so? I asked.

She knows who all the fans are, where they post things. She follows everyone. And if she thinks you might be good for something she wants—a story, some art, info—she'll send you a PM on Greenhouse. She's got it set up so she can send messages to you, but you can't send messages back to her. She gives you a link where you can upload your stuff to her. It's all anonymous.

Have you ever sent her anything? I asked.

Never ever, Lynn said. *I just know about it from talking to other people. No, wait. I tell a lie.*

I waited.

When you subscribe to her website, she asks you for your birthdate. Then, when that date comes up in the calendar, she sends you a digital card. One of those clever ones that you click on and they tell a story, with music. I got one on my birthday.

Did you save the card? I asked.

Yes, I've still got it.

Would you be comfortable forwarding it to me? Here's my email.

I didn't think she'd agree. But she was getting something in return—my personal email address. Not Gmail or Hotmail or any of the other generics I had at my disposal. My very own personal email address—which, quite honestly, I didn't share with a lot of people.

She replied a minute later, forwarding the entire notification from the greeting card company, which included a link you could click on to see your special message.

Thank you, I said, emailing her back. *I really appreciate your help.*

I followed the link and watched the cake being made and all the birds and animals in the forest gathering 'round to share morsels of the finished masterpiece and to sing "Happy Birthday." At the end of the animation was another link you could click on to forward a Thank You note to the sender.

I clicked.

Up came a nicely decorated frame with a blank space where you could enter your text.

Hello Castledancer, I wrote. *I'm extremely interested in talking to you about some items in the Picture Gallery on your Spicy site. Photos which were stolen from my parents in 1968. We're prepared to offer a cash reward for their safe return. Please contact me as soon as possible. Jason Figgis.*

I typed in my email address—the same one I'd shared with Lynn—and sent it off.

CHAPTER TWENTY

If I was expecting a quick reply from Castledancer, I was wrong. She'd obviously decided to take her time.

I wasn't feeling well enough to join Katey on a walking tour of Oxford she'd booked for that afternoon.

I stayed in bed, propped up with pillows, and got back to tracking down Annie Hobbs.

I'd narrowed my list down to fifteen females with the last name Hobbs who'd been born between 1942 and 1946. None of them had Annabelle as a first name, but all fifteen had "A" as their second initial.

I constructed quick profiles for all of them, using birth records, electoral registers, marriages, divorces and deaths, anything that Generations could provide by way of supporting material.

According to my mother, the last time she'd seen Annie, she was expecting a baby, due to be born roundabout the end of 1970 or the beginning of 1971.

So I did a search of the Generations website for babies who'd been born in the UK in 1970 to females whose last name was Hobbs, and whose father's surname hadn't been provided. There were eighteen of them.

I went through all eighteen, eliminating any that had been registered before the last quarter of 1970. That left me with four. I did a similar search for the first three months of 1971 and ended up with an additional eight possibilities, making an even dozen.

And then, working with those twelve children, I looked for possible maternal match-ups. I was making a huge assumption—that their mothers had not given them up for adoption and instead had kept them and raised them, either alone or, like my Granny Vera, with a new husband. But it was the 1970s and social attitudes towards single mothers were changing. And if I was wrong…it was back to the drawing board.

But I wasn't wrong. I was able to link all twelve children whose last name was Hobbs to their birth mothers. And of those twelve, only one had a mother whose middle initial was "A."

That child was Victoria Lillian Hobbs, born in January 1971, in Wandsworth, London. Mother, Louise A. Hobbs, who was a Christmas baby, born on December 25, 1944, also in Wandsworth. And I couldn't find any marriage registrations for Louise A. Hobbs—so it looked like she'd remained unattached.

And there she was, listed on assorted electoral rolls and voter registrations, always at the same address in the borough of Croydon Merton—which I looked up on Google maps and then Street View. It was a flat in Pollards Hill, one of those dreary six-storey brick-and-concrete structures that had sprung up in the post-war years, with outdoor walkways connecting everyone's front doors, and lifts that smelled of pee and were permanently out of service.

It's tricky trying to find voter information between the mid-1960s and the early 2000s. It isn't online at any of the family tree research sites or any of the other sites that provide names and addresses for a fee. The British Library has complete printed copies of every Voter List from 1947 onwards, but you have to go there in person to look them up and the registers are arranged by polling districts within their constituencies, not alphabetically.

Victoria Lillian Hobbs would have reached voting age in the early 1990s. I tried looking for her in the digitized electoral rolls that were available from 2002 onwards. But she wasn't listed.

My head was starting to ache.

And I still needed to track down a current address for Annie.

As it turned out, Louise Annabelle Hobbs's last known residence was Croydon's Mitcham Road Cemetery.

She'd died in 2015.

#

It was nearly time for dinner—which Mitch had arranged at a nearby Indian. Katey was back from her walking tour, which had been literary in nature and had filled her imagination with the likes of Oscar Wilde, T.E. Lawrence and John Le Carré.

I logged onto Instagram and composed a message to Jilly.

I've seen Lynn again. I'm more and more convinced she knows who Jackie Bolton is. As well as someone called Castledancer.

I told her all about the Spicy Pickled Figs website. And the stolen photos. And then I sent the message off.

Jilly replied about thirty seconds later.

You were conceived on that voyage aboard the Queen Mary, she said.

I was confounded. *How do you know that?*

You told me, my love. Six years ago. Don't you remember?

I had to admit, I didn't. But there were quite a few things that I'd forgotten about my relationship with Jilly.

Has Castledancer answered you? she asked.

Not yet, I said.

I'm certain she will. But you must be on your guard.

Is she Jackie Bolton?

I don't know, lovely. I'm still making inquiries. She isn't Lynn. You may trust me on that.

I've also had a conversation with my mother about Annie Hobbs. She was very resentful of mum's success. She died three years ago. She's buried in Croydon.

You really must talk to your grandmother, Jilly said.

I don't think I can manage it until the tour's over.

You must try and make the effort, Jilly said. *And you ought to do it sooner, rather than later, my love.*

There was something very urgent in her tone.

#

My grandmother lived in a lovely private residence that offered assisted arrangements in exchange for a generous monthly fee.

I had to let the phone ring a long time before it was answered. Granny Vera was somewhat hard of hearing.

"Hello, my darling," she said.

She always greeted me that way, and her voice was always warm and loving.

"Where are you now? Still rehearsing in that little village on the coast?"

Granny Vera's memory was as sharp as a knife—when it cooperated. Unfortunately, at the age of ninety-five, that memory was increasingly unreliable, and, coupled with dodgy lungs which often didn't provide as much oxygen as she needed, she was prone to lapses of confusion.

"Actually," I said, "we're in Oxford."

"Oh, that's a lovely little city!" Granny Vera exclaimed. "I once knew a boy from Oxford. An airman. He was shot down but he survived and after the war I met him again, quite by accident, of course I was married by then, and so was he, I met his wife as well as she'd come with him and they had three children, two boys and a little girl, ever so lovely they were, they'd all come to Battersea Park for the funfair and I was there as well with Mandy and Mitch and Frank, I think it must have been a Sunday. It was very soon after it opened, so 1951, Mandy was about ten and Mitch was five. It was all very futuristic and there were so many rides, and a roller coaster—it had that accident, didn't it—and I remember Frank didn't like the rides because they made him feel ill but he didn't mind the slide. It was on a big white tower and you had to climb up the steps to the top and then they gave you a mat to sit on and you rode all the way down, it curved around and around until you got to the bottom. Frank rode with Mitch and I went down with Mandy and I remember as we were waiting for Frank and Mitch I saw Aidan—I recognized him immediately—and he recognized me and it was so lovely seeing him again even though he'd lost an arm when his Hurricane crashed."

She stopped, not because she'd run out of breath, but because her brain had suddenly switched off and she'd forgotten what she was going to say next.

"Would it be all right if I came to visit you, Granny?" I asked. "I was thinking about the day after tomorrow. Sunday. Would it be convenient?"

It never wasn't convenient, but I always asked. I didn't like to show up unexpectedly, and the staff at the residence always appreciated a little advance notice.

"It would be lovely to see you, my darling," Granny Vera replied. "Do you think you might bring me some bars of chocolate?"

"I will," I promised. I didn't need to ask what kind. It was always the same—her favourite—Cadbury Dairy Milk Fruit and Nut. "Sunday afternoon, then."

CHAPTER TWENTY-ONE

It was Saturday morning—the day of our show—and I still wasn't well. My lungs hurt, my head ached, and my energy levels had scuttled away and were lurking somewhere under the bed. I supposed my trek over to New College the day before hadn't helped much, nor had our late night celebration at Janak's Indian Brasserie.

The entire band was there, plus our crew—Freddie, Beaky, Kato, Tejo and Neil—and even our caterers, Janice and Mary. We'd told jokes and exchanged anecdotes about other road trips, other tours. We were more than halfway through this one, and it felt like we were one big family. And I have to admit, a hot curry was right at the top of the list of things I was craving by that point. I hadn't been disappointed.

The evening was topped off by Beaky, who sang a cheeky song that included all of our names. Props to him for finding naughty rhymes for every single one of us.

I texted Kato with my requests for that night's setup at the College Playhouse.

I'll need my perch again, I said. *And a couple of extra bottles of water. And few more small towels?*

I knew the heat onstage was going to play havoc with my metabolism, especially with me still being on antibiotics.

Please, I added.

You don't want much, do you? Kato texted back, a few moments later.

Actually, if you could also move my foot pedals over to where I'm going to be sitting…

Where they usually were was hidden behind a wedgie speaker on the stage floor. It wasn't going to look all that great, but I didn't want to have to walk far to get my sound changes in.

Anything else?

That's it, I said. *For now.*

Don't assume you're getting special treatment because Beaky managed to rhyme Jason with mason at dinner last night.

It's not my fault the only thing he could come up with for you was potato, I said.

Eff off, Figgis.

I rang Neil to give him a health update.

"And would you mind cutting my spots a little?"

"Eyes bothering you?"

"They're OK for now," I said. "I'm just trying to avoid overheating and a killer headache from the glare and the noise."

The glare from the lights was one thing. The noise was another. The audience heard what we were singing and playing through the front-of-house system. Up onstage, there were amps and monitors and speakers that let us know how we sounded, individually and as a group. Plus there was the actual din from Rolly's drumming, which was fine if you were in good health, but if you happened to be at all fragile and he was having an enthusiastic night, it could all be very rough on the nerves.

"I'll write you a prescription for Co-codamol," Neil said. "That'll help."

I sent another text to Kato.

Can you move me a bit more stage left so I'm not in Rolly's line of fire?

I copied the text to the rest of the band.

Mum and Beth shared the front line with me onstage, so they needed to know where I was going to be in relation to them. Bob, on rhythm guitar, stood in the back, between Beth and mum, and Mitch, with his long-necked bass, was also in the back, on the other side of Rolly. My new setup would affect how all of them moved around during the show.

I waited for Kato to reply, but she obviously had better things to do.

I went back to sleep.

#

Castledancer decided to answer my message just before I left for our sound check. She didn't bother with an email. Instead, she sent me a greeting card, just like the one I'd sent her.

Hello Jason. I have to say I was very surprised to see you at SPF. As you may know, I'm cautious about who I allow in. And only one new person joined yesterday—so I will assume you are Paula McIntyre.

As it happens, I was going to contact you myself regarding the photos, but you beat me to it. I haven't quite collected my thoughts, but suffice to say, I am very curious about how much money your mother is willing to pay to have her pictures back. And I may have one or two other surprises for you.

Until next time…

#

I caught up with my mother at the College Playhouse's stage door.

"That was quite the website," she said.

"I hope you didn't look at the stories."

"Oh, I did. And the drawings."

I cringed. It's one thing to read about yourself being stripped naked and hung up by the wrists in a walk-in freezer, then being beaten by a dominatrix in a furry corset and earmuffs, then being abandoned until you're rescued by the daughter of a butcher (and coincidentally the sister of the dominatrix) who's lusting after you but lacks the courage to follow through until she cuts you down and attempts to warm you up by taking off all of her clothes as well and sharing her body heat with you on the freezer floor.

It's quite another when your own mother decides to acquaint herself with the narrative.

"I'd have relished a nice cup of hot chocolate and a cozy blanket," she said, confidentially, as we made our way backstage.

"I'd have relished a trip to the nearest hospital," I replied, unimpressed. "Did you contact the Thames Valley Police about the stolen photos?"

"Freddie did, yes. And we cc'd Constable Hutton from West Yorkshire and Constables Tucker and Fingal from Cambridge. We sent copies of all the relevant pictures and Thames Valley assured us they'd look into it. Though with a fifty-year-old robbery, I'm not sure they'll be assigning their top detectives to the case. Especially as it's only old photographs and they've probably changed hands dozens of times before landing at the doorstep of whatever-her-name-is."

"Castledancer," I said.

"I knew it had something to do with drawbridges and boiling oil poured from the parapets," mum replied. "Is she calling herself that after our song?"

"Right down to the boiling oil," I said, referring to Esme's revenge on her jealous sister, and Gertrude's unfortunate exit in the second-last verse.

#

The sound check went well.

Kato had arranged the stage exactly as I'd requested. Tejo decided to adjust my mic level a bit, as my voice clearly wasn't as strong as it should have been. From my point of view, I sounded like I was singing from inside an upturned saucepan.

On top of which, we'd planned on using the opportunity, with this show, to experiment with someone other than my mother taking over the lead for one of our two encores.

That someone was me.

"I Can't Stay Mad at You" was a Gerry Goffin/Carole King country and western/pop crossover that Skeeter Davis had made famous in 1963. It had a catchy beat and throwaway lyrics and the Figs had added it to their original repertoire mostly as inside joke about the starstruck fangirls who used to lust after all the men in the group.

The song was presented *a capella* at the end of every show, and although my parents had never actually made a recording of it, their audiences not only expected it to be included—they demanded it.

We'd carried on the tradition with our tour. Mum handled the lead at her mic while we all abandoned our instruments and gathered around a second mic to do the "shooby dooby doo bops" in the background. We had a little choreography to go along with it, too. Our audiences loved it, especially when we recreated the instrumental string section three-quarters of the way through with just our voices.

I quite liked the song and I was always humming it to myself on the bus. I guess that was what gave my mother the idea to switch out the singers, with me singing lead instead of her.

"That'll be interesting," Mitch said, "considering it's a woman moaning about her unfaithful git of a boyfriend."

"When I do it," I promised, "I'll be the unfaithful git of a boyfriend moaning about how his clever girlfriend got her revenge."

That afternoon was when we were scheduled to try out the new arrangement. But that was all planned before my cold had got demonstrably worse and turned itself into pneumonia.

"Are you sure you want to do this?" mum checked. "We could just carry on the way we always have, if you're not up for it."

"I am up for it," I assured her, bravely.

I mustered all of my energy and dragged my perch over to the solo mic.

I nailed it on the second attempt.

On the third run-through, mum got her choreography right.

On the fourth try, her backing vocals.

And I avoided collapsing.

We were all set.

#

It was a good thing I'd prepped for the lights and the noise during the actual show. I was incredibly hot, and halfway through our first set I developed the worst headache known to mankind and had to resort to Neil's magic tablets.

I don't know about you, but codeine has a very unworldly sort of effect on me—which resulted in me believing I was quite a bit funnier than I actually am, and departing from our banter in ways that hadn't been anticipated by the others, especially my mother.

I could see her looking at me, hands on hips, as I chatted with the audience from my perch. I'd gone off-script so much that she decided to let me stew in it, and didn't bother to answer me when I paused to let her respond—which left me dangling and resulted in a huge amount of laughter from the audience.

I slid off the stool and made out I was walking off the stage in protest—guitar and all.

More laughter as Mitch was sent to coax me back. I reappeared, sulking, to massive applause.

I sat down with very bad grace.

"Shall we continue?" my mother inquired.

"I think we'd better," I said.

"Are you sure you can remember which song comes next?"

"I've got it sellotaped to my guitar," I said, showing her—and the audience—my list.

"Right then—'Dancing in the Castle'."

"I think you'll find it's 'All in the Deep Dark Woods'."

Mum looked at me, so I slid off the stool again and carried my dad's Gibson Sunburst over to her and held it in front of her so she could read my list.

The audience erupted. I walked back to my perch, hiking my guitar over my head in a jubilant signal of victory.

Rolly counted us in and we launched into "All in the Deep Dark Woods."

#

I looked for Lynn in the foyer afterwards. I hadn't spotted her in the audience, but that didn't mean anything—sometimes her tickets landed her a front row seat, sometimes they didn't.

But I didn't see her in the little crowd of fans that came to chat with us, either, and to buy t-shirts and CDs and posters and have them signed, and that *was* unusual.

"She doesn't like you anymore, now that you've confessed to not having any interest in Harry Potter," Katey said. "I enjoyed the show, by the way. I'm glad I didn't stay behind and watch *The Great British Bake Off*. But I suppose now's not the time to tell you I'm not really into the sort of stuff the Figs play. It's far too 'jiggy' for my refined tastes."

"Good thing you're going home tomorrow," I replied.

"I'll always love you, of course. In spite of your musical delinquency."

I didn't have to remind her that the folky-pop songs that had made Figgis Green famous weren't my first musical choice, either. It wasn't something I could say out loud, surrounded by so many loyal fans. But my heart belonged to jazz. And I was really starting to miss my guys and our gig at the Blue Devil in Soho. Only two more weeks to go. Six more shows—and then I'd be on my way home.

The effects of Neil's tablets were starting to wear off. My head wasn't aching, but my body was, and on top of that, I had a codeine hangover and all I really wanted was to get back to the hotel and crawl into bed.

The last of the fans was trickling out of the front door and

Freddie was packing the merch back into its big plastic tubs when she waved me over.

"This arrived while you were onstage."

It was a small white envelope with my name written across the front.

"Thanks."

I tucked the envelope into my jeans pocket and went back to the dressing room to change into something fresh and not smelling of sweat for the ride back to the hotel.

While Katey and I were waiting on the pavement for a taxi, I got a text on my phone. It was Lynn.

Sorry I missed you at the show tonight, Jason. Any chance we can meet up at the Turf Tavern?

I looked up its location. Near New College.

It's closed, I said, noting the time. *Last call was at eleven. Can it wait 'til tomorrow? I'm dead on my feet and I really need to sleep.*

I'm so sorry, Jason…it's urgent.

"I'll go with you," Katey said.

Outside the Turf Tavern? I checked.

St Helens Passage. You'll see me.

Ten minutes, I said. *Just getting into a taxi.*

#

The driver dropped us off at the New College Lane entrance to the narrow little alley.

We're here, I texted. *Where are you?*

No reply.

There were still a few students about, making their way home after being shown the door by nearby drinking establishments. But the passage itself was dark and deserted.

Katey and I made our way in, using the lights in our phones to navigate through the canyon created by the high brick walls.

A few feet before the passage turned the corner I could see something lying on the pavement, blocking the way. It looked at first like a large bag of something, but when we got there, it turned out to be Lynn. Crumpled on her side, with her head resting on the pavement. She might have been asleep.

She wasn't, though. I checked. She wasn't breathing and she didn't have a pulse. And her skin was very cold.

CHAPTER TWENTY-TWO

I called 999 and then sat down on the pavement, bracing my back against one of the brick walls, near to where Lynn was lying but far enough away that I wasn't interfering with the crime scene.

I dug into my jeans pocket, automatically, for my cigarettes. And then I thought the better of it, and had a Fruit Pastille instead.

Katey went out to New College Lane to wait for the police.

Sorry I missed you at the show tonight, Jason. Any chance we can meet up at the Turf Tavern?

I'd received that message at 11:40 p.m. It was now a few minutes past midnight.

There was no way Lynn could have sent it. It was a chilly night, yes…but she couldn't have been alive twenty minutes earlier. I'd touched her face, her neck and her hand. Her skin was absolutely cold.

I shone the light in my phone over at her body. I could smell something peculiar. What was it?

My brain tried to recall where I'd encountered it before. Decades ago…in the Underground. And when I was a kid, when I'd fallen down and scraped my knee…

Disinfectant?

That was it.

Lynn smelled like Dettol.

#

It was a very, very long night.

Katey and I gave our statements at one of the Thames Valley police stations, Katey in one room, me in another.

It was a reasonably nice room—not a hard-edged place with a functional table and uncomfortable things to sit on and an institutional paint job like you see in TV police procedurals. This was more like a small conference room, with comfy office chairs and a friendly table and even friendlier walls with a couple of nondescript pieces of art hanging on them.

A witness interview room, I thought. Not the one they use for suspects.

It's funny how you focus on things like the nondescript art hanging on a wall when you're trying to put your thoughts together. Perhaps that's why they'd installed the two pictures, which seemed to form a pair. One was of the back of a woman sitting on her own in the sand at a beach, staring out at gentle waves. The other was of a large blue sun umbrella, stuck in the sand at the same beach, with a wicker picnic basket and a large pale blue blanket.

My first thoughts were, why isn't that bloody woman sitting under the umbrella? She hasn't brought any sun cream and she'll end up getting burned.

My second thought was, what's in that wicker basket?

Sgt. Dailey yanked my brain back from the beach. "And you got the text message when?"

I told him.

"But I don't think that could have been her," I said. "I think she was probably already dead by then. I think she was killed somewhere else and then her body was moved to St Helens Passage."

"You seem to be thinking a lot," said Sgt. Dailey.

"I'm a private investigator," I said. I suppose I was still in a bit of shock. "Not licensed. Not yet. And my sister writes crime novels. Taylor Feldspar."

I don't know why I said that, but it seemed to me, in my addled state of mind, to be a vitally important detail. I was immediately aware of how ridiculous I sounded.

"And she smelled of Dettol," I added, making things even worse.

"Your sister?" Sgt. Dailey inquired.

"Lynn," I replied, wishing I was somewhere else. "And if Lynn had been there in St Helens Passage all that time, her body would have been seen by students coming out of the pub. Whoever killed her knew what time our show finished. They knew when I'd be done with the Meet and Greet. Her body was put there so that I'd be the one to discover her."

I paused.

"And whoever it was knew my mobile number. Which Lynn very definitely didn't."

#

I drank five cups of coffee in the several hours I was at the police station. I didn't smoke any cigarettes. I finished my packet of sweets.

You know how you reach a place where everything in your body is demanding sleep? Like when you've been on a redeye flight and you haven't been able to drift off—and then you land and still have to get to your hotel, and in spite of all the caffeine in the world, you absolutely know that if you allow yourself the luxury of shutting your eyes, no matter where you are, you'll be unconscious in thirty seconds? That.

I told Sgt. Dailey everything I could remember about Lynn, from the time I'd first met her until I'd received those last texts.

"I don't expect you found her phone with her body," I said.

Sgt. Dailey would neither confirm nor deny my suspicion.

True, then.

I told Sgt. Dailey about everything else—the mishaps plaguing the tour, Lynn's possible acquaintance with Jackie Bolton, and the entity known as Castledancer.

By the time I was done, Katey had already finished giving her statement to the other officer in the other room, and had taken a taxi back to the hotel. She was blissfully asleep when I got there. I didn't even bother to undress. I crawled into bed beside her and I was out like a light.

#

I slept until noon, when Katey woke me up with lunch and the news that the rest of the Figs had gone on to Tunbridge Wells without me.

"Freddie's very helpfully arranged a late checkout for us," she continued, "but we absolutely have to be out by 2 p.m. And you're expected for dinner at Oakden Manor at 7 p.m. sharp. Don't be late."

"That last bit sounds like my mother," I said.

"It was your mother," Katey replied. "Oh—and Freddie left you this."

It was the envelope she'd given me in the foyer of the College Playhouse. The envelope that I'd tucked into my jeans pocket and then completely forgotten about when I went back to the dressing room to change. The envelope that Freddie had retrieved when she was checking all of our pockets before packing our clothes up to be cleaned.

Inside the envelope was a message from Lynn.

Dear Jason. I'm so sorry I had to miss tonight's show. Something came up. But I've left a package for you at your hotel's front desk. I think you'll appreciate it. I wish I could be at your concert in Tunbridge Wells but it's a posh invite-only. I'll see you in Croydon. Play well! (you always do!). XXX Lynn

I've encountered a few dead people since I've taken on PI work, and my reaction's never once changed. That individual was once alive. They'd breathed and lived, their heart was beating, they had memories and a voice and perhaps a family somewhere. Friends. A job. A purpose. And now that was all finished.

I liked Lynn—I really did. I might have lost my patience with her occasionally, but she was a nice person.

I'd seen the shell of her being, lying there in the passage, last night. Her spirit had been taken away.

And that had shaken me to my core.

I went downstairs to Reception and asked for my package.

It was a small cardboard box inside a plastic Tesco bag. The box had been fastened shut with about a hundred layers of sticky tape.

I took the box back upstairs and Katey got out her manicure scissors.

I'm not sure what I was expecting. A hand-knitted green scarf. A painted rock with fig leaves and a cute face.

Most definitely not my mother's alarm clock.

#

"You are absolutely having me on," mum said, over the phone.

"I'm not," I assured her. "Have you got to Tunbridge Wells yet?"

"We're just on our way to Oakden Manor now. Watch out for major roadworks near Oxted. Where are you?"

"Just checking out of the hotel," I lied. "I've got a couple of errands to run. I'll see you this evening. Clock in hand."

#

Downstairs at Reception, as I was settling my account, I asked whether anyone could remember what time my package had been delivered.

"I was on duty," said the clerk. Her name was Kylie and she was Australian. "It was roundabout this time yesterday. A short woman, bit on the heavy side, fiftiesh?"

That was Lynn, I thought.

"So, early afternoon. And if someone else came along after that—and it wasn't me—and asked for that package, would you have given it to them?"

"Absolutely not," Kylie replied. "I'd have needed to see ID. And if they weren't you, they'd have been right out of luck."

"And *did* anyone else come along and ask for it?"

Another clerk—Aslam, according to his name tag—looked over.

"Someone did, yes," he said. "Kylie was dealing with a guest. They tried—but as Kylie's told you—identification was required, and as they were most obviously not you, they were sent away empty-handed."

"Man or woman?" I asked.

"A woman, youngish, perhaps in her twenties. Her hair was long. Blonde."

I showed Aslam the photo of Jackie Bolton that Gillian had sent me.

"That is her, yes. I would swear to it."

"Thank you," I said.

#

I live in Angel, in Central London. My flat's on the first floor of a Georgian-era conversion near the tube station on Pentonville Road. I keep my car—an old silver Volvo V70 that has room for all my gear—parked nearby, in a paved-over space that was probably, in another era, someone's small private garden.

Katey dropped me off and I threw my all my bags into the back.

"I'll message when I've arrived safely," I said, kissing her goodbye.

"You'd better," she said. "I'm not accustomed to discovering dead bodies in isolated alleys. I may have to take tomorrow off work to recover."

I gave her another kiss. "You'll be all right," I said.

"How about you?"

"I'll be all right, too," I said.

"Wish you were staying in London, with me."

"I know. I'll call you."

"Promise?"

"Promise," I said.

#

Patchford House was in Hertfordshire, about fifteen minutes away from where my mum lived.

My grandmother had a beautiful room of her own, decorated with many of the things she'd brought with her when she'd given up her own home because she could no longer take care of herself and because she was terrified she'd wake up in the middle of the night in difficulty and there would be no one there to help her.

Granny Vera met me in the lounge, which had comfy armchairs with big, stuffed pillows, and long beige curtains decorated with large muted red and brown flowers, and doors which opened onto a patio and then a beautifully manicured lawn and gardens.

She was a part of that generation who never went anywhere without their face powder and rouge and lipstick, a pearl necklace and earrings. When I bent down to kiss her, I could smell her lavender soap and talc.

"It's such a beautiful day," she said, after I'd presented her with the three Cadbury Fruit and Nut bars I'd remembered to buy in the village shop. "Let's go outside."

Granny Vera wasn't as steady on her feet as she'd been in her younger days. She had one of those wheely walkers, which necessitated slow and careful steps.

I helped her with her long woolly cardigan, which she slipped on as insurance against the sudden chill when the sun disappeared momentarily behind clouds.

I helped her to sit down on a chair at a little glass-topped table on the patio.

And then I went back inside and got us two cups of tea from the "always on" buffet in the dining room, and some ginger snaps, and I carried everything back out to the table.

"The thing is…" I said, after we'd had the mandatory conversation about what I was doing, and how my mum was, and how my sister, Angie, was managing—living all the way out there on Mersea Island, which could only be reached by way of an ancient Roman causeway called the Strood. "I've been researching our family tree."

"How interesting," said my grandmother, handing me one of the chocolate bars, because she needed help peeling away the paper and foil.

I broke the bar into little squares, which Granny Vera immediately devoured, one after the other, after offering them to me.

"I was trying to locate mum's birth record," I said. "I had to do a lot of work. But I did eventually find it."

I showed her the copy of the certificate.

Granny Vera's eyesight was not what it had once been, but she could read properly if she had her glasses on. She slipped them out of a little soft case that she wore around her neck on a ribbon, and she looked at the document. The expression on her face didn't change at all.

"You see," she said, handing the piece of paper back to me when she'd finished, "I did ask your mother if she wanted to know the circumstances surrounding her birth, and she told me she didn't."

I looked at her.

"So she knew that Frank wasn't her real dad?"

"Of course. She's always known it. She was born in 1941 and I didn't marry Frank until 1943, nearly two years later, and some people might not have a memory of that, not a clear one, anyway, but your mother has an exceptionally good memory, always has had, and if you ask her, she'll tell you all about things that happened to her when she was very small. Some experts will try to tell you it's all some kind of trick, that you don't really remember it at all—it's something someone told you and you're remembering it second-hand. But if you ask her, Jason, she'll describe things the way she remembers them, because she was there and she's put those things into her own memory."

My grandmother paused to drink her tea, and to eat a ginger snap.

I could tell she was trying to organize her thoughts for me, but she'd forgotten where she'd left off.

"You married Frank in 1943," I prompted.

"Yes, that's right, and before that Mandy and I were living in my brother's house with his wife and their two children and we were ever so lucky to be able to be there even though it was only one room—Mandy and I had to share it—there was one little bed and a little cot in the corner and that was Mandy's—and my brother—your great uncle Peter—and his wife Cora had the big bedroom and there was another tiny room over the stairs and that's where their two little boys slept. Everyone was doubling up and people were living on top of each other because there was such a shortage of housing because of all the bomb damage. Anyway I had to leave the WAAFs when I fell pregnant—that was the rule, you couldn't continue—and I didn't really have anywhere else to go because my dad and mum wouldn't have me back so Peter and Cora took me in and then they let us stay after your mother was born."

She paused for another sip of tea.

"If you ask Mandy she'll remember that house because it had a little back garden with an Anderson shelter at the bottom. I used to put Mandy out in the garden in the morning. She had her reins on and I wound them through the rings on the pushchair so she couldn't climb out. She was quite safe. She'll remember that. She wasn't quite two. Frank came along in 1943 and he loved her immediately—as much as he loved me—and so I married him straightaway, because it was war time and people did things like that. You never knew if you were going to be bombed in the night and the person you'd gone dancing with had been blown to smithereens. Your mother was at our wedding. She'll remember that too, if you ask her."

I was stunned. I'd been afraid to ask because I didn't want to cause an upset, and all along, she'd known that Frank Green wasn't her birth father.

"Your mother loved Frank and accepted him as her father and when I decided she was old enough to understand what had happened, I asked her if she wanted to know who her real father was, and she told me that she didn't. As far as she was concerned, Frank was her dad, and that was that."

"So she never did find out?" I asked.

"Not as far as I know," Granny Vera replied.

"What was his name?" I asked, aware that my voice was shaking a little.

"Alan," my grandmother replied, after a moment. "I was in love with his younger brother, Lee, who was the most wonderful fellow you could ever wish to know."

"The airman at Biggin Hill," I said.

"That's right. Yes. I took you to meet him, didn't I?"

"You did," I said. "The dropping coin."

"He was a true gentleman. But he died, you see. He was shot down over Dungeness."

"I know, Granny."

"There's more of Lee in you than Alan. But there you are. Alan promised he'd marry me…but he kept delaying…and delaying…and after your mother was born I discovered he already had a wife and a child. And that he'd moved to London. So that was the end of that."

She finished her tea.

"Did Lee smoke?" I asked.

Granny Vera smiled.

"He did. But so did everyone. Even me. We were always hungry because of rationing and when you lit a cigarette it made the hunger go away."

"And was Alan a pilot?"

"Not at all. He tried to join up but he wasn't medically fit. He managed a printing firm. The family was originally from Norfolk, you know. Farmers. And another branch was stonemasons. And somebody told me, perhaps it was Lee, that hundreds of years ago, one of them contributed some carvings to Norwich Cathedral."

CHAPTER TWENTY-THREE

I wanted to drop everything and dive back onto the Generations website and look up Alan Merrifield. I would have sat in my car in the parking lot at Patchford House and researched him right there, but I knew if I did that, I'd be at it for hours, and I didn't have hours. I had to be at Oakden Manor in Tunbridge Wells by 7:00 p.m. or I risked the querulous eyebrows of Giles Jessop, the disappointment of the rest of the band, and the wrath of my mother—which was something you really never want to incur.

A phone call wasn't going to do the trick. Not even an abject apology about unavoidable delays. Short of a multi-vehicle pileup on the M25 or premature childbirth, nothing would excuse my absence.

I put everything my Granny had told me on hold, got back into my car, and drove like a madman so I could arrive at Giles Jessop's estate in Kent in time for dinner.

#

Oakden Manor had been in Giles's family for centuries. The descendancy came down through his mother, Gwendolyn Boswell-Thorpe, who had married Gilbert Jessop, the 17th Earl of Brighthelmstone, in 1938. Giles and his sister Arabella were silver-spoon war babies, but Arabella had disappeared—under somewhat mysterious circumstances—in 1965. Giles had inherited the lot—Oakden, a house in Mayfair in London, and Stoneford Manor—where mum and dad and the rest of the Figs had gathered to write and record their very first album, and, not uncoincidentally, where we'd assembled again to rehearse our Lost Time tour.

Oakden was three miles south of Tunbridge Wells, and it was surrounded by thirty acres of pastures and woodlands.

I'd looked at the website. You could have your wedding there, or you could just pay admission and come for the day and have a wander around the gardens with a guided tour of the house thrown in. You could have your lunch at a cafeteria in what used to be the old Stable Block—across the way from the old Coach House—and you could go into the shop next door and buy souvenirs to take home with you—tea towels, mugs, hand-made soaps, toys, local history books and, of course, home-made chutneys and preserves.

I drove up the long, lime tree-lined avenue from the main road. I could see our aqua and grey bus, our catering van and Kato's equipment van lined up in the gravel lot next to the Stable Block.

The house itself was Grade I listed and was built out of ashlar stone. The original Tudor wing off to the west still had its distinctive twisted chimneys. Facing me, the newer wing—which dated from the eighteenth century—boasted an amazing ornamental parapet that ran the length of the top floor, supported by balusters.

I parked my car and walked through the front courtyard and rang the bell. I halfway expected to be greeted by Mr. Carson from *Downton Abbey*—and being told, sternly, to go around to the tradesmen's entrance in the back.

The door was opened, instead, by a jovial young chap in a Savile Row suit.

"Good evening, Mr. Figgis. We've been expecting you."

It sounded like a line from a Hammer horror film and it made me smile. Though I'm sure that's not what the jovial young fellow intended at all.

"Do I need to change for dinner?"

"Not at all, sir—we're quite casual tonight. I'll show you to the dining hall and then I'll take your bags up to your room. Is your car locked?"

"It is," I said, handing him my keys. "Habit."

"And a very good habit it is, sir. This way."

He led me through a dark-wood-panelled entrance hall—lined with landscape paintings—to the dining room, which really was grand. It was much larger than the dining room at Stoneford Manor. There were tapestries and a further collection of landscapes on the walls, and an amazing display of portraits. The room had fireplaces at both ends, and in the centre of it all, a very fine rectangular table, around which the Figs' entire entourage had been seated: Beaky, Freddie, Kato, Tejo and Neil, and our two caterers, Janice and Mary, mum, Bob, Beth, Mitch and Rolly. There was an empty chair beside mum, which I assumed was for me.

The remaining two chairs were occupied by Giles Jessop and a woman I'd not met before. Her hair was swept up in a navy blue turban with an elaborate feather poking out of it, and her dress might have come from a vintage shop, all sequins and marine blue silk. She looked to be Giles's age.

The jovial young chap introduced me in much the same way a notable diplomat might have been announced as he arrived at a Victorian ball. "Mr. Jason Figgis."

A round of applause erupted from the table. I bowed deeply—to much laughter—then sat down beside my mother.

"Allow me to introduce my very good friend," said Giles, who was seated in the chair directly across from me. "Pandora Asquith-Jones. Jason Figgis. Also known professionally as Jason Davey."

"Lovely to meet you," said Pandora. The table was too wide to reach over and shake her hand, and it would have been awkward, anyway, with all of the silverware and china and sparkling glasses and vases of flowers. "I understand that, in your spare time, you're a private investigator."

"I am," I said.

"But you don't investigate murders."

"I don't," I confirmed. "I'd rather leave that to the police. I prefer to hunt down things that have gone missing. And people."

"He's very good," said my mother. "He's currently trying to get to the bottom of some odd mishaps…some threats we've been receiving."

"How fascinating," said Pandora. "I believe someone in Giles's family was involved in some sort of threatening behaviour in the 1600s—wasn't he, Giles?"

"Indeed," Giles replied.

"I can't quite recall who it was," Pandora said, racking her brain.

"A cousin on my mother's side," Giles said. "William Boswell, who was a colleague of Oliver Cromwell. And the object of the threatening behaviour was King Charles the First. Who ended up losing his head. Literally."

"I do hope it doesn't come to that in our case," my mother replied, as gentle and polite laughter rippled around the table. "Though you never know—perhaps the Mad Hatter in Leeds was trying to tell us something."

#

We had an exceptionally fine dinner—four courses—served on silver platters and in tureens by a white-gloved catering staff which, I was assured, had been hired strictly for this occasion.

"Usually we just putter about and do it all ourselves," Pandora said, confirming my mother's suspicion that she was Giles's current live-in love interest (and he'd apparently had many, over the years). "We have a housekeeper, of course, and Gerald, who's the butler-chief-door-answerer-general-fix-it-man-and-chauffeur, when required. And the people who look after the estate, of course, to keep it tidy for the visitors. Gardeners and cleaners and guides and shop assistants…actually, we do employ rather a lot of people, don't we, Giles?"

She seemed quite surprised at the totality of it all, once she'd actually thought about it.

"Necessitated by the opening up of one's private home to the public," Giles replied. "Which is, in itself, necessitated by the need to pay for constant upkeep, a leaky roof, unreliable hot water, and rampant woodworm."

I listened sympathetically, but I wasn't entirely convinced Giles and Pandora understood how different their world was from the world we'd all come from.

I was well-off, yes, but my mother didn't start out that way, and my dad certainly hadn't, and they'd always reminded Angie and me, as we were growing up, that we were lucky. And that we would be wise to consider that other people might not be as fortunate. And that we would also be wise not to cultivate an attitude that those who were not as fortunate or as lucky as us were any less deserving, or that we were automatically entitled to more.

I wouldn't say that Giles and Pandora had that kind of attitude…it was just that they couldn't possibly comprehend a life other than the one they were living. The leaky roof, the unreliable hot water and the woodworm were affronts to their established order. Along with the fact that they'd had to open up their home to daytripping families, wedding parties, and guided tours in order to pay for all the repairs.

Still...Giles wasn't lacking in cash. Our dinner was lavish, to say the least. Each of us was given a hand-lettered menu, explaining what we were about to eat. For starters, there was a prawn cocktail, which contained, in addition to the requisite prawns, lobster, cucumber, tomato and a sauce laced with brandy.

There was, as well, a hot soup—a velouté, if you want to be technical, made with roasted cauliflower and black onion seeds and truffle oil.

The main course was a roasted, boneless chicken breast, with whipped, mashed potatoes, baby carrots and tarragon gravy.

And for afters...a hollow sphere of chocolate and orange, filled with Clementine ice cream and decorated with a burnt orange syrup.

I would have taken pictures for Instagram, but I somehow felt it would be rude.

At the end of it all, sipping my Earl Grey tea from an exquisite Wedgwood cup and saucer, I was feeling well and truly pampered.

It was almost enough to make me forget about what had happened to poor Lynn in St Helens Passageway the day before.

But not quite.

Unfortunately, Lynn threatened to become the topic of after-dinner conversation in the drawing room, which was over in the Tudor part of the house, and reached by way of a series of other rooms called interesting things like The Great Boswell Hall and The Grand Entrance (because, in the sixteenth century, it had once actually been the only way in).

"I did read about that poor girl dying," Pandora said, to me, as everyone arranged themselves on antique sofas and in slightly uncomfortable, upholstered armchairs. "And I know it's not up your alley at all...but was it a murder?"

"It very much seems to be," I replied.

"She knew who stole your mum's clock," Kato said. "Didn't she."

"I believe she did, yes."

"That's why," said Kato. "Serious business. Colonel Mustard with the mic stand in the dressing room."

"I'm afraid I'll have to excuse myself," I said. I really didn't feel like taking part in a tour-themed game of Cluedo. "I'm still battling the vestiges of pneumonia, and I really need to go and lie down."

#

I wasn't sure how to address the butler.

"Gerald will do, sir," he said, as he accompanied me upstairs. "We're all on an informal first-name basis here, though if you wish to be very correct my last name is Benson. My father, Jerome, was in service, as was his father and grandfather and great-grandfather before him. You might say the occupation is very much in my blood."

My room was on the second floor of the eighteenth century wing. It featured an authentic four-poster bed and modern cream wall-to-wall carpeting, along with some very ancient armchairs, and original ceiling-almost-to-the-floor windows. And, of course, a fireplace.

Gerald had brought my bags up during dinner and had left them neatly at the foot of the bed. He handed me the keys to my car.

"Very nice Volvo, sir. Old, of course, but very useful for your purposes, I should think."

"Extremely useful," I said. I felt I ought to tip him, but there was no need. He was part of Giles's household staff. I really hoped he wasn't going to offer to help me undress.

"I'll say good night, then, sir...please do ring if you need anything."

Was there a bell, then? That tinkled downstairs to alert whoever was on duty in the kitchen that someone upstairs needed some help knotting a necktie or doing up their cuff links? Or getting into their pyjamas?

There was not, thankfully. A printed sheet had been placed on my pillow, and it contained the number of Gerald's mobile, should I require it in an "emergency."

The windows in my room didn't open, of course, and so I sneaked downstairs and outside for the ciggie I'd been craving for hours. Neil's medical advice aside, I felt I was well enough to indulge in my habit. I'd resisted all the way from Hertfordshire to Kent in my car.

I stood in the moonlight in the forecourt, gazing up at the ornamental parapet and its supporting balusters. After every fifth one I could see a little concrete pillar topped by a carved head. A gargoyle. Or—more correctly—a grotesque.

And one of those grotesques looked extremely familiar.

#

Back in my room, I checked Instagram on my phone while I waited for my laptop to boot up.

There was nothing from Jilly, and, for the briefest of moments, I had an awful thought—that mum was right, and Jilly had been Lynn, all along, and with Lynn dead, Jilly was also now permanently silenced.

Jilly, I typed. *Where are you? I know you must have heard about what happened to Lynn. I need to talk to you.*

I waited.

Nothing.

My laptop was up and running. I logged into The Greenhouse to see what they were discussing. Lynn's death, of course. Top of the list.

There were a lot of theories, some of them completely ridiculous and involving conspiracies and relationships that had no basis in reality. Others were quite thought-provoking, though, and really made me wonder.

She knew something…she kept hinting that she had information that would totally compromise certain people if she ever made it public…

Are you suggesting it was the Figs themselves that wanted her dead?

Not the entire band. Someone specific.

How can you say that about Mandy or Jason or any of them?

Not Mandy or Jason. Lynn had something on one of the others.

You can't just make statements like that without providing proof. What do you know?

I don't know anything. Forget I mentioned it.

I made a note of the person who was making those statements. Roving Minstrel 556.

I sent them a private message.

It's Jason from the Figs. I'm very curious to hear more about your claim concerning Lynn and what she knew. Can you PM me? If you need any verification of my identity, I'm happy to provide it.

I waited, but it was very late, and according to the Greenhouse logs, Roving Minstrel was no longer online.

I checked the news sources, national and local to Oxford. Lots of facts about the discovery of Lynn's body—though I knew the police had held back some of the details. And there were no new leads.

Right then. It was time to address Alan Merrifield.

But before I could log on to Generations, there was a knock on my bedroom door

It was my mother.

She poked her head inside.

"I'm assuming you're decent."

"If I wasn't, I'd be very surprised if you saw anything you hadn't seen before."

"Barring piercings and rings," my mother replied, coming into the room and closing the door behind her. "What's it called? A Prince Albert?"

"I do not know," I said, "because I do not have one."

"So you say," said my mother.

"And I never will," I added. "An earring was enough, back in the day."

My mother gave me a questioning look.

"Through my ear lobe," I said.

Mum spotted the Tesco shopping bag containing the brown cardboard box that Gerald had placed on my bed.

"Is that my clock?"

"It is."

"Might I have it back, then?" She picked up the bag.

"I was thinking," I said, "that we should probably give it to the Thames Valley police."

"Why, for God's sake? It wasn't at the crime scene. Was it?"

"It was at the hotel's Reception," I said. "But the person who left it there was Lynn. It'll have Lynn's fingerprints on if. But it might also have the fingerprints of her killer—if her killer was in any way associated with the theft."

My mother had been on the very verge of looking inside the Tesco bag. She stopped.

"And how did Lynn come to have my clock in her possession?"

"I don't know. That's what I'm trying to find out, actually. As Kato suggested, perhaps she knew the person who broke into your room."

My mother leaned over to talk to the Tesco bag.

"My darling Tony," she said. "It seems I shall have to wait a little bit longer before we're reunited. But at least I'll know where you are." She gave me a humorous glance. "Our son doesn't know about your secret piercing. I think we shall have to keep it that way."

"Excuse me?" I said.

My mother sat up straight and placed her hands in her lap and answered me with a look of pure innocence.

"I suppose if you want his ashes back," I said, "we could remove them. Carefully."

"Nobody need know," she agreed.

"The job requires a very tiny screwdriver."

"I have just the thing," said my mum.

She went back to her room, and returned with a little kit she kept for tightening the screws in the arms of the spectacles she wore for reading.

"Here we are."

Mum protected the clock from our fingerprints using one of the fresh towels Gerald had left for me. I unscrewed the clock's facing and gently pried the two sides apart.

Inside was a little plastic bag of white ashes, compacted into the hollow where the inner workings had once lived. I lifted it out, then carefully put everything back together and tightened the screws again. Mum returned the clock to its cardboard box.

"Tell Inspector Morse I'll require a receipt for that," she said.

"Absolutely," I promised, glancing at the little bag that was now in mum's hands. "Night night, dad."

Mum got up and came over to give me a kiss.

"Sleep well from both of us," she said. "Busy day tomorrow."

#

Of course, I didn't go to sleep. I logged onto the Generations website and did another search for Merrifield in my DNA matches. But nothing had changed. There were still only three matches, all fifth-to-eighth cousins, and all of them with fewer than ten cM in common with me.

Which was very odd, considering Alan Merrifield was my grandfather.

I went over to the general search page and typed in Alan's name.

He ought to have at least shown up in the 1939 Register that had been undertaken by the government at the start of World War Two. If you were still alive now, your name was blacked out. But he couldn't still be alive, I thought—he was older than Lee.

There was no record of him.

I decided to do a search for Lee, instead. That one paid off easily. There were all sorts of World War Two-related documents attached to Alan's brother.

And there he was, in the 1939 Register. Lee Merrifield. Birth date 19 April 1916. I looked him up in the GRO. Born in Loddon, Norfolk. Mother's maiden name Black.

In 1939 he was living in Norwich, unattached, and sharing a household with one Alan Hobbs, birth date given as 11 July 1914. A printing works manager. And his wife, Eva Mary, born 15 August 1916.

So. Alan Hobbs.

My grandfather's last name wasn't Merrifield at all.

I was so caught up in that lightning bolt of a revelation that it took me a full minute to process the fact that the surname of the person who'd put together Paisley Ascot, who'd been my dad's girlfriend before he'd decided he'd rather spend the rest of his life with my mother, who'd stormed off in anger the night he'd given her the birthday alarm clock, was also Hobbs.

Louise Annabelle Hobbs.

Late of Croydon Merton.

And current resident, since 2015, of Mitcham Road Cemetery.

CHAPTER TWENTY-FOUR

"What in the foul and pestilent congregation of vapours are you doing calling me at this hour?"

My mother was not happy.

It was nearly half-past two in the morning and she was throwing *Hamlet* at me.

I'd spent the previous two hours researching Alan Hobbs. I'd wanted to know why my grandmother was under the impression he was Lee Merrifield's brother.

Hints had flown at me from all over the place. Other people had created family trees that contained a lot more details about Alan than the ones I'd been able to track down.

I had the answer…and a lot more.

"I'm sorry," I said. "It's important."

"It had better be," my mother replied.

"I'm coming to your room." I paused. "Where is it?"

It was a long walk down the hallway of the eighteenth century part of the house and then a sharp left turn into the older, Tudor wing.

Mum was in her nightgown and had wrapped herself up in a cobalt-blue silk dressing gown with a giant dragon embroidered on its back. I recalled buying that for her when I was visiting Hong Kong after the *Sapphire* sank.

Compared to my room, hers was absolutely lavish. She had the requisite four-poster bed, of course—but also a Turkish carpet on the floor (gracefully displaying a few hundred years' worth of wear and tear), a beautiful fireplace with real chopped logs in the hearth, a china cabinet filled with what looked like a complete antique tea set, a chaise lounge upholstered in pink and red patterned silk, and an entirely new collection of tapestries, similar to what I'd seen downstairs, but on a much smaller scale, hanging on either side of the fireplace and on the walls on both sides of the bed.

Mum was absolutely in her element. She could have had a second career hosting one of those TV shows that explores Britain's historical houses.

But not in her current mood.

I set my laptop up on a Victorian writing table next to the fireplace.

"Sit down," I suggested.

She did, on the chaise lounge.

I pulled a chair upholstered in pink silk over from the window, which had gold-coloured curtains that matched the bedspread.

"Annie Hobbs," I said, "is—was—your sister. Half-sister."

My mother looked at me. She didn't say anything. I guessed she was probably processing what I'd just told her and trying to match it up with what she already knew—and didn't know—about the circumstances surrounding her birth.

"I've spoken to Granny," I said. "She told me who your father was. You don't need to know about him if you don't want to, but it's absolutely imperative that you know about Annie."

"Of course," my mother said, slowly. "Yes, of course. The letters."

"What letters?"

"The letters Annie sent me after the Figs were starting to really be successful. Always the same…moaning about her circumstances. Complaining that she was ill, or she was hard done by, she didn't have any money, she needed things she couldn't afford, she didn't know who else to ask and could I help her as she had nowhere else to turn. I owed it to her. I ought to look after her. We're family, she said. And family members have a duty to look after one another. I thought she meant, a family because we were all in Paisley Ascot together. And because your father had once been in love with her."

"You couldn't have known," I said.

"But she obviously did. She must have discovered we were sisters. Perhaps our father told her."

"I think it very likely," I replied.

"We did try to help her, at first. With money. And practical things for the winter. Pullovers and scarves and thick gloves. I told her where to go for advice about her benefits and other kinds of assistance. Job centres. Even places we'd heard were looking to hire someone with a musical background. Teaching gigs. We had to stop in the end, because she just didn't seem to want to listen. No matter how much money we gave her, or whatever leads we sent along, it was always the same. *Oh poor me.*"

"She obviously got it into her head that you were obligated to take care of her."

I pulled up my Alan Hobbs page on Generations.

"Do you want to know about your father?" I asked.

Mum thought for a moment.

"Bloody hell, why not. I expect he's long dead, anyway. Show me."

"There he is," I said, scrolling through his profile. "Born in 1914. His parents were Robert Hobbs and Eliza Frame, from Loddon, in Norfolk. They died in 1919 during the flu epidemic, when Alan was five. He went to live with his father's friend, Horace Merrifield. Horace and his wife Adele already had a three-year-old son."

"Lee," mum guessed.

"Lee," I confirmed. "There's the connection to Granny's dead airman. The family treated Alan like Lee's older brother."

My mother read the details in silence. I imagine it felt a bit like an earthquake to her...the same way it had to me when Katey had brought me the copy of mum's birth certificate.

"Here's Alan in the 1939 Register," I said, pulling up the actual copy of the thing, so my mother could see the names and details. "His wife's name is Eva, and Lee is living with them."

"Printing works manager," mum said. "Norwich."

"Yes. And then Alan and his wife moved to London, where both of his daughters were born. He eventually left them and emigrated to Australia. Where he met another woman and had some more children. He died there in 1994."

"I seem to be awash in half-siblings," my mother mused.

"I'm glad you can see the humour in it," I said. "His two daughters are Joanne and Annie. I haven't had time to track Joanne down yet, but Annie was born in Wandsworth."

"She always said that her dad was long gone. He'd abandoned them a few years before Paisley Ascot. So...Australia."

"Toowoomba," I said. "Queensland."

Mum was still taking it all in. "I think Annie's mum—what was her name?"

"Eva," I said.

"Eva had to go and live with Annie's sister."

"Joanne."

"Yes, Joanne. Otherwise she'd have been destitute."

"Are you ready for the next bolt of lightning?"

"Oh dear," my mother said. "There's more?"

I scrolled down the page and clicked on Louise Annabelle Hobbs's entry.

"Here's Annie. Never married. I looked—I really searched, before I rang you."

"She died in 2015," mum said, thoughtfully. "Shame."

I think she really meant it.

"Annie also had two daughters. Victoria, born in 1970—that's the one she was expecting when you last saw her. And Elizabeth, born two years before that. Their last names are both Hobbs. I haven't had time to find out much about Victoria. But Elizabeth's middle name is Lynn. And she married a guy named Sidney Wayland."

I paused, and waited to see if it would click.

It did.

"Lynn Wayland," mum said.

"Your lately departed niece," I confirmed. "And my lately departed cousin."

#

I went back to my room with my laptop.

But if I thought I was going to get any sleep, I had another thing coming.

As soon as I closed the door, my phone bleeped with an incoming text. It was from Castledancer.

Hello, Jason. I've now had time to put my thoughts together regarding your offer of a reward for the return of your mother's pictures.

How did you get my mobile number? I asked.

She ignored me.

Shall we say…£100,000?

Don't make me laugh, I said. *As much as we'd like them back…No.*

I assure you, Jason, I'm serious. £100,000 for 26 high-quality, professionally-shot black and white PR photos of Tony Figgis and Mandy Green. And another three which are not so much professional quality as compromisingly pornographic.

Sorry? I said. *Compromisingly pornographic?*

Do you really want to me to post pictures on my website of your mother and father, completely naked, having, shall we say, enthusiastic sex?

Where did these pictures come from?

I cannot say. Obviously.

When and where were they taken?

They were taken in Stoneford. In 1964. When your parents were obviously relishing love's first delectable, intimate passions.

And how do you happen to have them? I tried, again.

I don't think it would be in my best interests to reveal that, Jason. Suffice to say, I do have them. And the negatives they came from. I'm prepared to return them to you—along with the other 26 pictures—after you pay me the asking price.

How do I know they're genuine? I wrote back.

You don't believe me?

There was a pause, and then Castledancer texted me scans of the three pictures in question.

They'd been shot through a bedroom window. I knew which window, because I knew the house. It was the cottage my parents had lived in until just before I was born. I used to look at pictures of it when I was small. And I'd actually gone to have a real look at it before I ran away to sea. The owners had been only too happy to show me around.

The bedroom was on the second floor and the only way those photos could have been taken was with a telephoto lens on a camera being held by someone who'd climbed a tree about ten feet away and sat there, in the branches, watching.

And the two people in those photos were very definitely my mum and dad.

I would think you'd want to pay me the money, Jason, simply because you wouldn't want to subject your mother to the embarrassment of having those pictures circulating around the internet. Am I right? Because the moment they're on my website, they're fair game for social media. And you know what that means.

I did know what that meant.

I felt sick.

What's to stop me from reporting this to the police? I said. *Which I'm very much tempted to do right now.*

Do you know how quickly I can put these online, Jason? A couple of flicks of my finger. If I have any inkling that you've involved the police, I won't hesitate to act. And, as you well know, once something is "out there"...it's impossible to retract. So I hope you'll think very carefully before you do anything rash.

I won't involve the police, I said.

Excellent. We have the basis for further discussion. I'd like the money tomorrow.

My bank's in London, I said, *and in order to arrange for that amount of cash quickly, I'd need to go there. I'm in the middle of a tour and I'm in Tunbridge Wells and I can't easily do that and come back in time for our next show. Which is tonight.*

That is a dilemma, isn't it, Jason. But I'm sure you'll be able solve it.

Are you Jackie Bolton? I asked.

Who?

How did you get my number? I asked again.

Castledancer didn't reply.

Jackie Bolton has my number, I said. *I rang her when we were in Cambridge and I got her voice mail. She answered me back with a text and then she blocked me. I've never shared my mobile number with you. And I didn't give it to Lynn Wayland, either. Jackie Bolton's the only one who's ever known what it is.*

I am not Jackie Bolton, Castledancer replied. *I shall talk further with you in the morning. Sleep well.*

As if.

I went back online and did a deep dive into Jackie Bolton. I refused to believe there was no information about her anywhere.

True, she didn't have a social media presence, and she didn't show up in the electoral rolls or anywhere else I'd have expected her to leave a footprint. But she'd worked for a firm that had provided catering for a popular music festival. And like an unsuspecting murderer, I was sure she'd left clues. I just had to find them.

I typed "Crafty Knaves and Dodgy Wenches" into Google, along with "A Fine Mess."

Three pages into the results, I found a posting that someone named John Cox had made on Facebook. It was from 2016, and the picture showed the interior of the VIP tent, with a handful of musicians chowing down.

The accompanying text said: *Working at Crafty Knaves and Dodgy Wenches. Excellent music. Even more excellent food, if I do say so myself. Please drop by and say hello!*

The posting had three likes and two comments. The first of the likes was from a guy named Gordo in Miami Beach. The second was from a sheepdog named Lola who lived in Perth, Scotland. The third was from someone named Jackie Wooley.

I clicked on her name and was taken to her Facebook page.

Her profile photo was a fancy cake, decorated with flowers and birds and squiggles, all made out of pastel-coloured icing.

Her birthdate was 11 Oct 1994. Her postings were set to private—but her friends list wasn't. She had about four hundred of them, which wasn't too bad. I was prepared for 1,500, but she apparently wasn't that popular.

I scrolled down through the lot of them, looking for anyone else with the same last name, Wooley. There was only one: Vicky.

Vicky Wooley's main purpose in life appeared to be to complain about the people who lived on the same housing estate as herself. They were, according to her postings (and there were many, in multiples), fraudsters, hoaxsters, bullies, illegal immigrants, lazy layabouts on benefits with chandeliers hanging in their sitting rooms and half a dozen mobile phones in their pockets (most of them stolen), thieving gits and pagans who made her feel like a refugee in her own country.

She was also obsessed with a male stripper she believed was sending her secret messages on Twitter, and equally occupied by a drug-sniffing police dog who had his own Facebook page and was providing updates on his daily life at one of London's airports.

She adored *Strictly Come Dancing*. And she despised her not-much-missed and thoroughly repulsive ex-husband, George, who she'd married in 1992, and who'd walked out of the marriage three years later (dodged a bullet there, George).

She really was a piece of work.

She was forty-eight years old and she was Jackie Wooley's mother.

I went back to Generations and typed Vicky's information into the search field. That gave me her Civil Registration Marriage Index entry…and her full name.

Which was, of course, Victoria Lillian Hobbs.

CHAPTER TWENTY-FIVE

I didn't sleep well.

On top of everything else, there was that fireplace at the foot of my bed.

I hadn't bothered to close the curtains and we were in the middle of the countryside, so there were no street lights. Just the moon, casting a pale silver beam through the eighteenth century window panes and onto that black square opening in the wall with its white stone surround.

I don't know about you, but when I was a kid, at bedtime, my imagination used to run rampant. Clothes hanging on hooks became the silhouettes of evil, lurking men. Open cupboard doors were the portals to dark, forbidden caverns housing unspeakable entities. There was a fireplace in my bedroom, but it wasn't unfriendly. If wood or coal had ever been burned in it, the leavings were long gone. Everything had been swept clean and painted over, and it was a repository for my boxes of Subbuteo, all neatly stacked, one on top of the other.

Our entire house was heated with hot water so, in fact, the only working fireplace was down in the lounge, and it was more of a conversation piece than anything functional. Though it did provide a lovely warm blaze on a winter's night, especially at Christmas.

The fireplace at the foot of my bed at Oakden Manor took me back to my monsters-in-cupboards childhood and the prospect of hideous deaths having been committed within Oakden's centuries-old stone walls. I felt an uneasy chill. And when I turned my head slightly to the left, I immediately knew why.

There he was. Again. Lee. Sitting in the armchair next to the fireplace. Still wearing his cap with its winged badge, and his thick white crew-necked sweater and his grey flying jacket and grey trousers and fleece-lined boots and yellow inflatable lifejacket.

He was smoking.

And then he spoke. "Hello, Jason. I shouldn't worry."

He sounded like Noel Coward in *In Which We Serve.* A clipped accent, 1940s.

"I shouldn't worry about what?" I asked.

"Anything, much, really. It'll all be sorted out. In the end."

Then he smiled, and I will swear on my mother's well-thumbed copy of *The Complete Works of William Shakespeare* that, in that moment, in that pale moonlight, his face was once again exactly the face of the Green Man in Norwich Cathedral.

He raised the hand that was holding the cigarette, and, with a confident smile, gave me a thumbs-up.

And then he dissolved away, into the darkness.

I blinked, and saw only the empty armchair.

Was it a dream?

It certainly didn't seem like one. I could have sworn I was wide awake.

But in the morning, staring at that black cavernous square beyond my feet, I honestly didn't know.

My phone had been recharging overnight on a George III mahogany kneehole desk beside my bed. I checked it to see if there was anything from Jilly.

There wasn't.

I really didn't want to believe that, all along, she'd been Lynn. But it seemed more and more like that was the case. I tried to work out, in my head, how she could have known everything about me that Jilly did. And how she could have known everything about Jilly.

Lynn had been a self-confessed fan for a very long time.

Six years ago, on board the *Sapphire*...could that have been her? Masquerading as Jilly's constructed personality? Sending me Twitter messages from wherever she was in England?

I'd enjoyed entertaining the idea that I had my very own personal guardian angel. The realization that she was likely just an ordinary human being with a very creative imagination made me feel sad.

I'd always been a little bit in love with her.

I felt empty.

I navigated over to The Greenhouse to see if Roving Minstrel 556 had answered my private message.

They had.

Hi Jason. We all know you're Cold Fingers, LOL. You don't have to prove your identity. How can I help?

Of course. That was me told. No such thing as presumed anonymity with this bunch.

I read your posts about Lynn, I said. *You were saying she was hinting that she had information that would compromise someone in the band. And that someone specifically wanted her dead.*

Roving Minstrel 556 took a moment before replying. *It's just that she said something when we were in Cambridge. After you fell into the river. We were all in the pub and she said something like, that's enough. She couldn't deal with them anymore.*

She couldn't deal with who anymore? I asked.

She wouldn't say. I didn't know what she was talking about. I did ask. And she just shook her head. And then, when you had to cancel the show, she was very upset. Not at you, not at the band. She said she should have stopped her.

She should have stopped who? Jackie Bolton?

She wouldn't say. Who's Jackie Bolton?

Lynn never mentioned her?

Never.

How about Jackie Wooley? I asked.

Never heard of her, either.

How about anyone with the last name Hobbs?

I've got nothing, Jason. Sorry. Actually, Wooley sounds familiar, now that you mention it.

Why?

I don't know. I'm thinking I've heard it somewhere before. I can ask around.

If you don't mind, I said. *But be careful.*

Yeah, no worries.

Where did you get the impression Lynn had compromising information about someone in the band? I asked, again.

There was a moment of silence. A very long moment.

When we were in Oxford…we were meeting up in a pub. The Ancient Porter. Some of the Figs were in there too. Mitch, Rolly, Bob and Beth. Not you or Mandy. I saw Lynn come in and she looked over at where they were all sitting and she seemed really frightened. I went into the loo and she came in too and she said she'd just done something that could get her into a shitload of trouble. And I asked, what kind of trouble. And she wouldn't tell me. In the end she said, I can't stay, I've got to go. They'll kill me if they find out. Who's 'they' I asked. But she just shook her head. And then she left, really quickly. So I sort-of made the assumption.

That it was someone in the band? I said.

Yes. Because of the look on her face when she came in. When she saw them sitting there.

To say I was stunned would be an understatement.

Mitch was my mum's brother—half-brother, as it turned out, but still. Rolly was my dad's cousin. Bob and Beth were the two outsiders, the newcomers, the two I knew the least well. And one—possibly more—of them had terrified Lynn?

What day was this? I asked. *What time? Can you remember?*

Yes, it was Saturday. Around 2 pm. We had lunch in the pub and stayed on.

Saturday. We'd performed that evening. Lynn's body had been discovered in St Helens Passage that night.

The thing that Lynn had just done, that she worried would get her into a shitload of trouble, was leave my mother's clock for me at Reception at the Radcliffe Hotel.

Do me a favour, I said. *Please don't say anything else on the chat group.*

Oh don't worry, Jason, I won't. So who's the guilty Fig? My money's on Beth. The last to join, and we know so little about her…

Beth's a lovely person, I said. *I can't believe she'd have anything to do with this.*

Do you think I should tell the police what I know?

A nightmare scenario flashed in front of me. Mitch, Rolly, Beth and Bob being hauled in for questioning. Unspeakable disruptions to our schedule. All triggered by some vague words from the murder victim, and some very big assumptions from a fellow fan.

But Lynn was dead.

And her killer was still at large.

I think you should, I wrote. I typed in Sgt. Dailey's contact information at Thames Valley Police. *And please let me know about that last name. Wooley.*

I will, Jason. Thanks for the chat.

Thank you, I said, and I added a thumbs-up emoji to my message.

#

My bedroom shared a bathroom with the three other rooms on the second floor of the eighteenth century wing of Oakden Manor. The fittings were exceedingly ancient, although the taps and the plumbing and the inside workings of the toilet had obviously been modernized.

I had a shower and shaved, and then I went downstairs to see what was on offer for breakfast.

There was a sign in the dining room: **Please help yourself!** And, on a long side table, someone—was it Gerald?—had laid out a selection of rolls and croissants, butter and marmalade and jam, bread and a toaster, and a little buffet of hot things kept warm with tins of flaming Sterno and large, removable lids. I investigated, and discovered sausages, bacon and scrambled eggs. There was a basket of teabags, and a kettle, and a coffee-maker with single-serve pods, along with a handwritten apology good-naturedly acknowledging that none of this was environmentally friendly but the only way forward when there were eleven guests staying in the house and no formal plans for breakfast.

At the end of the table was a further sign, this one from Giles, suggesting that anyone who was interested should meet up at 11:00 a.m. in the forecourt for a grand tour of the house, followed by lunch at one.

It was only half-past eight, and I had the dining room to myself. I guessed the rest of the band and the crew were still asleep—particularly my mother, who I'd kept up until half-past three.

While I ate my breakfast, I checked my emails and texts.

A reminder from Castledancer about the £100,000 and another dire warning about what would happen if I failed to come through with the cash. I sent a message back:

I'm just about to talk to my bank manager in London. I'll arrange to have the money available to me in Tunbridge Wells later today. I appreciate your patience.

I posted a picture of my breakfast to my Instagram friends, along with a comment about that night's upcoming gig, and promising more pictures closer to event time.

And then I rang my sister in Mersea, and asked to speak to her husband, Tom, who was a retired copper.

"What do you think I should do?" I said, after I'd explained the situation with the photos of mum and dad.

"What do you think this person's motives are?" Tom countered. "Usually when someone's being blackmailed with the threat of exposing sexually compromising pictures, it's a former lover or someone who's trying to get something more—more compromising photos from the victim, or getting the victim back into a relationship. Or money. This appears, on the surface, to be more about simple extortion. This person doesn't seem, to me, anyway, to have any personal stake in the pictures. They're simply trying to extract some cash out of you."

"The blackmailer's set herself up to be a huge fan of Figgis Green," I said. "She has a website. Exclusive photos. Fan fiction. Worldwide adoration."

"She can't be much of a fan if she's intent on exposing your mother and relieving you of £100,000," Tom replied.

"My thoughts exactly. And if she did put those pictures up on her website, she'd risk losing about ninety percent of her followers."

"Who's to say she doesn't have even more of these compromising photos, and the demands for money never stop."

"If she's behind all the other things that have been going on with this tour," I said, "it's not about extortion at all. It's about revenge."

"You could get an injunction," Tom said.

"The minute I do that, those pictures will be online."

"Well, from my perspective, if it's all about revenge, she wants to enjoy seeing you—and your mother—suffer. If there's no indication of that…where's her personal payoff?"

"It's almost as if the money's incidental," I said.

"You may be right. In which case, it's not a matter of *if* she'll put those photos online…it's when. She may be timing it to cause maximum damage." Tom paused. "I think you know what you need to do."

"I do," I said, my mood sinking. "Thanks, Tom. Would you mind putting Angie back on the line? There's something I need to discuss with her, as well."

#

After my conversation with my sister, I rang Thames Valley Police, and asked to speak with Sgt. Dailey.

I didn't tell him anything about Castledancer's photos. Or what Roving Minstrel 556 had told me.

But I did bring him up to date on everything I'd discovered about Annie Hobbs—including the fact that Lynn Wayland was her daughter and Annie was my mother's sister. And that there was a deep resentment on that side of the family because of a perceived wrongdoing that dated back more than fifty years.

Sgt. Dailey noted it all down without much more than an occasional appreciative acknowledgement. I had no idea how much he and his investigative team had already discovered on their own.

"Have you found out how Lynn died?" I asked. "I didn't see any signs of violence. No wounds, no obvious bruises, no marks."

"The coroner hasn't been able to make a determination yet," Sgt. Dailey replied.

"What about the Dettol smell?"

Sgt. Dailey made noises that indicated he was consulting his notes.

"None of our people smelled disinfectant. Must have been gone by the time we got there."

"The thing is," I said, "the principle ingredient in Dettol is Chloroxylenol. Which is a derivative of phenol. It's also related to creosote. The wooden sleepers in the Underground used to be preserved with creosote and that's the smell I remembered while I was waiting for the police to arrive."

Sgt. Dailey didn't say anything.

"Lynn was a Type Two diabetic," I said. "Insulin dependant. And if you've ever been around someone who's just injected insulin, you can smell it. The insulin. Because it's preserved with phenol."

"So…you're suggesting…what?"

"I think Lynn might have been given a massive insulin overdose. And I think whoever did it accidentally spilled a sizable amount of it on her body. Maybe a vial broke. Or a needle. I don't know. Were you aware she was a diabetic? Did she have anything with her that would have given you a clue? One of those medical bracelets…glucose tablets…?"

Sgt. Dailey was silent. A no to that, then.

"You should tell your pathologist about Lynn's diabetes," I said. "And tell them to look carefully for multiple injection sites. They'll need to excise the areas around them to test for an excessive amount of insulin. Immediately. Insulin degrades quickly at room temperature so you'll have to act fast if you want to preserve evidence."

"This is a bit of a random leap," Sgt. Dailey replied. "And you seem to be uncommonly familiar with the process."

"I told you," I said, "my sister writes crime novels."

Sgt. Dailey laughed. I wasn't sure if he held a very dim view of crime-writers, or if he was genuinely amused.

"I promise we'll look into it," he assured me.

"Quickly," I added.

"Quickly."

"One more thing," I said, before I let him go. "Lynn left a package for me at my hotel's Reception the day she died. It was a clock that was stolen from my mum's room in Cambridge a few nights earlier. I'm pretty certain she wasn't the thief. I think the thief is probably the woman who calls herself Jackie Bolton. Her real name's Jacqueline Wooley. She's Lynn's niece. I was thinking that if Jackie's fingerprints were on the clock, that might help you solve the murder."

"Are you able to bring the clock in?"

"Not today," I said. "I'm in Tunbridge Wells and I'm playing a gig tonight."

"I'll arrange for someone from Kent Police to pop over and pick it up," said Sgt. Dailey. "If that's convenient?"

"That would be great," I said.

After I disconnected, I sat for a few more moments in the dining room, composing, in my head, the words I was going to say when I rang my mother.

Right then.

Ready as I'll ever be.

"Good morning," I said. "You know how you were joking earlier that the only reason you invited me along on this tour was to look after you?"

"I'm not going to like this, am I?" my mother replied.

"I've got something to show you," I said. "And no, I don't think you're going to like it at all."

CHAPTER TWENTY-SIX

The conversation with my mother took half an hour, and I was extremely relieved when it was over.

Mum rang her solicitor, and I went back to my room.

I sent a private message to Dan, the moderator at The Greenhouse, and explained what I wanted to do. I waited for his answer. It arrived about ten minutes later.

Go for it, Jason. We're absolutely disgusted. And we've agreed to kick Castledancer off The Greenhouse and permanently ban her.

Don't do it right away, I said. *I want her to see what I'm posting. And everyone's reactions.*

If that's what you think is best. All our best wishes and thoughts to you and your poor mum.

Thank you, I said.

#

Music is not my only creative talent.

I opened up Photoshop, and, in each of the three pictures Castledancer had sent me, I preserved mum and dad's bedroom, their bed, their heads and shoulders and the bottoms of their legs and feet.

But where their bodies were, I applied some very judicious smudging.

And overtop of each of the three photos, I placed some text, in bright red caps.

DISGRACED FAN CASTLEDANCER ATTEMPTS TO EXTORT MONEY FROM FIGS FOUNDER MANDY GREEN

WHO IS CASTLEDANCER AND WHY IS SHE THREATENING MANDY AND JASON WITH THESE SHOCKING PHOTOS?

MANDY GREEN CONDEMNS CASTLEDANCER'S VILE ATTEMPT TO SMEAR THE MEMORY OF HER BELOVED TONY

Then I uploaded the three pictures to The Greenhouse, and wrote an open message to the group.

I'm sharing these, I said, *so you know what kind of a person Castledancer is. She contacted me the other day with the unedited versions of these photos, demanding £100,000 or she'd release them online.*

These pictures are extremely graphic and I can't begin to tell you how angry this makes us. No doubt Castledancer believed she could intimidate us into buying her silence. She was wrong.

And then I added a fourth picture, which I'd created myself, showing a Google Earth shot of the cottage where my parents had lived in Stoneford, and the garden surrounding it. I highlighted one of the trees with a large red arrow, and added a text box.

THIS IS WHERE THE PHOTOGRAPHER WAS HIDING

Then I drew a dotted red line to the upstairs floor of the cottage, and added a second text box:

MANDY AND TONY'S BEDROOM WINDOW

If you've got any sense of decency, I wrote, *you'll let Castledancer know what you think of her, on this forum. You'll demand the return of your artwork and stories. And you'll unsubscribe from Spicy Pickled Figs.*

I clicked "Send"...and off it all went.

I could have waited for Rose Saker to pick up the story. But that was assuming she made a habit of regularly checking The Greenhouse. We were long gone from Cambridge and the Figs weren't really news anymore—although this bombshell was shortly going to change all that.

No, I thought, this deserves something extra.

Something very special.

I rang up an editor I knew at one of the London tabloids. I'd been at school with him, and although it had been decades since we'd played together on the school's football pitch, we still had a friendly, if slightly wary, connection.

"Mike," I said. "Jason Figgis. How are you?"

We exchanged pleasantries.

"I've got a story you might be interested in," I said.

#

It was nearly eleven when PC Lewis Mansbridge from the Kent Police rolled up in his car and was greeted at the front door by Gerald, who quickly escorted him up to my room.

"Sorry to disturb you, Mr. Figgis. The local constabulary."

"Thank you, Gerald," I said, feeling very Earl of Grantham-ish.

"Very good, sir."

Gerald departed, closing the door behind him.

I handed over the Tesco bag containing mum's clock. "Sgt. Dailey's explained everything?"

"Got it all," said PC Mansbridge. "Lovely house, isn't it? The wife and I did a tour in the summer. She wanted to see the attics where the servants used to live. But we were told they were off-limits. Not structurally sound, apparently. Still—plenty of other things to explore. How the other half lives, eh?"

"Indeed," I replied.

"You playing that show here tonight?"

"We are."

"Not my kind of music, I'm afraid."

"Nor mine," I said, confidentially. "To be honest."

PC Mansbridge laughed. "I'm a big fan of Disco. The Bee Gees. KC and the Sunshine Band...Boney M."

"Bloody Russians," I said, but I'm not sure he got my joke.

#

After PC Mansbridge left, I still had a little time before Giles's tour of the house. I put the receipt for mum's clock into my wallet, and went online to see what I could find out about Jackie Wooley. aka Bolton.

I had her birth date and I knew her mother's maiden name. And that got me her birth registration record on Generations.

I did a quick search to see if she had any siblings—and she did. An older sister, named Erin, born two years before her, in 1992.

I went back to Facebook to search through their mother Vicky's postings and pictures.

And bingo…there she was. Jackie Wooley. It was a selfie Vicky had taken with her daughter in 2015, at a local marathon run where Jackie had competed. Vicky had very helpfully tagged both of them. And Jackie looked very fit. Fit enough to paddle a getaway canoe. Fit enough to run up and down hotel stairs. And fit enough to race across rooftops and climb down onto balconies.

She had dark brown hair and it was shorter than in the photo Gillian had sent me. But it was very definitely the same young woman. Absolute confirmation that Jackie Wooley had deliberately changed her appearance and was, indeed, Jackie Bolton.

I saved the picture and then sent it over to Sgt. Dailey at Thames Valley Police, along with an explanation.

And then I went downstairs.

Gerald was on duty in the forecourt. Over by the old Coach House, I could see a collection of lorries and vans parked on the gravel drive, and the base camp belonging to the crew that was filming that night's show, set up on the central lawn.

"Busy day," I said.

"A great deal of hustle and bustle, sir," Gerald replied. "All very much taken in stride. Although the film people have been a bit of a nuisance this morning, roaming all over the house with their cameras. Extra footage for the program, I've been told. Adding more colour to the event and, at the same time, tempting the viewing public into a possible visit."

I smiled.

We were joined, in short order, by the rest of the band and all of the crew. And, of course, Giles and Pandora.

And over the next two hours, we were introduced to Oakden's history, from its new front entrance (constructed completely from hand-hewed sandstone), to the dining room ("All of the wood in the walls has been invaded by worms," Pandora said, "and we've just spent £90,000 having this tapestry restored...") and, behind the dining room, the original eighteenth century kitchen with its flagstone floor and a massive fireplace ("Because we're Grade I listed," Giles said, "we had to be careful not to alter its general structure, although Pandora did have the new AGA cooker installed.") ("I simply could not deal with what was in there before," said Pandora. "If I'm expected to prepare my own meals, I must insist on the best.").

We were then taken through Great Boswell Hall, with its Indian carpet from Agra and its dark oak wall panels and a huge blue and brown Japanese-looking tapestry ("It was terribly threadbare after hundreds of years in Giles's family but it was mended to perfection by a dear little man in London who was recommended to us by that American woman who has that program about stately homes on the television.").

And past The Grand Entrance, with all of its portraits of ancestors, lovers of ancestors, dukes and countesses and nieces of dukes and countesses and friends of dukes and countesses and influential writers and artists and members of parliament, along with a king or two.

And then, finally, we were guided along to the Tudor rooms, the original part of the house that dated from the 1560s.

Everywhere, there were wide plank floors and fabulous carpets ("Rather threadbare, I'm afraid," said Pandora, leading us over them, "and in dire need of refurbishment.") and more and more portraits of ancestors, friends and lovers ("That would be Caroline," said Giles, "the woman who bore four illegitimate sons with my sixth great-grandfather—four! Can you imagine! And none of them entitled to anything!")

"Although," Pandora added, confidentially, "he did apparently acknowledge them in his will, along with Caroline, who was a good deal younger and rather more attractive than Giles's sixth great-grandmother, and this caused an immense scandal and a rift in the family that still hasn't healed to this day."

"Imagine!" said my mother.

She was admiring the drawing room's massive fireplace which featured, above the mantle, an impressive carving of the family crest, flanked on both sides by ancestors accompanied by great winged birds, all of them sitting on top of what looked like, from a distance, dragons' tails.

"Shall we have one of these installed in my lounge, Jason?"

"On the wall over the TV," I said.

"Fire-breathing dragons perched on a pair of matching Fender Strats," said Mitch. "I'm in."

"Everything in Tudor times was designed to show off one's status and power," Pandora continued. "And so we have this extravagant ceiling..." We all looked up. "And, naturally, the original windows..." We all looked over. "...and then, later on, every house was required to have its own classical sculptures and friezes and, of course, cabinets filled with curiosities collected from all over the world, civilized and uncivilized."

I would have liked to have lingered in the drawing room, with its armchairs and sofas, its grandfather clock and still more portraits of countesses and earls and several dogs. But we still had the library to visit, and all of the bedrooms on the second floor, and then the most interesting part, to me, anyway, the top floor, where, outside, I'd spotted that amazing parapet that ran the length of the front of the house, and all those gargoyles.

But my hope of going out to investigate the carvings was immediately dashed by Giles.

"Ornamental only, I'm afraid," he said. "The parapet was never designed to be functional. You'd need to clamber through one of the windows. Utterly impractical."

"And, of course, if you did venture out," Pandora supplied, "you'd risk putting your foot through the ceiling of the room below, as the entire thing's rotten to the core and in desperate need of remediation."

"I was wondering about one of those carvings," I said. "From the ground, it looks like it's almost an exact replica of the Mad Hatter from St. Peter's Church, in Winchcombe."

"You have excellent eyes," said Giles. "It's a copy. The architect of this part of the house was apparently a great fan of the thing."

"You ought to have brought Keith in from the bus," my mother said, nudging me. "A kindred spirit."

I had to content myself with a remote viewing through the windows. And, of course, the Mad Hatter of Oakden was facing in completely the wrong direction.

In spite of that, I could easily pick him out as he leered over the forecourt—I knew what he looked like from the back, with his medieval hat and the two wing-like humps growing out of the tops of his shoulders. He was quite large, easily twice the size of his counterpart in Leeds. And about four times bigger than Keith.

I pulled my little Lincoln Imp out of my pocket and held him in front of my phone, so that he was framed, through one of the windows, by the back of the Mad Hatter. I took a photo of the two of them, then wrote up a short explanation and posted it to Instagram.

Just a little taster. The Imp has found a friend!

CHAPTER TWENTY-SEVEN

Castledancer was, of course, incandescent.

And her fury was compounded by the fact that I'd completely ignored all of her texts—and there were many.

I had read them. I just hadn't bothered to respond.

Mike's story was up on his paper's website, along with a statement from my mother (which I'd written), and my doctored photos.

And a lot of people had read—and reacted to—my posts on The Greenhouse.

I want a word with you, Castledancer said, when I finally made up my mind to acknowledge her.

No thanks, I said. *You'll be hearing from my mother's solicitor. And the police. I doubt they'll have much trouble tracking you down. The last time I looked, blackmail was still a criminal offence. Have a nice day.*

Castledancer wasted no time in answering.

You're going to be very sorry, Jason.

I didn't bother with a reply.

I was starting to feel a little bit nervous, though.

I was pretty positive that Castledancer was, in some way, connected to Lynn, and whoever had killed Lynn was still out there.

And I had a really nasty feeling that it might have been someone she knew extremely well. Jackie Bolton—or Wooley—was at the top of my list. She was elusive. She'd made herself nearly invisible. She was good at changing her appearance. She could talk her way past security guards and she was clever—she knew how to slip in and out of places without being noticed.

Oakden had been closed to the public in order to allow the film crew—and us—to set up in the old Coach House in advance of our gig. Nobody else was allowed in, other than Giles and Pandora and members of their staff.

From my bedroom window, I could see the marquee tent where the film people were gathering for their afternoon break. A catering van was parked on the gravel drive, its big side windows propped open and a selection of snacks lad out in wicker baskets on a long table below.

I went downstairs, lit up a ciggie, and walked over to the van.

"Jason Figgis," I said, introducing myself to the woman in the window. "I'm with the band."

"Hello," the woman said. "Would you like something to eat? We have fresh fruit, biccies, protein bars…endless tea and coffee…"

"Thank you," I said. "No. I was curious though…we had a catering crew set to tour with us but they had to cancel at the last minute. I was a bit worried about one of them…she seemed short of money and I was hoping she'd found herself another gig…you haven't got anyone named Jackie Bolton on board, have you?" I paused. "Or Jackie Wooley?"

"Afraid not," the woman said. "Just me and Roy—my husband—doing this show. And my sister Pru."

Roy was busy in the back of the van but turned around at the mention of his name, and waved. Pru was tidying up the tables in the tent.

"Ah well," I said. "Thanks."

I wondered if she could hear the relief in my voice.

"You're welcome! I'm hoping we can pop in later and watch your show. We usually do TV and film sets. Strict rules about who can go where. Nice change."

"See you there," I said.

I finished my ciggie on my way back to the house. And then I checked my Instagram.

I had a new message.

It was from Jilly.

My love. I'm so sorry I haven't been in touch. I was unavoidably detained having to deal with my Guardian Angel recertification. There was a backlog in the administrative offices and then, of course, some of the staff decided to stage a slowdown to protest unholy working conditions…

I didn't care how ridiculous her explanation sounded. Jilly wasn't Lynn. And I was so happy to hear from her, I'd have believed absolutely anything she said.

Lynn's dead, I said. *She returned my mother's clock…and then someone killed her.*

I know, lovely. She's here. I've seen her. But I haven't spoken with her. It's too soon. I do have something to tell you, though. You asked me, in Cambridge, why, if I was watching the river, I didn't do something to help you. And I told you that I did do something. What I did was urge Lynn to act. She couldn't see me, of course, and she couldn't hear me. But I spoke to her conscience. And I believe she did listen. I believe everything she did, from that moment on, involved setting her own interests aside—and those of others—and turning her thoughts towards helping you.

I think that's what got her killed, I said.

Nobody is more aware of that than me, Jason. Questions were asked here. That's why my recertification was held up.

Who were—are—these 'others' that Lynn was concerned with?

You must know the answer to that by now.

She was afraid of someone in the band, I said.

And then I told her about the day Lynn went into The Ancient Porter in Oxford, and saw Mitch, Bob, Rolly and Beth, and confessed to Roaming Minstrel 556 how frightened she was.

I don't believe it could possibly have been any of them, my love. Perhaps it was someone sitting nearby, and your friend was mistaken about who Lynn saw.

I think it was someone who's connected to Annie Hobbs, I said. *She's related to me, Jilly. Annie Hobbs was my mother's sister. Half-sister.*

Was she? Jilly countered. *That does surprise me.*

And Lynn was Annie's daughter.

I do believe that to be true. And I shall ask her about all of this, when I'm given the opportunity.

Why can't you just ask her now?

I was aware of just how stupid our conversation sounded. Jilly was as human as I was. And for me to pretend that Lynn's spirit was with her, and accessible, but not just yet, was just…fuckably ridiculous.

Be careful, Jason. I'm very worried about you. I feel you are surrounded by danger…

You're my guardian angel, I said. *Isn't it your job to look after me? To shove me out of the way of speeding cars? To rescue me from plummeting gargoyles?*

It is my job, said Jilly. *I told you that when we first met. I'm with you for life. If your shoelace hadn't come undone in Leeds, that piece of falling masonry would have hit you squarely on the head and probably would have killed you.*

How do you know about my shoelace?

There are some things which I'm able to influence, Jilly replied, *and some things which I am not.*

I didn't know what to say.

I was reminded of that film, *Sliding Doors*. Where a two-second delay made all the difference in the world to Gwyneth Paltrow's future.

Have you, by any chance, looked into the family history of Pandora Asquith-Jones? Jilly inquired.

No, I said. *Should I?*

I should if I were you, yes.

Why? Is she trying to kill me as well?

Jilly responded with a laughing emoji. With tears rolling down its face.

Please be careful, my love, she said. *And remember. I will always be watching over you.*

#

I certainly wasn't feeling very confident about my safety. Or my mother's.

I'm not sure what it was. The fact that Castledancer had told me I'd be sorry. That Vicky Hobbs Wooley—Annie's daughter, Lynn's sister—was so filled with rage that it obscured her concept of reality. That her own daughter, Jackie, was still out there somewhere, unaccounted for, a loose cannon.

And now Jilly's warning.

I'd always listened to her when I was working on board the *Sapphire*. Even though she was wrong nearly half the time.

She'd been right when it had really counted.

I still had an hour 'til I was needed for a run through of "Sultans of Swing" with Giles, Beaky, Mitch and Bob.

I tried to distract myself with my grandfather.

There were no relatives in my DNA results who had Hobbs in their histories.

I found three of Alan's Australian sons on the Generations site. They'd made it known in their profiles that they'd done a DNA test.

They'd added little pictures with spiralling chromosomes to their entries, identifying links back to their ancestors.

Those three sons were my uncles, my mother's half-brothers. And I ought to have had a huge number of DNA strands in common with them.

But I had nothing.

It made no sense at all.

Reluctantly, I turned to Pandora Asquith-Jones. If Jilly wanted me to investigate her, she had to have a good reason.

A romp through archived society pages from the 1960s (courtesy of the British Library) provided a good starting point. Pandora was a close friend of Giles's twin sister, Arabella, and their friend Portia Mainwaring, whose father was Lord Wintle, a British ambassador who'd been posted somewhere in the thick of a coup.

Pandora's nickname in the 1960s was "Binky," derived, somehow, from her middle name, Bridget. She was the daughter of an existential poet named Alden Webster who was serving time in prison for setting fires, and a mother who worked as a cleaner. She wasn't what anyone would call "landed gentry" at all, in spite of being best mates with Arabella and Portia. In fact, they seemed to have befriended her in order to thumb their noses at their parents' well-established social hierarchy.

And, she'd also once been engaged to both Giles and his brother, Jeremy, who was a racing car driver in France (though not at the same time). Both engagements had ended acrimoniously, with accusations flying from both sides.

Pandora had gone on to have an affair with the husband of Apollonia Johns-Maxwell, whose mother was a fourth cousin to someone who'd married into the Royals; as well as Pierre Potter, an American actor who'd been blacklisted for being a Communist, who'd relocated to England where he'd found work as a talking milk bottle on a children's radio program.

Pandora had eventually married the late Brian Asquith-Jones, a well-placed photographer who'd also happened to be a Lord. But her days of wedded bliss were numbered: Lord Asquith-Jones was found drowned on his estate in Dorset, having accidentally tumbled into an ornamental pool after a night of heavy drinking.

Pandora had spent the next chapters of her life gracing the pages of *Hello!* while she promoted her country home, her favourite charities, and her series of romantic novels, which were all apparently dreadful but which sold thousands of copies on the strength of their "inside" glimpse at titled households.

It appeared, too, that Pandora had regretted her decision to abandon Giles all those decades ago, and was now making up for lost time in his exclusive company. Giles Jessop, she proclaimed to the *Daily Mail,* "was always the only real, true love of my life."

If nothing else, I thought, those details would greatly amuse my mother.

I went over to Generations. Pandora Bridget Webster was an extremely unusual name, so there was only one result. And there she was, born in 1942 in Norwich.

For some reason, that last name—Webster—was sticking in my brain. I had to think, and then I realized what it was. All three of my distant Merrifield cousins also had Webster in their trees.

What were the chances?

Why couldn't Jilly just come out and tell me things? Why did she have to send me on obscure fact-gathering missions?

I typed "Webster" into the search field for my DNA results.

I wasn't prepared for what came next.

It was just like that ad on the telly, when the hints come flying at you from all sides and leaves start exploding exponentially on trees. There were Websters everywhere. And they all seemed to have originated in Norfolk.

And their common ancestor was a gentleman by the name of Charles Webster.

A stonemason.

CHAPTER TWENTY-EIGHT

Oakden's Coach House was a beautiful old building, an eighteenth-century barn built of hand-hewed stone, with a roof made of flattened slate. And when Giles had undertaken its most recent restoration, making it ready for wedding breakfasts, after-wedding parties, dances and workshops and conferences, he'd stripped off years of unsympathetic improvements, exposing the original interior walls as well as all of the overhead trusses and cross-beams.

He'd also overseen the installation of a state-of-the-art professional sound system—which was what we—and the film crew—were going to plug into for our show.

I went inside.

Kato, wearing her favourite fashion statement—black jeans, a sleeveless lilac sweatshirt and steel-toed boots—was up a ladder, hanging a decorative Figgis Green banner from one of the cross-beams.

Rolly was changing his snare drum head. He'd mentioned on the bus that it was sounding a little flat. The down side was that it took two or three performances to break a new head in, and we'd all tried to persuade him to wait until after that night's show. Unsuccessfully.

Neil and Tejo were consulting with the film's director and their camera and sound people—they'd been to our show in Oxford, so they had a good idea what to expect that evening.

Mum, Beth and Pandora had conspired to act as an impromptu audience for our run-through of "Sultans of Swing," and had seated themselves in chairs directly in front of the stage.

We'd added the song to the end of our first set. Acoustic guitars are notoriously difficult to mic, so we'd decided to make it easy for Tejo by using guitars that had fitted pickups already wired for sound. Beaky had brought along his own 1935 Martin D-18. And I was playing my dad's 1969 Gibson J-160E.

The five of us made ourselves comfortable on our stools, and I counted us in.

If you don't know the history of "Sultans of Swing," Mark Knopfler was inspired to write the song after watching a Dixieland jazz band playing in a mostly-empty pub in east London. Dire Straits initially recorded it as a demo in 1977, and they ended up signing a deal with a record company who had them re-record it for their debut album in 1978. It was officially released as a single in January 1979.

It's pretty much a textbook song in 4/4 time, with six-and-a-half verses, punctuated throughout by a chorus—which is instrumental, no lyrics—and there are two solos, the famous long one in the middle and the shorter one at the end, which leads straight into another chorus that fades the song out.

Beaky and I had arranged it so that Mitch, Bob and Giles played the bed of the tune, the same way it sounds on the record, but with acoustic guitars, not electric. And then Beaky and I took turns picking out each verse's melody. When I played, Beaky fingered the lead guitar part you can hear Mark Knopfler playing on his '61 Strat. When Beaky took over the lyrical lines, I reverted back to lead guitar.

In the middle of the song, I performed the first solo, and then Beaky played the second one, at the end.

It was actually incredibly difficult to pull off. The lead lines were all tricky, and the whole thing relied on perfect cooperation between all five of us—and none of us were used to playing as an ensemble like that. On top of which, "Sultans of Swing" wasn't originally written for acoustic guitars at all.

But our arrangement did sound truly magnificent.

One run-through, and Giles had nailed it.

"You've been practising," I said, impressed, after Beaky and I'd ended on a brilliant arpeggio'd duet and we'd all strummed a solid final and sustained unified beat that would have made George Martin proud.

There was loud applause and cheering from the front row.

"Of course, dear boy," Giles replied. "Every waking moment. In the library. Inflicting daily impromptu concerts on the visitors."

"I won't say anything about you having a daytime job and doing all right," Mitch quipped, as I propped my guitar up in its stand and got down off the stage to have a further word with Tejo about Giles's mic.

#

Afterwards, as I was walking back to the forecourt, I was waylaid by Freddie.

"Got something for you," she said, presenting me with a little flash drive. "CCTV from the parking lot in Norwich. Perhaps you'll be able to spot whoever was responsible for the flat tires on the bus."

"Have you had a look?"

"I have not," said Freddie. "The courier's only just dropped it off."

"Have the police got a copy?"

"They do," she confirmed.

I took the flash drive upstairs to my room and plugged it into my laptop.

I could see our three vehicles arriving, all around the same time—the bus, driven by Beaky, the catering van—Janice and Mary—and the equipment van, with Kato behind the wheel. One of the other cameras recorded where they'd parked—beside each other—and then all four of the crew got out. Janice, Mary and Kato chatted briefly while Beaky did his walkaround, checking the bus. Then they left the lot on foot. The camera aimed at the exit showed them waiting on the pavement, and then a taxi arrived and they all climbed in.

I sped through all of the footage from the camera that was aimed in the general vicinity of the bus. Lots of coming and going, vehicles, people. No unusual activity. Night fell, lights came on…and the clarity of the picture diminished significantly. The parking lot wasn't particularly well-lit. But the lights that were there provided enough visibility that I was able to see two individuals walking into view at 1:52 a.m. on the morning of Tuesday, September 25.

One of the individuals was wearing the same clothes she'd worn in Cambridge, on the hotel's CCTV. Jackie Bolton in her blue hoodie and baggy track trousers. The other individual was taller, and was also wearing a hoodie that obscured their head and face. But, I thought, female—from the way she was walking, and the shape of her body—athletic, solid, well-toned. Both women were wearing gloves and carrying some kind of implement—large screwdrivers, I reckoned. I could see that the second woman's gloves were black and had a kind of neon orange stripe outlining the fingers.

And both women appeared to know what they were doing. After checking to make sure there were no witnesses nearby, they split up, one approaching one side of the bus, the other taking the other side. Then, they employed their screwdrivers to push aside the valve releases in the tires.

And, when they'd finished, they checked again to make sure they were alone, and then nonchalantly sauntered out of the lot to the road. As the second female left, she peeled off her gloves and stuffed them into the back pocket of her jeans.

I ran the footage from the entrance/exit camera to see how they'd arrived. No luck there—they were on foot. And the same for their departure—they walked out, turned left, and kept going.

I wondered if that second female was the same person who'd let Jackie into the stairwell at the Eagle and Lion Hotel in Cambridge. It certainly wasn't Lynn. And it wasn't her sister, Vicky, either. Both women were very heavy-set, and decidedly not athletic-looking.

I was craving another ciggie.

I pulled out the flash drive and put my laptop to sleep, and went downstairs and walked over to the gravel lot in front of the Coach House to light up.

I checked my phone for messages. I was impatient to hear back from Roving Minstrel 556, but she hadn't sent me anything. So I composed another message to her.

When you were in the pub in Oxford, do you happen to recall anyone else sitting near the band? Anyone who might have been familiar to you, that Lynn could have seen as she came in?

I waited to see if she'd answer me.

Not online, obviously.

I heard a shout.

"Oi! Figgis!"

I turned around.

"Kato," I acknowledged, as she caught up to me.

"Got a little tip for you. You know that Mad Hatter gargoyle thing?"

"The one up on the parapet, the one that came down in Leeds or the one on the bus?" I said.

"All three," Kato replied, with a grin. "Anyway, there's a fourth. A twin of that one up there. Used to sit on the opposite corner but it got taken down when they did some repairs."

I'm sure my eyes lit up. "Where is it now?"

"In the attic." She indicated the Tudor section of the house, to our left. "Under the roof where the servants used to live."

"And how do you know about it?"

"How do I know about anything, you twat?"

I must have looked sceptical.

"Gerald the All-in-One Butler showed it to me," she said. "You interested?"

"I've heard the attic's structurally unsound," I said.

"Nah," said Kato. "They only say that because they haven't done any work on it to make it look good for the punters. Coming?"

I walked back to the forecourt with her, and then we went inside and upstairs, all the way to the top floor, and then along to the older west wing of the house.

We stopped in front of a massive oak door.

The door creaked rather theatrically as Kato swung it open, and then she switched on a light, which revealed a further staircase. This one was extremely narrow and steep, with wooden steps and no handrails, and it twisted around a corner at the top.

"Mind how you go," she said, over her shoulder, leading me up.

I shoved my phone into my pocket as I needed both of my hands free to steady myself against the stone walls. The stairs were worn down by servants' shoes, and were narrow on the left and wider on the right. It all reminded me of medieval castles and stone turrets, where knights had once defended their realm with battle-drawn swords.

I could hear my phone pinging and I could feel it vibrating against my thigh. I stopped at the top and pulled it out of my pocket. I could see Kato just ahead of me, walking under a huge bare wooden beam that supported the steeply-pitched roof.

It was Roving Minstrel 556.

Hey Jason. You really jogged my memory there. I had to think but actually, the pub wasn't that full and there weren't any others sitting close to the Figs. They'd pushed two tables together. Bob, Beth, Mitch and the woman who sells your merch were at one of them, and Rolly was sitting with two of your crew—

one looks after your lights and the other takes care of your equipment.

Thanks, I texted back. *Freddie, Neil and Kato.*

Kato, said Roaming Minstrel 556. *That's it.*

I glanced up at Kato.

I was asking around about that last name, Wooley. And someone said, Erin Wooley.

She had a pair of black gloves with orange stripes outlining the fingers shoved into the back pocket of her jeans.

Which didn't mean anything to me at all and then they said, the Figs' equipment girl, that's her name. Erin Wooley.

My heart dropped into the pit of my stomach.

"Fuck," I said, out loud, but my expletive didn't go anywhere because someone was behind me and they threw a bag over my head and twisted its bottom tight around my neck and then shoved me onto the floor.

My phone went flying out of my hands.

I landed on my stomach. I tried to roll over and fight back but whoever it was—there had to be three of them—had my arms and legs pinned with their knees. And then they yanked my hands behind my back and used what felt and sounded like plastic cable ties to lock my wrists together. And my ankles. And then they dragged me along the floor and into a room and slammed the door behind them.

I could hear the floor planks creaking as they lifted me up bodily and sat me on a hard wooden chair. They fastened my hands to its straight back with more cable ties.

And then they pulled the bag off my head.

The room was just large enough to house two narrow metal bedsteads under its eaves, a rudimentary wooden dressing table and a small wash-stand. It had one small window and no fireplace and it was very cold and smelled strongly of wood rot.

There were two women standing in front of me. One of them was Kato.

"Aka Erin Wooley," I said.

"Yeah," Kato said, as if I'd been some kind of idiot not to have figured it out before.

I was pretty positive Freddie, who took care of the tour contracts and the pay, probably knew Kato's full name, but nobody else associated with the band did. She'd insisted on being called Kato right from the start, while we were still in rehearsals, and we'd never bothered to inquire further.

"And Castledancer…?" I guessed.

"Also," said Kato, taking aim at my left leg with her work boot and landing an excruciating kick on my already-bruised calf. "You fucking shitface."

"How did you get the *Queen Mary* pictures?"

"Mother," said the woman who was standing next to Kato. She looked about fifty, with a fat, round face and long dark brown hair pulled straight back into a tight ponytail.

"You're Vicky?" I guessed.

"That's right, clever clogs," she replied.

"'Mother' being Annie."

"God rest her dearly departed soul," Vicky replied.

"We knew about the pictures because she'd told us," Kato said. "And then we found them when we were going through her things."

"Mother stole 'em," said Vicky, a touch of pride in her voice. "Broke into the house and helped herself. And why not? She deserved every bit of what Mandy had. It should have been her. Not your bleedin' mother."

"What about the other pictures? Was it Annie who climbed the tree with her camera?"

"She was good at that," said Kato, with one of her grins. "In her younger years."

"And when you lot heard the Figs were getting back together, you came up with your plan," I guessed. "To make life miserable for my mother. And me. For the sheer joy our suffering would bring you. The big payoff being those last three photos. Sorry I wrecked your fun."

"Oh no," said a third woman, stepping in front of me. Blonde—artificially. I could see her dark roots. "We've only just begun to have our fun."

"Jackie Bolton."

"Hope you liked the mussels," she said.

"I suppose you thought they'd kill us."

"Not at all. But I did relish the idea of both of you doubled over the toilet in seriously agonizing discomfort. And then, of course, the show had to be cancelled. Even better."

"Which one of you killed Lynn?"

None of them was in a mood to confess. It didn't matter. Each was as guilty as the other, as far as I was concerned.

"She was your sister," I said, to Vicky.

"Yeah, and me and Jackie's aunt," said Kato.

"It wasn't like we was close," Vicky replied, defensively. "We never knew her, did we? Not 'til five years ago, when her old man kicked off. And she decided to go and live with Mother. What a surprise. And here's me thinking I was her only daughter. Family secrets, eh?"

"Granny'd had her two years before mum was born," Jackie said. "And she arranged an informal adoption, with a friend. Who took her in and raised her."

"It was no adoption at all," Vicky said, resentfully. "Seeing as Mother could visit her anytime she liked and I was none the wiser. Lynn grew up with advantages. We was struggling to put food on the table and all the while her majesty was living the high life down the road."

"And she was a rat," said Kato.

"She was going to ruin everything," said Vicky.

"Well," I agreed. "She did return mum's clock."

"And that was the final straw," said Jackie.

"Yes, after you tried unsuccessfully to get it back from the hotel's Reception," I said. "The best you could hope for was to shut Lynn up so she couldn't say or do anything else to betray you."

I looked at Kato.

"You were the 'inside' person who let Jackie into the hotel that night. You had a party in your room. Lots of coming and going. I saw you go into the lift on the hotel's CCTV. You went down to the hotel's cellar—there weren't any cameras there. And then you went into the stairwell, climbed up one flight, and held the exit door open for Jackie. Then you went back to the cellar and took the lift back up to your room."

"You'd have made a good PI," said Jackie.

"I am a good PI," I corrected. "You weren't wearing gloves and you left your fingerprints on the second floor stairwell doors in the hotel, as well as the panic bar on the exit door to the roof. And you were carrying the clock when you ran out of the hotel. That clock's got your fingerprints all over it, too. And now the police have it."

"Liar," Kato said.

"Am I? You obviously missed PC Mansbridge when he popped by this morning. If you lot have any common sense at all, you'll let me go. The police can link Jackie to Lynn's death. I've given them everything I know about her. There'll be a warrant out for her arrest.

Don't make it worse for yourselves."

For the briefest of moments, I thought I'd got through to Jackie.

But no. She held up her phone—it was pale blue plastic and cheap—and took my picture.

"For the collection," she said.

"Those burners have rubbish cameras," I said.

Jackie shrugged. "It doesn't have to be good. I'm sure your mother'll recognize you."

And then she disappeared behind me.

"Tell you what we're going to do," said Kato. "You know how Lynn died?"

"Insulin overdose," I said.

"Yeah. We've got the same planned for you."

"Lynn didn't die fast," I said. "Type 2's use slow-release insulin. She got groggy. It must have taken hours."

I knew I was right. Angie'd told me all about insulin after I'd spoken to Tom. She'd researched it for one of her novels.

"Yeah," said Kato. "Hours and hours. Lucky you."

"I'm going to be missed downstairs," I said, trying not to panic. I could hear my heart pounding. My adrenaline was urging me to fight, to try and escape, but logic was telling me I wouldn't get far. Not strapped to a chair, with my ankles tied together. My only hope was to try and reason with them.

Fat chance of that.

"You won't be missed until the sound check," Kato replied. "And by that time I'll be long gone as well."

"My sister's going to drive as far away from here as she can," said Jackie, coming around to the front of the chair again. She was carrying a handful of what looked like fat pens. "And when I send her pictures of you—dying—she's going to forward them on to your mother. And then we're going to leave, Jason, and with any luck we'll be long gone before the police can come up with any kind of clue as to where we've been…and where you are."

"You really won't get very far."

"Won't we?" Jackie said. "I'd say I'm pretty good at making myself disappear. I've learned a few things over the years. There are ways and means. And that extends to my sister and mother, too."

She handed the burner phone to Kato, and then removed the lid from one of the fat pens. I could see the main part of the pen contained a glass vial of clear liquid.

She screwed a needle into the end of the vial and pulled off its protective plastic top.

Then she twisted the bottom of the pen, dialling it up to its maximum dose.

"Lynn used to inject her insulin into her thigh," she said, "but we'll spare you the embarrassment." She pulled up my t-shirt and exposed my stomach. "She also used to use little packets of alcohol swabs, in order to make sure her skin was squeaky clean and there was no possibility of contamination or infection."

Jackie stabbed the needle into the fatty tissue on the side of my stomach. It stung like blazes. And then it really hurt as she pressed the bottom of the pen and slowly forced a full dose into me.

"I don't think we'll need to bother with that," she added, as Kato snapped pictures.

I could see the little dial on the pen's side rotate down as all of the insulin was pushed out.

Eighty units.

She yanked the pen out of my side and dialled up another dose and stabbed me again.

And then a third time. And a fourth time.

Until all three hundred units were gone.

And then she got another pen.

"Enjoy the ride," said Kato. "Fucktard."

CHAPTER TWENTY-NINE

I had no idea how much time had passed.

Jackie was explaining to me how she'd managed to save up enough insulin to cause an overdose.

"Lynn was prescribed thirty-five units a day," she said, conversationally. "Divide that into three hundred and you get eight doses in a pen, with twenty units left over at the end. Which Lynn was throwing away. But we picked them out of the rubbish."

"One at a time," Vicky added. "Every day for two years. Saved 'em all up, all for sodding Mandy. That made me very pleased indeed."

"And then," said Jackie, "I had an idea. I realized that losing you would cause your mother to suffer much more than if we killed her. The best revenge. Ongoing. Never-ending."

"But we had to use the insulin on Lynn instead," Vicky said. "Change of plans, but there you are."

"And all those little dosages weren't very efficient," said Jackie. "I had to break the pens open and empty them into a bottle and use an old-fashioned needle."

"You spilled a lot of it on her," I said.

"She would keep struggling," said Vicky.

"And then," said Jackie, "afterwards, we found out Lynn had just got a new three-month supply in. Two boxes. Weren't we the fortunate ones?"

She held the empty boxes up so I could see. Five pens in a box. 3,000 units. All of it, by that time, in me.

My stomach felt like a pin cushion.

I could smell the phenol.

Jackie had made so many punctures, the insulin had dribbled down my front and made my jeans wet.

#

It might have been a slow-release, long-acting version of insulin, but I was having a non-diabetic reaction. I had normal blood sugar levels and they were going down, rapidly. I was light-headed. The room was beginning to spin. It felt like I was getting drunk. It had been a long time since I'd been legless at a party.

Kato had gone.

Jackie was sending her pictures.

Kato was messaging my mother and relaying all of my mother's responses back to Jackie and Vicky.

They were delighted.

#

There was another gap in time. I couldn't recall what had happened. I knew where I was. Just not when.

"All the things Mandy could have done to help Mother and me," Vicky said, "but would she? No."

"She didn't know," I whispered.

"'Course she bloody knew," said Vicky. "Mother wrote to her. Went to see her and asked her. Many times."

"Didn't know she was her sister," I said, trying to form the words, trying to force them out. "Just thought she was a fucking pain in the arse."

"She had a responsibility!" Vicky shouted. "She was family! She could have done something to help! But she didn't care! Neither of 'em bleedin' cared!"

I didn't say anything.

Couldn't.

"As usual," said Vicky. "Expect nothing off the relatives."

"Listen," I whispered. "I had no idea you existed. Neither did my mother."

"That's a laugh," said Jackie. "You saying my grandmother was a liar?"

"If it wasn't for Mother's friends," Vicky echoed, "who was always there to help her find a bit of work, hoovering peoples' homes and scrubbing their toilets, we'd have been done for. After the music people turned their backs on her. After *your* mother…" She gave the side of my head a clout with her fist, sending the room swimming. "…made sure *my* mother would never see the inside of a recording studio again."

"I don't think she did," I said.

"You're either very stupid," Jackie replied, "or very naive."

She bent down so her face was level with mine.

"Your mother knew all about that song, though, didn't she?"

"Which song?"

"'Dancing in the Castle.'"

"I don't understand..."

"Grandmother told us Tony wrote 'Dancing in the Castle' with her," said Jackie. "And then, when Figgis Green was huge, so high in the charts, everywhere you looked, Figs, Figs, Figs…Mandy and Tony froze Grandmother out. Never gave her the credit she was due."

"They owed that to Mother," said Vicky. "They owed her a share of that song. But Mandy didn't want to know. So there we was, condemned to that miserable ground floor council flat. Next door to drug addicts and thieving gits. Defrauded my identity, they did, the bleedin' pagans. Our civil liberties was violated by a bully running her motorbike underneath our kitchen window. Fraudulent bleedin' tax evasives stealing the petrol out of my car."

#

I couldn't breathe.

I couldn't stay conscious.

I was starting to shiver, uncontrollably.

"We'll be leaving you in a minute," said Jackie.

Her voice was distant and hollow-sounding.

She was at the other end of a long, long tunnel.

"So we'll take one more picture for Mandy and then we'll say bye-bye."

I struggled to stay awake.

I could feel everything dropping.

Blood pressure.

Breathing.
Heartbeat.
My face felt odd.
My skin.
Clammy.
Like when you're sweating but you're cold.
Your skin's wet.
I was shaking.
Cold sweat.
Bad taste in my mouth.
"Not even Hobbs," I said.
I think I laughed.
"What's he saying?"
"Not even Hobbs," I repeated, more slowly.
My mouth wouldn't work.
"No Hobbs DNA," I said.
My tongue wouldn't move.
"Webster. Mum's dad. Webster. Not Hobbs."
It was getting so hard to breathe.
My head flopped back.
I opened my mouth.
Must keep air coming in.
"We're not even…"
Must keep eyes open.
"…related to you."
And then…I saw Lee.
He was standing over me.
Looking down.
"Help me," I whispered.
He smiled.
He touched my face.
Gentle fingers.

#

I was somewhere.
Maybe I was dead.
I felt as if I didn't have a body anymore.
But I could still hear my heart.
And I could still hear my breathing.

Knocking. On the door.
A voice.
"Jackie. I must speak with you."
Male.
Clipped.
Old-fashioned.
"Jackie. I'm afraid it's quite urgent."
Whispers in the room.
"Who is that?"
"How does he know we're here?"
Panic.
Knocking.
"What do we do?"
"Don't open the door!"
"Jackie. Vicky. Stop being so silly. This is all so frightfully ridiculous."
Door creaking open.
Cold air.
Cigarette smoke.
Falling…falling…

#

Footsteps.
Another voice.
"PC Lewis Mansbridge…Kent Police…"
Hands all over me.
Another voice. Female. "He's still alive, sir.
Cutting the plastic straps.
"Empty insulin pens on the floor."
"Anybody got any sweets? Fizzy drinks? Anything with sugar?"
"Can you swallow this, Jason?"
Orange juice.
Spilling.
Another voice.
"Ambulance on its way."
More orange juice.
"Don't put anything in his mouth if he loses consciousness."
Stay awake.
Swallow.

Not enough.
Dropping…

CHAPTER THIRTY

I was comatose and verging on death by the time they carried me downstairs and outside.

They pushed an IV line into my arm and loaded me up with a glucose solution. They gave me injections of glucagon.

But by then, the damage had been done.

I was having seizures and convulsions.

My heart couldn't function anymore, and it stopped beating.

They performed CPR on me in the ambulance.

They got me to the hospital, where the doctors took over.

They got paddles onto my chest and zapped me.

Twice.

My heart jolted me back from death.

#

Hours and hours later, I regained consciousness.

The doctor checked me for brain damage.

"Patients who've overdosed on massive amounts of insulin usually recover with no lasting side-effects," he said, cheerfully. "It's a surprising statistic. Tell that to your sister."

I didn't recall mentioning my sister was Taylor Feldspar, best-selling crime novelist. But perhaps I had.

"I've read all her books," he added, patting the side of his white jacket. I could see the outline of a paperback in his pocket.

I laughed.

I was given packets of glucose gel and about a hundred bottles of fruit juice.

I fell asleep again.

I dreamed about Lee.

"It just jolly well wasn't your time, old chap," he said, clapping me on the back.

It was the same voice I'd heard in my room at Oakden Manor…and the same voice that had summoned Jackie from the other side of the door.

#

When I opened my eyes again, my mother was sitting beside my bed, reading emails on her phone.

"Care for an orange juice?" I asked, hazily.

"Welcome back," mum said, and I could see the absolute relief—and love—in her eyes.

"Hello Cleveland," I replied.

My middle hurt horribly. I tugged at the neck of my hospital gown and looked down. My stomach was covered in massive, dark bruises.

"What in all of *King Lear*'s filthy, hundred-pound, worsted-stocking knaves were you doing in that attic?"

"I was invited to look at a gargoyle," I said. "By Kato."

"Our now-missing and on-the-run equipment manager."

"She wasn't arrested?"

"The police seem to be having a difficult time locating her. She left in the equipment van. Fortunately, she'd already done our stage setup and there were no instruments inside. But I shan't ever forgive her for the messages and the pictures she sent. That was…"

My mother paused.

"Indescribably cruel."

She shook her head.

"I'm just so glad I didn't lose you. I don't know what I would have done, Jason."

I reached over and took her hand and squeezed it tight.

"Someone was watching over me," I said. "It wasn't my time."

Mum placed her other hand on top of mine and we stayed like that for long moments, not speaking. There was no need.

"Who rang the police?" I asked, finally. "How did they know

where to find me?"

"I did, of course. As soon as Kato contacted me. But they'd already been alerted."

My mother took my phone out of her bag and gave it to me.

"It must have been knocked out of your hand and when it landed it was jarred into automatically dialling 999. They rang you back several times. And when you didn't pick up, they sent PC Mansbridge out to Oakden Manor to investigate. He'd apparently been there earlier. It took him quite a long time because he couldn't quite get a fix on where your phone actually was. He did find it in the end. Wedged in between two dodgy wooden Tudor floor planks in the attic."

"Thank you," I said.

"And your recharger. I collected it from your room."

I plugged it in. There was still a sliver of battery left. I checked my messages.

There were about a thousand from Katey, panicking because she couldn't reach me. My voice mail box was full.

Nothing from Jilly.

Of course.

"And the police arrested Jackie and Vicky?" I checked.

"They booked Vicky for battery, assault occasioning actual bodily harm, false imprisonment and making threats to kill. To start with."

"What about Jackie? She was there too." I stopped. "But I have a vague memory of her leaving…"

"She didn't go far," said my mother. "Just as the police arrived, we heard a monumental thud in the forecourt. Everyone rushed outside. And we discovered one of the stone carvings that had been up on the balustrade had fallen down. The copy of that one in Leeds. It just crumbled away from its pedestal and crashed into the forecourt. It struck that young woman. The caterer. She was killed. Her head was crushed."

I didn't say anything.

"Bad luck with those Mad Hatters," said my mother.

#

I fell asleep again.

I had vague recollections of waking up to a nurse changing the glucose drip in my arm and checking my blood sugar readings with one of those stabby things diabetics use on their fingers.

My brain may not have been permanently damaged, but my ability to think still felt impaired. I felt like I was in a kind of dream state—that briefest of moments you're sometimes aware of as you're drifting off to sleep—and its boundary was very very hazy.

I recall opening my eyes again, and seeing someone else standing beside my bed. It was the tall, dark-haired woman who'd spoken to us in Sheffield. Kezia Heron.

"Thank you for your warning," I said. "It all came true."

"As I predicted," she said, with a beautiful smile. "I have the gift. As do you."

"I don't think I do," I said.

"You share my blood. You need only listen to what's inside."

"I share your blood? I don't understand."

"My ancestors are Romany. I will be married soon, to a man who comes from Ireland. He is not of our tribe, but my parents are willing to allow the exchange of our vows because of our love. His name is Ronan Figgis."

"That's my last name," I said. "My dad was Tony Figgis."

"You share my blood," Kezia said, again.

She bent down, and kissed me on the cheek. She smelled of woodsmoke and forests.

"We are all wanderers on this earth. Our hearts are full of wonder, and our souls are deep with dreams."

I drifted back to sleep.

#

Later, as my sugar levels were slowly returning to normal, I was visited by Giles, bearing a bunch of green grapes and a Get Well Soon card from Mark Knopfler.

"We'll reschedule," Giles promised me. "He's looking forward to it."

"After we reschedule Croydon," I agreed. "And Cambridge."

"Your tour manager sends her love," Giles chuckled.

#

On Wednesday, my mother returned. I was wide awake by then. A nurse had pricked my finger and tested my levels, and taken out my IV line. They'd stopped giving me orange juice. But they were keeping me in one more day for "observation."

"We're full speed ahead for Brighton on Friday, if you're up for it."

"I will be up for it," I promised. "Have they found Kato yet?"

"Not yet. But you'll be pleased to know Freddie's got us a new equipment manager. Her brother."

"I have no problem with other relations," I said. "As long as they're not yours."

I paused.

"Did dad write 'Dancing in the Castle' with Annie?"

"Don't be ridiculous. Annie couldn't have thought up a lyric if her life depended on it."

"Music?" I said.

"She was famous for banging a tambourine," my mother reminded me.

"The germ of an idea…?"

"Where's this all coming from?" mum asked.

"Something they said to me. Jackie claimed that Annie co-wrote the song with dad, and you stole it."

My mother laughed. "If they'd bothered to do any research at all on the subject, they'd have discovered that your father and I lifted the entire premise of 'Dancing in the Castle' from a seventeenth century ballad that originated in Norway and made its way to Scotland and England where it was recorded by half-a-dozen Celtic folk-singers in the mid-1950s before we had a go in 1965."

"Ha," I said. I felt uncommonly relieved.

"Don't tell me you believed them."

"Never a doubt," I assured her.

My mother had some additional news.

"I went to see your grandmother yesterday."

"And…?" I said.

"It seems what she told you wasn't entirely truthful. Alan Hobbs wasn't my father, after all."

"That makes sense. Who was it, then?"

"Her airman. Lee Merrifield."

"Not physically possible," I said.

"It is. I was actually born on May 13, 1941. Not, as it states on my birth certificate, July 13."

I was trying to work out the dates in my head. My mother saved me the trouble.

"I looked into one of those reverse conception calculator things online," she said, "and it means I was actually conceived roundabout August 21, 1940. Ten days before Lee was shot down."

"Why on earth would Granny change your birthday?"

"Because she was an unmarried woman with a baby facing a very bleak prospect. Lee had died. She'd been forced out of the WAAFs and her parents had practically disowned her. But Alan had begun a relationship with her and she believed he would marry her if he knew she was carrying his child. Desperate times. Desperate measures."

"He was already married."

"She didn't know that. She gave birth to me and kept it quiet for two months. Then, once she'd done the official registration, she went looking for him…and discovered the truth."

I shook my head.

"Still can't be," I said. "We haven't got any close Merrifield relations. Eighth cousins only. Everyone's ten cM or less."

I could tell my mother had no idea what I was talking about.

#

I checked for messages from Jilly. But she didn't get back in touch until Thursday, while I was standing on the pavement, beyond the hospital grounds, waiting for Giles, who'd very kindly offered to collect me and drive me back to Oakden to retrieve my bags—and my car.

I'm so glad you're all right, my love. But I knew you would be.

I dug into my jeans pocket for my cigarettes.

There they were. Next to my two little talismans—my whale tail, and my Lincoln Imp. They were never leaving my side. Ever.

You cut things rather fine, I said. *I was technically dead.*

I shook out a ciggie and put it into my mouth and lit it. I dragged in a lungful of smoke.

I coughed.

I'm so sorry, lovely. But I did make sure you were brought back. It wasn't your time.

My ciggie tasted awful.

That's what Lee said. I saw him, Jilly. I heard him.

I took the cigarette out of my mouth and stared at it.

I know, Jilly said. *He's been watching over you ever since that day at Biggin*

Hill. How do you think you became my practicum at Guardian Angel school six years ago? You have your grandfather to thank.

I dropped the lit ciggie onto the pavement and stubbed it out with the bottom of my shoe.

How can he be my grandfather, Jilly? I don't have enough Merrifield in my DNA.

I picked up the squashed ciggie and shoved it back into its packet.

My love, when Lee's mother, Adele, was sixteen, she worked as a kitchen maid for a family who owned an estate near Loddon, in Norfolk. Adele and Edward, the family's eldest son, fell in love. But the family would not approve of their relationship—and, in fact, threatened to disown Edward if he married Adele. She was dismissed on the day she discovered she was carrying his child.

I was standing next to a cycling path sign, and beside the sign was a blue rubbish bin.

The family's name was Webster, I guessed.

I looked at the bin.

Yes, my love. I expect you have rather a lot of Websters in your tree.

An entire forest, I said.

I looked at my packet of Benson and Hedges Gold.

The family employed a gardener named Horace Merrifield who had always carried a soft spot in his heart for Adele, even though she'd rebuffed his earlier advances. He knew she was expecting Edward's child, and proposed to her anyway. She accepted. And when Lee was born in 1916, he was given the last name Merrifield. So now you know.

They were distantly related, I said. *The Websters and the Merrifields. The Websters were descended from a family of stonemasons.*

George Webster, Jilly confirmed. *Who, many centuries ago, carved a Green Man boss for the interior roof of Norwich Cathedral.*

I smiled.

I could see Giles, approaching in his car. He drove past me, looking for a place to stop.

I must go, I said, to Jilly. *But I need to ask you one more thing. What do you know about Kezia Heron?*

I think, said Jilly, without hesitation, *that you'll discover the Herons were a Romany tribe which, in the 18th century, expanded into northern England. And that is where Kezia was born, in the early 1800s. And where, some twenty years later, she met and married an Irish fellow named Ronan Figgis.*

The 1800s? I said.

Yes, my love. You've been spending all your time focusing on your mother's side of the family. Did you not stop to think there may have been a reason why your father was so fond of that song, "The Gypsy Rover"? You must look up Ronan Figgis in your family tree. And Kezia Heron.

I was incredulous.

Did my dad know about his heritage?

Have a safe journey, my love, Jilly replied. *I shall see you in Brighton.*

I threw my packet of cigarettes into the rubbish bin.

See you in Brighton, I said, sending her a smile, a heart and a kiss.

ABOUT THE AUTHOR

Winona Kent was born in London, England. She immigrated to Canada with her parents at age three, and grew up in Regina, Saskatchewan, where she received her BA in English from the University of Regina. After settling in Vancouver, she graduated from UBC with an MFA in Creative Writing. More recently, she received her diploma in Writing for Screen and TV from Vancouver Film School.

Winona has been a temporary secretary, a travel agent, a screenwriter, the Managing Editor of a literary magazine and a Program Assistant at the School of Population and Public Health at UBC. Her writing breakthrough came many years ago when she won First Prize in the Flare Magazine Fiction Contest with her short story about an all-night radio newsman, "Tower of Power." More short stories followed, and then novels.

Winona began her Jason Davey Mystery series in 2017 with *Disturbing the Peace*. Two more novels followed: *Notes on a Missing G-String* and *Lost Time*. *Ticket to Ride* is the fourth book in the Jason Davey series, and her tenth novel overall.

Winona lives in New Westminster, British Columbia where she is on the board of the Crime Writers of Canada and an active member of Sisters in Crime–Canada West.

Please visit her website at www.winonakent.com for more information.